Write is Wrong

Write is Wrong

A Psychological Mystery

Claire Cabot and
Susan Baumbach Parry

Contact: Claire CabotAddress: 103 Hart Road, Beverly Farms, MA
Email: clairecabot@cabotfamily.com

This book was printed in the United States of America.

To order additional copies of this book, contact:
Xlibris Corporation
1-888-795-4274
www.Xlibris.com
Orders@Xlibris.com
86064

Contents

Dedication

"This book is dedicated to my beloved husband, Sam, whose encouragement and good humor will always keep me writing." Claire S. Cabot

"For Madeline and Hunter; may they grow up great!" Susan Baumbach Parry

The characters in this book are fictional. Any similarities to the living is coincidental.

Chapter One

Getting Online

Memphis was unseasonably hot and steamy on this early June evening in 2007 and so was Jake Proctor as he paced back and forth in his small apartment. The single window unit air conditioner strained audibly to cool the place down but was less than adequate.

Jake had thought of moving many times but knew he needed to keep the image he'd carefully cultivated. When he did have to move on, anyone questioned by authorities would say things like, "You must be mistaken, officer; I can't imagine Jake doing anything like that. Why, he was the best neighbor I ever had," and so on.

To beat the heat and try to settle down, Jake wrapped a cool, damp towel around his neck, grabbed a Diet Coke, turned a floor fan on full blast in his direction and sat down at the computer. While it was booting up, he rolled a joint and thought about where he'd surf to get his Internet kicks that night.

As the marijuana began its mellowing effect, Jake stared at the USPS priority package that lay open next to his computer. The return address caught his attention; the package had been sent by a handwriting analyst and below the logo a website was listed: Handwriting-Traits.com He'd already visited every "girlie" site and then some. It was time for something new. Could handwriting analysis relieve his neurotic behavior? Oh, what the hell, he'd give it a try.

The website was immediately impressive, it claimed people could *change their behavior* by altering their handwriting. It showed a photo of the owner . . . a young blonde. But Jake thought her name . . . Adelaide Stubbs . . . was ridiculous and homely as hell. "Why didn't she change it, for god's sake? Broads could be so clueless about what turns a man on," he muttered to himself.

He figured Stubbs was around 40. In his experience, that was a good age for a woman. Hell, Jake himself was now in his 60's, and his sexual appetite hadn't waned one iota. "Last woman I slept with thought I was only in my early 50's for chrissakes," he chuckled to himself. He'd smoked another joint by now and was feeling very loose and adventuresome.

Although the pot slowed him down a bit, and he had to do things with great deliberation, Jake managed to corral pen and paper and write out a sample of his handwriting to send to the Stubbs broad. The instructions specified providing at least a page, but he got so into it, he ended up with a two pages.

He wrote out a check for $250 but paused before putting it in with the sample. *I don't want this woman knowing my name,* he thought. He tore up the check, opened the phone book and pointed to a name: Hunt. *That's as good as any, I'll get a cashier's check tomorrow.* He wrote Jake P. Hunt on the return address. According to the pretty lady's website, he would receive his analysis within two weeks upon receipt. It was going to an address in Massachusetts, so he figured it would take at least three days to get there.

Things had cooled off a bit, by the time he had addressed the envelope and found a stamp. He felt like getting out of his smoke-filled apartment for some fresh air. Plus he needed some more smokes. Since he no longer drank, pot and cigarettes were a big priority in his daily life . . . running out of either put him dangerously on edge.

Chapter Two

An Afternoon of Fishing

It was a hot summer morning when Adelaide Stubbs, affectionately known as "Addie" to friends and family, looked out the kitchen window of the yellow Victorian house she shared with her second husband Butch. The red geraniums she had planted in May looked slightly wilted. She took the watering can from underneath the sink, filled it from the tap, and proceeded to the outside terrace where she drenched the flowers with water. Mousetrap, their black and white cat, who was sleeping on the garden chair raised his head slightly to watch her.

Addie felt delighted with her situation in life. Two years ago, she married her childhood sweetheart, Butch Stubbs. After raising two children and twenty years between marriages, Addie was blissfully happy with her new husband.

She poured herself a glass of ice tea, glanced at the copper pots on the wall, and made a mental note to remind the cleaners these needed some attention. Walking through the long narrow kitchen, she ascended the back staircase to the attic where she and Butch shared their office. The room was of ample size with good light and during the winter, when the trees were bare, there was a far off view of the ocean. Their two computers were sitting beside each other on a long built-in desk. The dormers had bookshelves overflowing with a wide variety of volumes on many subjects.

A telephone was within arm's reach of Addie and Butch when they were sitting at their computers. The fax and copy machine with reams of copy paper in different weights was on the table at the north end of the room.

Addie was a handwriting analyst. In addition to working for corporations she was writing a book analyzing the handwritings of the American Presidents. She had considered the idea of this book for a long time and was trying to fit it in between assignments from her commercial clients. Currently, she was writing an analysis of George Washington's handwriting. *What a stellar character,* she thought.

Butch was seated at his computer.

"I love having you semi-retired, do you know that? I also like having our computers in the same room. It creates an office atmosphere, and I don't get lonely." Addie went over to Butch and gave him a kiss. Butch looked up at her and laughed.

"Oh hi honey. What are you working on today? I'm amazed at how many e-mails I have when I check every day," Butch focused on the computer screen. His white hair was the only clue to his age of sixty-five, otherwise his lean frame looked like a fifty year old.

"I am going to write the conclusion to my analysis of George Washington," responded Addie. She turned on her computer and pulled out the sample of Washington's handwriting. "What a fantastic person he was. Man, I wish I could have met him!"

"I totally agree," said Butch. "By all accounts, he was very charismatic. I too would have liked to meet him. Do you realize he never took any money from the Continental Army? It is even more incredible when you realize the war lasted for eight years." Butch had been a History major at Dartmouth.

"No, I didn't realize that." Addie was staring at the sample of handwriting, checking her data a final time before writing the conclusion.

The foreword slant of George Washington's handwriting indicates that he was a man of action and deep sympathy; a person who cared deeply about his fellow man. He set the archetype not only for our nation's presidents, but also for the American character. As is evident by his long flowing 't' bars, he had an enthusiasm for life and a passion for new discoveries. Although he never considered himself an intellectual, George Washington had an astute mind and excellent organizational skills noted by the well-balanced loops in the letter 'f.' Washington was an outstanding manager who understood human nature. He was diplomatic and had a sixth sense of how to get people to perform at their fullest capacity. He was stubborn to the point of being resolute; note the triangular space in his 't's. Washington was not without his own sense of ambition and self-betterment; what more American characteristic is there? He improved his own lot in life and helped others do the same.

After lunch, Addie went into the village to the Post Office. Founded in 1653, Manaport was a small New England town on the coast North of Boston. The early settlers soon became discouraged with the rocky soil and gave up farming for fishing. The village was noted for its eighteenth century houses; among them the famous Caleb Tansin home, long prized for its exquisite proportions and architectural detail.

Two weeks earlier, Addie had sent a Priority Mail package that had never reached her daughter-in-law in California. She asked the man at the window to have a word with the Post Master. She was ushered into an office at the end of the building. The Post Master was standing at his desk speaking on the phone. He was about five foot ten, slightly built with reddish blonde hair. His conversation seemed to be of a personal nature. When he saw Addie, he quickly told the other person he would call back later.

"Good afternoon, may I help you?" He asked.

"How do you do? My name is Mrs. Stubbs. I mailed a package two weeks ago to my daughter-in-law in San Francisco, but it still has not arrived. I wondered if you could please find out what happened. I mailed it Priority, and I was assured the package would arrive in two days. Here I have the receipt." Addie took the receipt out of her pocketbook. "May I keep a copy of this, please?"

"Sorry, but we would have no way of tracking this. Unless, was it insured?" asked the Post Master.

"I didn't think it would be necessary to insure a package sent through the United States Post Office. I've lived in developing nations where you couldn't count on the mail but I didn't think it was necessary in my own country. Where does the mail go from here?

Could you call the next spot, and ask them if it got over there?"

Addie could feel her face getting red and her heart beat increasing.

"Oh yes, that's a good idea. I'll call over and see. But there can be a problem in that the packages go through machines and sometimes get crushed so badly we can't see who they are from." The Post Master was beginning to shift from one foot to the other. "Our shipments for the West Coast first go to a clearing house in Reading Mass, and then on to Memphis, Tennessee."

"I sent it Priority mail, and you are telling me it could have been crushed? That's unacceptable!" Addie raised her voice trying not to sound as angry as she felt.

"I know how you feel. I am glad you came to report this. Really, I am. I would feel the same way. Some people wouldn't have even bothered. Let me look into this for you." His blue eyes avoided her cold stare.

The Post Master was younger than Addie. She could not help but feel her age in situations like this. The postal service had always performed accurately when she was a little girl growing up in Manaport. She took a deep breathe. She knew if she got very mad that would not help.

"Thank you very much. I do appreciate any help you can give me. I enjoy coming to this Post Office and you have always given me good service. But I am distressed for obvious reasons. The package contained a very pretty green glass necklace I bought in Venice."

"Of course, I understand," the Post Master responded.

Addie thanked him again for his promised efforts and left the Post Office. She thought to herself, *I'll come back in a week if I don't hear anything from him. I wonder if I should write my Congressman? or actually, I guess the Post Office comes under the FBI if it is an interstate violation; better give the guy a chance. He doesn't seem very competent, but I can see he is trying to do a good job.*

It was towards the end of the afternoon by the time she returned to the house. Adelaide stopped at the end of the driveway and collected the mail. She then drove up the hill to the house. Butch was sitting on the porch outside waiting for her. He had shorts on, and Adelaide knew that meant he was interested in taking the boat out fishing. Butch was waving and blowing her kisses. He held Federal Express envelope in his hand. "Hi Sweetheart, you got a Federal Express Package. It is addressed to 'Handwriting-Traits' and looks like another job. Pretty soon you'll be able to support me."

"Hi Honey, you look like you'd like to go out fishing for a little while." Adelaide gave him a kiss and took the envelope out of his hands. "Wonder who this is from, must have picked up my address from the website. She examined the letter and quickly assessed the copy. Rarely, had she seen handwriting indicating such a disturbed person. She instantly felt troubled. The contents of the letter were extremely sexual and vulgar. Her face changed from a cheery countenance to one of fear.

Butch looked at her. "Sweetheart, are you alright? What's wrong?"

This letter; the subject matter is terrible. My gosh, I have never seen anything like it. Oh, this is scary." Adelaide shook her shoulders and shuddered. "Here read this." She handed the letter over to Butch who quickly looked over the pages.

"This guy is sick. Forget about him. Let's catch the rest of the daylight, see if we can catch some blues and forget about this creep." He handed her back the letter more focused on fishing than the perverted text.

"At this point, I'd love to leave the working life problems and recharge my batteries on the high seas. We haven't had much good fishing this season." Adelaide pulled open the screen door and walked inside the house. She wanted to change her clothes, grab a sweater, and put on topsiders.

The Stubbs loved to be on their boat *Seaworthy*. Manaport has a well-protected harbor where the tides ranged from ten to twelve feet. Butch drove the boat slowly out of the channel. They passed large, weather-beaten, gray-shingled houses with green lawns. There were three islands offshore: Mason's, Darby, and Cooks. When Adelaide had been a young girl, she had swum from the Yacht Club to Mason's Island with a swimming class. She had always wanted to do this again, but never had. She took a deep breath. "Hmm, I love the smell of that salt air. Gosh, it is gorgeous out here. This is just what I needed. That handwriting sample made me very nervous." She put her arm around Butch who was standing at the helm. He gave her a quick hug back.

"Now, I will teach you how to catch some bluefish. It is all skill of course, but I can give you some good pointers. I have had years of experience! We will troll with two rods off the back of the boat. Bluefish usually swim in schools. So, when we get a strike, reel in the other rod. When I have landed Mr. Blue, we will try and get that other rod back in the water as fast as possible." Butch was standing behind the wheel laughing. "Why don't you steer? Just head right for that buoy, and I'll get the fishing rods out." He disappeared below deck. They went beyond the islands. The shoreline ran forever at their backs, and they could see the skyscrapers of Boston far off in the distance.

They trolled slowly. There was a lot of activity on the water and other boats were also out looking for blues. Butch spotted one of his friends and picked up the receiver of the short wave radio. "This is *Seaworthy* come in: *Second Chance*. Over"

The sound of the radio crackled. "Hey Butch, how are you? Have you had any luck? Over." They could see their friend Jerry in the other boat. He appeared to have two other passengers.

"Yeah, we caught a few." Just at that moment, the rods on *Seaworthy,* which had been sitting upright in the holders on either side of the boat, began to spin. "Just got a hit, over!" Butch threw the throttle into neutral and quickly grabbed the reel. "Addie reel the other line in and get it out of the way!" When a fish is on the line, there is enormous activity on any boat. Butch reeled in and lifted his rod. "Keep your rod tip up and keep pressure on the fish; wind when you can, and pump the rod occasionally." Adelaide could see the excitement on Butch's face. The fish jumped in the air revealing its size. "He's a nice one," laughed Butch. The fish swam towards the boat in a zigzag fashion trying to rid itself of the hook. He got closer and closer to the boat. Butch grabbed the gaff and snared the fish skillfully. With one graceful motion, he lifted the bluefish into the boat. Gasping for breath, the fish flailed about on the cabin floor. Butch picked up a metal bat and hit it over the head. He removed the hook and placed the fish into the cooler. "We'll weigh it later. Let's get the lines back in the water. The next strike belongs to you. See if you can catch one." They quickly cast the reels behind the boat and Butch pushed the throttle forward. Within seconds, the reel spun out of control. Addie grabbed the reel.

"Oh my gosh, this fish is so strong. I can barely hold the rod. What do I do now?" Butch put the throttle into neutral. "Keep your rod tip high, and then try to reel in."

"Oh my gosh, I think this is really a big one. Gads, he is putting up a big fight. You need to be strong. This is so thrilling." Adelaide got energized when she caught a fish.

"Keep your rod tip high, honey." Butch repeated. "That's it, reel when you can."

They fished until the early evening bringing in almost six, nine to ten pound bluefish. It was a good day of fishing. They motored into the lee of Mason's Island. "This is the time of the day when all good fishermen get to have a beer!" Butch said with a smile.

"And this is the time of the day, when all good fishermen's wives, get that beer!" Adelaide disappeared below deck and came up with two cold beers from the galley.

"I'll clean the fish after I finish 'me wee tipple!" Butch took a hefty gulp of brew. "We did very well for ourselves out there." After finishing his beer, he took a long wooden board from under the port seat compartment. Next, Butch took a filleting knife and inserted the long thin tip behind the gills of each bluefish. Quickly, he ran the knife to the end of the blue fish and threw the entrails and bones overboard. The end of the day was approaching and the sun had turned into a large orange mass reflecting off the water with fleeting dashes of light. They brought *Seaworthy* into the harbor just as darkness approached.

The Stubbs grilled the freshly caught bluefish on the terrace that night. Butch had made himself a martini and Addie was sipping a glass of wine. The moon hung low in the sky.

Their house was surrounded by woods and very private. Mousetrap was sitting near them on one of the wooden chairs under the umbrella.

"God, do I ever love this place," said Butch looking around the yard. "You feel as if you are in New Hampshire or Maine. Yet we are forty minutes from an international airport and downtown Boston."

"We are two of the luckiest people in the world Butch." Addie looked at him dreamily. "In some ways, the really hard work of our lives has been done. We have cared for our aging parents and raised our children. We have four kids between us, and will always worry about them, but it is really up to them now. This chapter of our lives is for us. I am so glad I have the time now to work on the book analyzing the handwritings of American Presidents. I was also thinking about that handwriting sample I received today. Within our profession, we emphasize the content of the material is not important. That writer appears severely disturbed but very bright. Perhaps I can help that person by doing the analysis. It is difficult, however, not to be alarmed by the content. I feel so conflicted." Addie took another sip of her wine.

"And I feel romantic, ha, ha, ha," Butch laughed, reaching over to give her a kiss. They chatted long into the night in the soft glow of the moonlight.

The next morning Addie rose early and had breakfast with Butch. She excused herself from the breakfast table without finishing the morning newspaper. She wanted to analyze the disturbing letter as fast as possible. She did not like to look at handwritings of troubled people for very long. It made her feel anxious, as if she was close to the abnormal energy of another person. Years ago, Addie had gone to a psychic who understood her sensitive nature and encouraged her, when confronted with an abnormal personality, to build an imaginary wall around her and mentally bounce that energy back at the other person.

Addie carefully enlarged the size of the letter on the copy machine and measured one hundred strokes. She plotted the results on the last page of her graphoanalysis worksheet. The perspectograph demonstrated a graph of red and purple; a highly impulsive and feeling individual. *Well, she thought, this person cares deeply. Gosh, but he is so depressed. He needs professional help so badly.* She wrote up her four-page report and then picked up the phone to call Federal Express for a pick up. She sent the report to the address on the outside of the envelope at 31 Mercer Street, Memphis, Tennessee. *Now isn't that ironic,* she thought, *the clearinghouse for the Post Office is in Memphis as well as this person; strange coincidence.*

The phone rang and Addie answered: "Hello, Adelaide Stubbs, handwriting analyst." There was silence. "Hello, Hello, may I help you?" The receiver clicked.

Butch walked into the office in his tennis clothes. "Who was that?"

"Oh nothing, guess it was a wrong number. It was on my office line." Addie answered.

"Any heavy breathing?" laughed Butch.

"No, thank god." Addie smiled. "We have a party tonight. I'll pick up your shirts at the cleaners."

"Excellent, why don't you meet me at the club for lunch?" He gave her a kiss.

"I accept with pleasure." Addie returned the kiss with a big hug.

"Have fun on the courts. I'll come over in a bit and take a swim before lunch."

Chapter Three

Old Friends Reunite

Meanwhile, across many miles in Lakeside, PA, Babs Baker was finishing a gardening project and reveling in the glorious midsummer weather. The methodical activity allowed her mind to wander and she found herself reminiscing and wondering about old friends with whom she'd lost touch. Approaching her 65th birthday in a few months, Babs increasingly thought about what she wanted to accomplish with the life she had left. The desire to renew friendships was gaining priority on her long list of "want to do's," and she decided that before the day was over she would pursue contact with at least one long ago pal.

While she walked the dog, she decided whom.

"That's it! . . . Adelaide," she thought, as Sam, her lab puppy-in-training, walked obediently at her side. This was the first of their twice daily, 20-minute loop around the cottage-style neighborhood where she'd lived the past 16 years. People called Woodhurst quaint and quaint had become very desirable, especially when there was beach access, low taxes and low crime: a real neighborhood reminiscent of the 50's. After the walk, with Sam settled in his crate, Babs thought again about her plans to locate Adelaide, wanted to clean the domestic decks, and free up the time to do so ASAP.

Lunch was next, so she yelled down the basement stairs to alert her husband, George, that if he could break away, there'd be some lunch above stairs in about 20 minutes. "Great," he responded: "I'm hungry as a bear." And he was nearly as big as one, at 6' 6" with the distinctive Baker barrel chest and long arms. Babs, at a relatively diminutive 5'6" and medium build, always feeling safe haven when he wrapped his arms around her.

She and George were both married for the second time and would celebrate their 15th anniversary the following May. Babs marveled at their marital 'endurance' as somewhat miraculous since their interests and personalities appeared so opposite. But, she realized, at the core where it really matters, they shared the same values. And they didn't argue about money. How many couples could say that? As George would often quip, "We don't *have* enough money to argue about." If anything, they were frugal and occasionally might disagree on just *how much* to penny pinch on this or that.

However, there were a few exceptions, however. One was the boat . . . George's only admitted extravagance Bab's couldn't quite appreciate; just as he couldn't appreciate her indulgence in gourmet cookware. Well, it's pretty simple. He loved all things boating, she loved all things culinary, and as their family and friends would tell you, they were each quite expert in their area. George was never prouder of Babs than when she performed kitchen magic for dinner club get-togethers. And Babs literally glowed when George captained the boat with grandchildren onboard, breaking his usual "hands off" stance to let the curious twins enjoy taking the helm, talking on the shortwave, honking the horn.

During lunch, Babs and George thumbed through sections of the newspaper without conversation until Babs asked if George would be next "on duty" for the dog so she could spend a little time on the computer.

"Well, I suppose, but I can't get much done in the basement if he's underfoot. What's it worth to you, anyway?" he teased.

"Actually, a lot, dear. Lately I can't stop thinking about old friends I've lost track of, and I've decided to try finding one of them today. "Her name's Adelaide . . . Cooper was her maiden name. I don't think I would have mentioned her to you though. We were housemates in Boston with four other women in the early '60's in Boston. Actually, I was better friends with a mutual friend; that's how we met. Anyway, Adelaide was pretty tied up romantically with her future husband then. So I didn't see much of her, but she always fascinated me. Bright, fun, charming, witty . . . so many things I felt I was not at the time. After I lost track of her, I'd hear occasionally about her from others. That she lived in and traveled to exotic places, was a freelance writer, had three children, got divorced. And that's where we left off, about 20 years ago!"

"Catch your breath, hon. Can't believe you just said all that without air. Sounds like you're on a mission, so I'll keep an eye on Sam. Good luck finding your friend, but remember, you owe me . . . . so wear something sexy when you're done!"

"George," she admonished, blushing.

Upstairs in their postage stamp-sized office/guestroom, Babs fired up the computer, feeling a little nervous about her pending search. Up to this point, she'd only occasionally looked up information, and it was mostly medical to allay or heighten fears about her aging parts and faculties.

"Ok, here we go," she murmured to herself, as she typed in finding people I've lost touch with in the web search bar and pressed go. In what seemed a nanosecond, her effort was greeted by a web page titled, "Simplifying your People Search." All it said you needed was a last name to get started, and that any additional information would narrow the search.

Unbelievable, she thought, as she then entered both "Adelaide" and "Cooper" in the appropriate fields. Click, and, another nanosecond later, there was more information showing that name connected with someone age 64, plus a list of possible relatives and several cities/states where she has resided. "Bingo!" Babs yelled. "I can't believe it's this easy. Then she clicked on the "more details" field and learned that for just $9.95 she could obtain a report on her friend that would include phone number which is all she really needed. On the other hand, maybe she should just call information at each of the cities listed and find her that way. It'd cost a lot less. But she'd be under a different name, wouldn't she? If only I could remember her ex-husband's last name, or knew if she married again.

"Oh, for heaven's sake," she scolded herself, "quit nickel and dimming get the damn report, and just spend $10 less on dog toys!"

A few minutes and a debit card charge later, there was all the information she needed to connect with Adelaide, aka "Addie." What time was it now? Mid-afternoon. Too early to try? "Nah," she said as she dialed.

The ring tone seemed endless, and when she was about to give up, a female voice answered breathlessly, "Hello."

For a moment Babs thought she got the wrong number due to the unfamiliarity of it all. But she quickly recovered and said, "Adelaide Cooper Stubbs?"

"Y-e-s-s-," Addie offered hesitantly.

"Oh my gosh, I've found you! Addie, this is Babs from our '60's Boston days. Remember me? The housemate with the stuffed animal I slept with that you used to tease me about unmercifully?"

"What an incredible surprise! Of course I do! I've thought about you so many times and the other girls who shared half that two family house. We just lost track along the way. How'd you find me? What's going on?"

"I don't know," said Babs. "I've just been thinking about old times lately and missing connections with people who helped shape me along the way. You came to mind as you were a role model at the time."

"Really", said Addie. "That's hard to believe but wonderful to hear. Thank you."

"Hey, is this a good time to talk? Or should we make a later date to catch up? Do you even want to?" Babs, hoped she didn't sound too eager. She had always felt Adelaide possessed more maturity and self control.

But Addie leapt at the opportunity for reconnection. With unbridled enthusiasm, she suggested they block out an hour in the coming week for a lengthy catch up phone conversation. Addie would place the call. In the meantime, they agreed to make respective lists of what they wanted to be sure to ask/share, etc . . .

After they set the date and hung up, Babs immediately wrote the time on her wall calendar on the kitchen bulletin board where she'd be sure to see the reminder.

In the days leading up to the call with Addie, Babs found herself surprisingly preoccupied anticipating of their talk. In their initial brief conversation, she already felt a 'simpatico' element; as though they had something to share dormant all these years. She loved Addie's energy and zest for life and imagined in the future they would find common ground and even share a few secrets about growing old gracefully.

On the appointed day and time, the two women had an exchange that went well beyond the allotted hour. They just couldn't turn off their enthusiasm and interest in each other's lives. It was an exhausting shared energy, but they both loved it and so kept going until they hung up agreeing they just had to get together . . . . and soon! They both used e-mail and decided to communicate that way to set up their visit.

Babs knew she couldn't afford the time or money to travel to Boston, she hoped she could persuade Addie to come to her. From what she gleaned, the Stubbs lived very comfortably. No boasting on Addie's part, mind you, but just some references that gave Babs the impression the air in Manaport was a bit more rarified than the air in Lakeside.

It turned out, Addie's husband Butch, an insatiable sportsman, would be away fishing with friends in a few weeks. Indeed, that seemed the perfect window for Addie to travel to Lakeside for their reunion. They tentatively set the date for the weekend of July 28th, pending spousal approval, flights, and so on."

Babs had warned Addie that Lakeside had few direct flights, and definitely none from Boston. She suggested she fly into Cleveland or Buffalo, each city less than two hours away. "I can easily pick you up either place and don't mind a bit, in fact, I insist!" said Babs. "We can drive along the lake coming back, and you'll get a flavor for this under-appreciated part of the country.

One more phone call cemented their plans. Addie would fly into Buffalo mid-morning July 28 and depart early afternoon on the 31st. "You're sure that's not too long, Babs?" Addie asked. "Of course not just bring some throat lozenges 'cuz I'm sure we'll be doing a lot of talking!"

In the days leading up to July 28th, Babs reviewed the many things she had learned about her old friend via phone and e-mail. Eclectic odds and ends, like she still wore the same size she did in college. She was a staunch Republican. She looks forward to her first grandchild in the spring. She is athletic . . . . swims, rows crew, and cross-country skis. Her current husband was her childhood sweetheart. Her first husband was a disappointment. She's active in her church. For many years, she sold real estate to support herself as a single parent. She also wrote and sold travel articles, and started a cookbook, which is still in progress. But the thing that most caught Bab's attention was Addie's interest in handwriting analysis. She was a certified graphologist and had her own website, for heaven's sake. Figuring out what makes people tick through their penmanship. Imagine. It fascinated Babs, and she was eager to learn more when Addie came.

Meanwhile, Babs checked out the website: Handwriting-traits.com. And here was Addie, looking very professional with the same cherubic face and wispy curls Babs remembered. Granted the face was older, but she looked good . . . . damn good in fact! Hardly a wrinkle either or was that camera filter doing its magic?

A few days before Addie was due to arrive, George was taking advantage of good weather to do some outdoor projects. His regular contribution to the neighborhood was to mow the common areas within a two street

CLAIRE CABOT AND SUSAN BAUMBACH PARRY

radius. A few grateful residents offered to pay for the gas and once in a while someone gave him a few bucks. But he was just happy to do it. The activity fed his need for order, and he liked to be outdoors. The mower was the smallest of riding mowers so George loomed large at the wheel; in fact, watching him out the window Babs thought of clowns she'd seen as a child piling out of miniature cars at the circus.

When he came in from mowing around lunchtime, he caught Babs looking intently at her reflection in the dining room mirror. "What's the matter; see a ghost?" he quipped.

"Very funny, dear George," she said. "Actually, I'm feeling a little nervous about Addie coming and perhaps just a tad inadequate."

"*You*, inadequate? Why you're one of the most confident, self-reliant women I've ever met. That's why I married you. *And*, you put up with me; that's the most amazing thing!"

"There's some truth in that," she agreed, feeling now a bit more lighthearted. "You know I did recently make a list of things about myself I was proud of; 'think I should probably read it again?'"

"Could you share it with me?" asked George "I'm really interested."

Babs got the list from her desk, sat down at the dining room table with George, cleared her throat, and began:

Things I am Proud Of
(in no particular order)

1. *Raising a son by myself with zero financial support*
2. *Buying a house by myself*
3. *Going from an hourly to a management position in my career without a degree*
4. *Quitting smoking for good after 10 tries*
5. *Running my own freelance business*
6. *Being a recovered codependent now helping others*
7. *Being a hospital volunteer and children's literacy mentor*
8. *Having the stamina to be a nurturing nanny to 3 children, 3 days a week*

"Whoa, whoa, whoa . . . . back up a minute," George interrupted. "Those are all great, except what's this one about being a recovered codependent; I don't get that at all."

"Oh come on, George, that's about my first marriage. How I enabled his drinking and other stuff. It's nothing I enjoy talking about, as you know." Babs quickly added.

"How well I do know, dear," George responded with a sigh of resignation. "Now, how about reading me the rest of your list."

"That was it, honey. There isn't any more," Babs said, feeling pleased that George thought there would be.

"Well, what about the children's health fair you run every year? Your fabulous cooking and those holiday coffee cakes you send to everyone? I'm sure there's more I'm forgetting, too." praised George. "While I might complain about the time you spend on things, I'm really proud of you, you know." He then leaned toward her, lifted her hand and with a princely gesture, kissed it.

That was a close one, Babs thought to herself later as she put the list away. *If George only knew the extent of my former codependent life, he'd be scratching his head in wonderment that I ever 'got my shit together.*

Chapter Four

The Stubbs Make Travel Plans

"When are you leaving for the Icelandic fishing trip?" Addie was looking over her calendar in front of her. Butch was pouring intently over his favorite box of flies.

"On July 28th. We'll just be gone a few days. I especially hate to leave you in the summertime, but my brother's fiftieth birthday is a milestone. There are going to be several friends of his from Harvard and no wives." Butch picked up a large fly and examined it carefully.

"Well if you are going to leave me for a few days I am going to fly to Buffalo and visit my old house mate, Babs Baker. There are no direct flights to Erie, so I will fly to Buffalo, Babs will pick me up, and we'll drive to her house. It was so much fun to speak with her; I am really looking forward to seeing her again. She was such a neat girl. That was so nice of her to track me down.

Do you remember the party we had at Atherton Road when we were in college? It was the spring of my senior year. Babs was the gorgeous blonde haired girl dressed in a sexy, French, strapless, black waitress dress with a thigh length skirt and a red flower in her hair. The party was a mop scene. I remember it clearly, as if it were yesterday. We had five girls living in half a house in Brookline and each person invited twenty-five people who in turn must have invited twenty-five people. We had such a huge crowd; it is amazing we weren't arrested!" Addie laughed.

"I think I do remember that party; it was a good one. Mind if I turn on the radio? I want to listen to the weather report." Butch picked up the remote control.

"There have been a series of packages disappearing from the United States Post Office. If you, or anyone you know, have any information regarding this subject please contact the Reading Post Office." The radio stated. Addie was sitting straight up in her chair.

"Did you hear that? Did you hear that? I think there is a conspiracy. God, what is this country coming to? The U.S. Postal Service used to be a sacred institution, and now you can't even send a package through the mail!" Addie's voiced was slightly raised and she was speaking quickly.

She picked up the phone and dialed information. Information gave her an 800 number, which led her through a wide variety of recorded services. Finally, she dialed zero in frustration and waited for a Post Office operator.

"Hello this is Adelaide Stubbs calling from Manaport, Massachusetts. At the end of May I mailed a package to my daughter-in-law in San Francisco that never arrived. I just heard a report on the radio that anyone knowing anything about thefts from Reading, Massachusetts should notify the Postal Service." Adelaide said with controlled calm.

"I am sorry M'am, I am not familiar with any thefts." The man on the other end of the receiver had a strong Southern accent. "M'am, you must go to your local Post Office."

"Where are you located, Sir?" Addie inquired.

"I am sorry M'am, I am not at liberty to give out that information because of Postal Regulations. If you have filed a report with your local Post Office, that is all you can do." He sounded as if all he wanted to do was get her off the other end of the telephone.

"I know you are trying to do a good job." responded Addie. Patience was not one of her virtues. "Isn't the Postal Service part of our government? My immediate reaction in this post 9/11 era is one of deep concern, what if I was shipping a bomb through the postal service? Isn't it important to our national security to have an accurate tracking system? How many packages do you ship a day?" Addie was now fascinated by the logistics of the postal system.

"I am sorry M'am, I don't have that information at my finger tips but I do know that we ship more packages than any other mail carriers." Now the postal employee was sounding exasperated.

Addie realized that her conversation was going nowhere. "Thank you very much, I guess I will just have to physically go down to the Post Office *again*."

"Sorry not to be of more help, M'am, but that is the best solution." The voice at the other end of the phone sounded relieved.

Addie hung up the phone. "Do you believe that? What is this world coming to? I remember when we were young, and my sister Lydia was at camp. Those were the days when the postman came to the door and handed you your mail. Lydia was really home-sick. You knew my mother, who used to broadcast every family event to the entire universe. Well, the Postman knew Lydia was homesick because my mother and father were writing her letters everyday, and Lydia was writing them all the time. The Postmaster called my mother one afternoon and said: 'Mrs. Cooper, it looks like there is another letter here from your daughter. We are about to close, but if you drive to the post office right now, I'll wait for you.' Now that was service!" Addie looked at Butch.

"Oh I agree. Hang them all, that's what I say. That's why I like to go fishing and get away from it all." Butch looked at her and gave her a kiss.

"Are you teasing me?" Addie laughed.

"Why would I tease the woman I love?" Butch laughed.

It was early evening. Butch was sitting on the terrace with his martini and Addie was spreading some smoked bluefish paté on crackers. "Try this. I read a new recipe for making the paté. Let's see if we like it as much as the other recipe." Butch took a bite of the cracker. "Hmm. That's interesting."

"You hate it!" laughed Adelaide. She then took a bite. "I agree with you, its okay, but we are striving for perfection here. I like my old recipe where you mix the smoked blue fish with mayonnaise, lemon juice, and a tad of horseradish." She took a sip of her wine, and changed the subject. "Why do you think it is that when we all get older we are fascinated with our past? I was thinking about Babs and our college days. We had so many funny times."

"I think you think about the past because you have one." Butch looked straight at her with his incredible blue eyes.

"What do you mean exactly?" She looked at him quizzically.

"Well, when you are five years old, there isn't that much to look back upon is there?" Butch stroked Mousetrap.

"When I was writing for *The Good News Newspaper,* I wrote a feature article about a Chinese restaurant. The owner had swum from Mainland China to Macao. Where, incidentally, I have been and can't image how he survived; it is a very long distance. Anyhow, he said being in America for him was like winning the Lottery. He felt there is so much opportunity here. Somehow, we got talking about birthdays. When I told him I was about to turn sixty he said to me, 'Oh Adelaide, your life will begin again.' For me, that has been so true. I reconnected with you, the first boy who invited me to the movies, and now we are married. The other day I heard from Babs after all these years which is so wonderful, and now I am going to see her. Maybe we just have more time to reflect. We don't have to work as hard, we have no children at home, and we have taken care of our aging parents who have dropped off the twig." Adelaide was thoughtful.

"Dropped off the twig? Dropped off the twig?" Butch roared with laughter. "Where did you hear that expression?" He took another sip of his martini.

"It is an English expression. I learned it from watching one of their sit-coms. I think it is so funny." Addie tried to speak in a British accent. "I say there Mabel, do you think you will be dropping off the twig any time soon?" It did not take very much wine for Addie to be silly.

Butch added. "The English are very good at using colorful language. I feel that way about people from the South." Butch stood up and turned on the grill. He started dancing to the sound of the music on the radio. "May I have this dance?" Addie leapt up, and they twirled around the terrace in giggles.

They rose early the next morning. "It is so much easier to wake up early in the summer than in the winter, isn't it?" Addie was sitting at the breakfast table. Mousetrap was about to pounce on the counter and take his morning stroll across the kitchen table to check for tidbits of food. Addie was eating her usual large bowl of fruit and drinking a cup of green tea. Butch was eating an English muffin and reading *The Wall Street Journal.* He turned the page and said, "Sweetheart, I'd like to invite a few people over for dinner the second weekend in August. How does that work with your schedule? I would like to have the wives of our fishing team over after the tournament." Butch was getting himself another cup of tea.

"Sure, it would be fun to have a group for dinner. Hopefully, it will be a nice night and we can eat on the terrace. I have been working so hard I would enjoy some serious cooking. I find messing around in the kitchen very relaxing. I am going to miss you when you are in Iceland." Addie looked at Butch and smiled. "Can we coordinate our trip to the airport? My flight leaves at 11:00 a.m."

"I think we take off at 9:00. Several of us are taking the same flight. You could stay in the Continental Lounge, if you don't mind, and then we could take one car seeing how we are returning the same day. Do you mind waiting a couple of hours?" Butch added two teaspoons of sugar to his tea.

"Not at all, I will bring a good book. In many ways, I look forward to plane rides to have several uninterrupted hours of reading time. I just checked our schedules; I am afraid you will also have to wait an hour for my return flight on the other end. You should have a very interesting trip, and I am so looking forward to seeing Babs after all these years. Maybe one thing we could do is . . . ." Addie stopped and looked at Butch who was laughing.

They both finished her sentence in unison: "rent a house in Iceland and invite all of our children!" Addie always wanted to rent a house wherever they visited and invite the children.

Addie perused the paper. She liked reading book reviews. "Oh Gosh, here is a memoir about a woman who came from the Mid-West and went to college in Boston. If my memory serves me correctly, Babs's birthday is next week and she always loved biographies. I think I will send this to her for a surprise."

The doorbell rang. "Hmm, wonder who that is?" Addie got up and went to the front door. To her surprise, a man standing in a white shirt and grey pants was holding a Federal Express envelope. He was about five feet ten with brown receding hair. Adelaide noticed that he had carefully combed the hair from one side of his head to the other to cover up his bald spot. His left hand held the large white envelope.

She could see a blue and red tattoo peeking out from under the face of his watch. The design appeared to be a multi-pointed star. Adelaide was fascinated by tattoos and even more curious about why and where people got them. It was normal for her to conduct a quick, in-depth examination. However, she felt slightly uneasy with this man and decided minimal contact was important. She also noticed the smell of stale cigarettes on his breath.

She glanced quickly at his vehicle, which was not a Federal Express truck, but a black Chevy pickup truck.

"Do I need to sign for this?" Adelaide looked at the driver.

"No, that isn't necessary M'am, thank you." The driver had a decidedly Southern accent.

"What happened to your Federal Express truck?" She asked curiously.

"It has broken down, M'am. It is in the shop, but my boss felt it was better to make the delivery rather than wait until later today. The envelope is next day delivery." The driver was smiling, but his blue eyes were cold and piercing. Adelaide was an astute observer of people and she didn't like the looks of this guy. He wasn't their usual Federal Express delivery man.

"Well, making the delivery really is the most important thing. You were so correct about that. Thanks very much." Addie took the package and didn't bother to close the front door. It was warm out, and after breakfast she planned to water the new hanging plants she and Butch had just bought the other day. The delivery man hesitated briefly and looked through the screen door into the hallway of the house.

Addie walked back into the kitchen for her second cup of tea with Butch. She looked at the envelope that had just been delivered and her heart sank. "Oh god damn it. Here is another sample from Mr. Wacko. I thought I had gotten rid of him." She looked at the check for $250 and recognized the address on the upper left hand corner. There was a note written by Mr. J.P. Hunt with a request for an analysis of his brother's handwriting. Addie was frightened; this handwriting also showed a very disturbed individual.

She stood in front of Butch. "Oh my god, I just got another handwriting sample from that weird guy, sending me his brother's handwriting, which is just as disturbed as his. I almost think he wrote it himself and is just playing with me. I think I am going to mail the letter and check back and tell him that I feel his brother needs professional counseling, and it would not be fair to take his money." Addie plopped herself down in the chair and was looking upset.

"I think that's probably a good idea." Butch looked at the letter. "Yeah, that's the right decision. He is trying to form some type of relationship with you now. Good decision; end the communication."

Jake drove away chuckling to himself. She looks older than the picture on her website. Bitch. That is so typical of a woman, isn't it always? Hiding the truth, he took a long drag on his cigarette. The good news was that she didn't have a dog, and she lived at the end of a long, private driveway. He felt strangely triumphant. He had taken a flight last night from Memphis to Boston, rented a truck, and made the delivery. He couldn't help but think that he was one hell of a smart guy. She even smiled at him like there was nothing wrong. Nothing wrong at all, and no lousy barking Fido. He'd call into work saying he was sick today and spend the weekend in Boston, then take the plane back to Memphis on Sunday. The excitement of stalking was worth the price of the airfare.

Chapter Five

The Villain—Past and Present

Jake Proctor (born Lee Jacob Roberts) was in a manic mode and loving it. He felt rocket-fueled and dangerous, and the high from such boundless energy was intoxicating. *Better than booze,* he thought, which he hadn't touched since accumulated DWI's landed him for 30 days in the clink a few years back.

Soon after that fiasco, he left his third wife and moved out of state with a new identity; a feat made amazingly simple thanks to, what he liked to refer to as the graveyard gamble. All it took was a trip to a local cemetery where he looked at tombstones until he found one with all the credentials he had learned to look for during his brief research.

First of all, you choose someone who died in their early teens because they wouldn't yet have a driver's license or other tell-tale identification. The bonus for Lee-turned-Jake was he found someone with his given middle name; not that it was useful. But he liked the connection, and it helped him feel that he wasn't leaving his prior self *altogether* behind.

From there, it was as simple as using the name and date of birth of the deceased and requesting a copy of that person's birth certificate through the state's Department of Vital Statistics. This part of the process proved a little unnerving initially as he didn't know whether he'd have to provide additional identification to back up his request. Apparently that requirement remains curiously inconsistent state to state even today, and getting a birth certificate verifying he was Jake Proctor ended up being a piece of cake.

Once armed with the birth certificate, Jake easily obtained a driver's license and social security card . . . all he really needed to establish his new identity. He then spent a few weeks on the road deciding where he might like to settle, and Memphis, Tennessee came out the winner. The next step was to find work, and soon, since he was running low on funds. He'd been a freelance writer with a vacillating income and had never been too good with finances anyway.

New identity in hand, along with a supply of want ads, Jake ended up getting a job in Memphis with the U.S. Postal Service in their package division. Memphis was a major hub in the northeast corridor and if he kept his nose clean, job security would be a given.

As Jake acclimated to the work, he became increasingly bored but soon discovered ways to feed his need for challenge with selectively stealing packages. He especially watched for possible drug packages because they were his abuse of choice since he no longer drank. Pot was his favorite, always had been, because it worked best to calm the relentless demons.

On one particular day, a July scorcher, he was keeping cool in his modest air-conditioned apartment, gloating over his latest postal "find." He had no idea what was inside; it was the outside of the box that had him excited. He had no idea who the people were it was addressed to, either. That wasn't it. What riveted his attention was a return address still vaguely visible from the box's previous use. It read:

Babs Baker
228 Bayview Drive
Lakeside, PA 16505

He hadn't thought about her in years and was surprised she was still there. The last name was different, but the address was the same. Now he found himself thinking about her intently, and the old memories bubbled up. "What a fool that bitch made of me," he hissed.

Initially he had cared about her, but that caring turned to indifference and finally hate. He wasn't proud of how he retaliated, but he wasn't sorry either. In fact, he now enjoyed thinking about all the things he had done to make her suffer . . . and actually wished he had done more.

With nothing particular planned for the day, Jake fired up a joint and let his thoughts of Babs take flight. He imagined reappearing in her life and what fun it would be to strike terror in her "little miss sunshine" demeanor.

Hell, we're both in our 60's now, he thought, *but I bet she still has that same aggravating Pollyanna personality. What did I ever see in her anyway?* He knew what he saw in her; someone to use and manipulate, someone to feed his narcissism, an escape route from his boredom in other relationships and a new bridge to burn later.

When the high wore off, Jake was ravenous, but there was little to eat in the house. So he lit a cigarette then braved the 100 degree temperature outside for the five minute walk to the neighborhood deli. There he saw several familiar faces and nodded in recognition, hoping no one would strike up a conversation; he wasn't in the mood. He was still focused on Babs and didn't want his diabolical thoughts interrupted.

"Hey Jake," said a big moose of a guy as he came in the door and spied him sitting in a booth. "You alone? Mind if I sit with you?" He slid in across from Jake without waiting for an answer.

It was Stan Farrell, about the only person Jake didn't mind talking with if his thoughts of Babs had to be sidelined. Stan was really the only friend Jake had made since moving to Memphis. The rest were just acquaintances: other co-workers, his barber, people like that. And he liked it that way; especially since he wasn't really Jake Proctor at all. Only Stan knew about his past and true identity. He trusted Stan with that knowledge because Jake knew things about Stan that were also outside the law.

"Gee, don't look so glad to see me," quipped Stan.

"Hey, Stan, no offense. I've just got some stuff burnin' in the 'ole brain right now," Jake said, while nervously tapping his fingers on the table. The tapping was an unconscious habit he had and particularly annoying to Stan.

"OK, quit the tapping, and let's get Rosie over here to take our order."

Once they placed their order, the two men simultaneously leaned toward each other, and, in hushed tones, Stan told Jake briefly about his latest score. Stan worked at the Memphis hub as well but in a different section than Jake. His expertise was in "scoring the impossible" as he put it and reselling it as hot goods. This time it was a plasma TV.

"How the hell did you manage to cop something so big?" Jake asked in awe.

"If I told you, I'd have to kill you," Stan responded with a sly grin.

35

And then their food arrived. The deli was filling up with customers seated in close proximity. So, they limited the rest of their conversation to safer subjects like baseball, the current heat wave, and so on. Later, back in his apartment, unable to sleep, Jake's thoughts returned to Babs. He began counting her injustices during the two years they lived together just as someone less resentful might count sheep to get to sleep.

1. Hid my liquor or poured it out.
2. Often left me at the bar without a car.
3. Told my boss I was too hung over to come to work after I called in sick.
4. Refused to let me screw her if I was drinking.
5. Went ballistic when she found out I went to see an old girlfriend when I'd told her I was meeting a buddy to go hunting.
6. And the straw that broke the camel's back . . . . arranging an intervention to get me to stop drinking. Involving my family, my best friend, my boss.

They bought her bullshit until I set them straight. Then I got as far away from that bitch as I could. Already had someone else to keep me warm anyway.

That was years ago, but even with all the time gone by, Jake felt jarred into a renewed, fresh animosity toward Babs and was glad he was going to take action.

As he finally edged toward sleep, his thoughts drifted to his daughter, the one bright star in his life. They kept in touch. He longed to see his three grandchildren but realized that was unlikely while protecting his new identity. But Lauren sent pictures. He hadn't seen her for 10 years . . . just before she got married. They lived in Colorado. Any good in Jake was reflected in his love for Lauren, and he had been a good parent to her, his only child. Heck, Lauren, his mom, and sisters were the only women he ever really loved. The rest he basically came to hate for one reason or another.

Take Judy. At first, she made commuting a dream. Back when he was in the corporate world, he'd pick her up for work. On the way she'd perform discreet sexual favors in exchange for a good performance review. He was her boss after all. But things turned sour when she got a boyfriend and shifted her sexual allegiance.

Then there was Carolee. She was a travel agent and got them tickets everywhere at no cost to Jake. Traveling together was somewhat tricky since he was married at the time. But they managed. His wife always thought he was on long business trips. Until one time there was an emergency at home, and Carolee answered the phone in their room. That was the end of Carolee. How could she be so stupid and not think to say his wife had reached the wrong room?

The list went on. But in review, Babs surfaced as the worst.

The next day at work Jake was surprised by the volume of packages. It wasn't a holiday, but the pressure was on to keep things moving without any bottle necks. Like UPS and Fed Ex, timing was everything, and employees were evaluated on their ability to be fast and efficient. Jake excelled in this regard and was proud of his speed and accuracy. That's why he rarely heard from his supervisor. But on this day, he did.

While intently sorting, Jake felt a tap on his shoulder. It was Terry looking disgruntled.

"Jake, can you shut down your line for a minute? I need to talk to you," Terry said.

"Sure thing. What's up?" said Jake cheerfully while hiding the foreboding he suddenly felt. They went over to a nearby break area, away from the noise of the sorters, and sat down. Terry began, "We've been tracking a problem with un-received packages over the last several months, and they all seem to be in your section. So we're talking with everyone on each shift in the section to see figure out what's going on.

It's kind of like looking for a needle in a haystack, but we've got some irate customers who want answers, so I hope you can help."

"I will if I can," Jake graciously replied.

"Well, it's a little complicated, but here's what I need you to do," Terry added. He pulled out a checklist with dates, destinations, and other information about missing material that Jake was to match to his processing during the same time period.

"Can do," said Jake. "When do you want it back?"

"Well, if you can, work on it at home tonight and get it back to me tomorrow," Terry said.

"No problem," Jake replied.

Cunning mastermind that he was, Jake had covered his tracks well. He knew all missing packages were ones he had absconded, but he also knew how to manipulate the records to show the packages had actually gone to a different sorting area and were lost there. "Whew! Sorry Terry I'm afraid you'll be working on this for a long time. *Hope it doesn't cost you your job*", he chuckled to himself.

A week later while smoking a joint and wondering what to do for the day, Jake was startled by a loud knock at his apartment door. Who could it be? So few people even knew where he lived.

To his relief it was only his immediate neighbor Sonja wanting to know if his power had gone off like hers. (*Not bad*, he thought, as if seeing her for the first time; *in her 50's, shapely, nice smile.*) It had been a long time between women for Jake and he was admittedly aroused. But the price of involvement would be burdensome, and he was getting better at squelching any sexual desires. Mustering his self-control, Jake said "No, we've got power here, Sonja. Anything I can do for you?"

"No, I'm OK; I called the electric company and expect help anytime now. Thanks anyway."

"OK, if you have any more problems though, please let me know," offered Jake.

"I will, and thanks," responded Sonja as she turned around and walked away.

It was now late evening and Jake was ready to turn in. It had seemed to be an especially long day, more emotionally than physically. So many thoughts about the past, he couldn't wait to erase it all with a good night's sleep.

Chapter Six

Lakeside, Pennsylvania

The Bakers lived in Lakeside, a small town outside of Erie, Pennsylvania. Addie sat on the plane reading her guidebook and glanced at a map of the city. She continued to read and learned that the French founded the city in 1753. Interestingly enough, the ships used by Admiral Perry to defeat the English in the War of 1812 were built in Erie. Perry's flagship the *Niagara*, continues to be on exhibit. Addie was an insatiable history buff and thought she might be able to persuade Babs to visit the Maritime Museum. Erie's Importance as a major shipping port, rather than diminishing over time, increased in fact.

Addie lay back in her chair and glance at her watch; forty more minutes. *If I remember correctly, Babs's family came from Germany, in the mid 1800s to work in the shipping business. I think she wrote a paper about it. Her father had been a real estate tycoon and helped develop the area around Liberty Park. He was a sweet man,* thought Addie. *Seems to be, he became a painter in retirement; that family was very talented. Babs was always writing or painting something . . . . I hope I recognize her when I get off the airplane.*

The plane landed with a slight jolt. The passengers all clapped. In post 9/11 there is always a great feeling of relief to be on an airplane and have it land safely. Addie quickly refreshed her lipstick and looked out the window.

Disembarking went smoothly. The passengers filed out quickly. Before she knew it, she was in the terminal looking wildly around for Babs.

"Here I am!" called Babs. She looked just as Addie had remembered; blonde and trim with a generous welcoming smile. "Oh my gosh, I can't believe that we are actually doing this. It is so great to see you!" They gave each other big hugs. Addie knew instantly she had made the correct decision to come to Erie. After all, what is more important than friends and family?

They drove into town talking at once, jumping from one subject to the next, covering everything from books which had influenced them, children, religion, their mutual education, old classmates, the present, and their wonderful husbands for whom they were eternally grateful.

Babs drove down South Shore Drive. Addie was impressed with Lake Erie and its vastness. "I am so used to looking at the ocean, but this expansive stretch of water gives you the same feeling of endlessness. What a wonderful area. Do you do a lot of sailing?" Addie looked at Babs whose eyes were focused on the road.

"George loves to sail, and yes, to answer your questions directly, we do. Finishing our sailboat has taken a little longer than we expected. George is very handy and loves working on making the boat—just right—if you get my drift." They gave each other knowing glances and chuckled.

Babs took a right onto Lincoln and a left on Bayview Avenue. The Bakers house was near the corner and had a view of Lake Erie and Ferncliff Beach. The interior of the Baker's house had an open floor plan with lots of glass to take advantage of the view. Over the fireplace in the living room, was a beautiful watercolor of a tropical flower. Addie looked immediately at the painting. "Oh Babs, I bet your father painted that. You sent me a Christmas card with that image about five years ago." Addie had majored in Art History and quickly assessed people's pictures first when she entered someone's house.

"You are so right, thanks for remembering." Babs went over to the stove and turned on the kettle. "George will be home in about half an hour, would you like a cup of tea?"

"Absolutely, I am a tea addict and haven't had a cup of coffee for twenty years. I can't wait to meet George. I am so happy that we have both found two such good men at this chapter in our lives. You were single for quite a long time too, weren't you? It is hard to be a single parent, but worse for children to have a household where everyone is fighting all the time." Addie sat at the kitchen table, wound the tea bag around her spoon tightly, and then removed it. She took a deep breath and inhaled the steam. "Hmmm, this is good tea."

"There is a great little shop connected with the Erie Art Museum that carries specialty teas and I couldn't resist splurging." Babs hauled out a cookie jar and offered Addie a chocolate macaroon she had made herself.

"This recipe came from my great-great-grandmother who came to Erie in 1835 from a small town outside of Munich called Diessen am Ammersee. It was rumored that her father owned a bakery and she ran away from home because her father did not approve of her boyfriend. The star struck couple eloped and fled to Erie, where my great-great Grandfather had a job in the shipbuilding industry. My great-great-grandfather did very well for himself, and later, my great-great-grandmother reconnected with her father who found it hard to admit he had made a mistake, but soon came to love his grandchildren. Gosh, there are a lot of greats in there." Babs laughed the way Adelaide always remembered her laughing in college.

"I am fascinated by family cultures. Most families have memories associated with food even if it is Twinkies." Adelaide chimed in.

"What do you think you'd like to do while you are here? I figure we can sail and do the beach thing for a couple of days. There is a music festival at Presque Isle on Sunday all day long which might be fun. If it rains, we could visit either the Maritime Museum or the Erie Art Museum. There really are quite a few options. There is a special exhibit at the Erie Art Museum of someone named George Ohr who was called the mad potter of Biloxi." Babs was looking at the paper.

"My god, George Ohr? I would really like to see his things. I read an article about him not too long ago. He was very eccentric and gave up creating ceramics in 1908, after thirty years. He misguidedly felt that the Smithsonian would recognize his collection and buy the entire body of work. Sadly, he died without recognition. Then, in the late 1960's, an antique dealer rediscovered his pottery and other people interested in ceramic art have became very enthusiastic about Ohr. So yes, at first I thought I might like to go to the Maritime Museum, but I will leave that for a time when Butch comes to Erie with me. If it is ok with you I would like to go to the Erie Art Museum. But Gosh, I just like being with you. We have so much to catch up on." Addie laughed and smiled at Babs.

"Oh, I hear a car. George will bring in our new Labrador puppy, so be prepared. His name is Sam and he has a tendency to jump up. George likes to take him down to the boatyard to keep him company when he is working on sanding the bottom of our boat. We will take you out for dinner tonight. So, we were going to have Sam get as much exercise as possible. You and I might take him for a little walk later if you're up for it."

Addie leapt at the chance. She loved to walk any place and also enjoyed getting a feel for a city at ground level. George entered the room, with a puppy barking loudly.

Babs gave George a big kiss. "Here is the love of my life, my dear husband George. Sam now settle down, settle down, good doggie." George was a large, good-looking man with receding hair and a kind face. He extended a big hand towards Addie who smiled in return. Addie's first reaction, *he must have played football in high school.* She instantly liked him. Having met Babs's first husband, she knew Babs had made an excellent second choice.

"I am just delighted to meet you George. I feel as if I already know you from the e-mails Babs has sent me about your combined activities."

George smiled and said "Oh gosh, don't believe everything Babs tells you!"

Addie bent over and petted Sam. "You are a good watchdog, aren't you boy? Yes, you are. Good boy."

"I'd like to take you two ladies out for dinner tonight. I am going to have to go to a Yacht Club meeting tomorrow night and I thought you two gals could really catch up. There is a good restaurant in Lakeside we reserve for special occasions called the Colony Pub and Grill. You can get one of our Lake Erie fish, or a great steak." George was smiling.

"Oh honey, that is so nice of you. We would love to do that. Any excuse to go to The Colony Pub and Grill is a good one in my book. That would be really fun, and then tomorrow night we could go to a movie or just schmooze around here depending on what you would like to do." Babs looked at Addie.

"I would enjoy just spending time talking to you and having a quiet meal at home. After all, we have decades to catch up on." Addie laughed.

"How did Sam behave at the boat yard?" Babs asked George.

"He did pretty well for a puppy. His favorite trick is picking up my hammer and running away with it. Eventually, he will be well trained, but now he has all of the super puppy instincts."

Babs and Addie had another cup of tea and exchanged pleasantries with George. He had served in Vietnam under General Tilson. Addie was curious about his experience but reserved her questions until she felt she knew him better. So many Vets of her generation disliked discussing their time there. They all lost college friends during that painful era. Clearly,

George had a good sense of humor, and Adelaide could see by the way that Babs looked at him that she adored him.

At four o'clock in the afternoon, Babs and Addie took Sam to Liberty Park for some exercise. Addie asked Babs if George liked to talk about his experience in Vietnam. From the look Babs gave her, Addie instantly knew she had made the correct decision not to ask George any questions about that period of his life.

"Vietnam was a terrible time in our history. It is very difficult for George to talk about it and I have just learned to respect that. He lost one of his best friends, Harry Shadwell, going up a ridge. I actually dated Harry before I dated George. He was so good looking; graduated from West Point with full honors. We were really just good friends, but that brought the war home to me. Such a waste and now we are going through it with Iraq." Babs had Sam on the leash as they walked swiftly around the Park.

"Oh, it is so painful to think of all those boys and their families." Addie took a deep breath. "The one thing about our generation, however, is we were activists. Students were very involved with the issue of fairness in race, as well as the war." The two spent the next hour chatting and walking through the trails of the eight acre park.

"Addie, tomorrow night when we are schmoozing around the house, I'd like to show you some handwriting samples. There are a couple of people I am curious about. How on earth did you ever get interested in that?" Sam started eating some unidentifiable piece of brown block. "Sam, stop that!" Babs gave a yank to the leash.

"When I was married to John, he decided to start his own import/ export business with Africa. So, we came back from Liberia to live in Connecticut. Our children were young, and I had no skills to get back into the market place. So . . . I decided I could be helpful to John by reading periodicals about that continent. There was an interesting article in one of the trade publications about a firm who always used a handwriting analyst when hiring personnel.

Years later, after I was divorced, I had the opportunity to manage a very small manufacturing company. It was obvious to me some people are intrinsically better at their jobs than others. I learned a lot.

After that experience, I got my certification as a handwriting analyst which took about two years. Handwriting analysts consider handwriting analysis to be like looking into someone's brain. You can track about 100 different traits. The combination of traits in each individual is also unique. In addition, best of all, there is no difference between male and female handwriting which is why it is such a good employment tool. During the Bush, Perot, and Clinton presidential campaigns, I had a lot of fun analyzing their handwritings on television. George Bush, Sr. is reported to have used handwriting analysis to learn more about Saddam Hussein."

It was about 7:30 by the time George, Babs and Addie got to the Colony Pub and Grill. The wine flowed and they laughed about silly things they had done in college remembering parties, stressful nights when papers were due, the first time they saw the Beatles on television, and the day J.F.K. was shot. Addie often wondered when she met an old college or school friend how much of her personality had adapted to the attended learning institutions. The sixties were formative years, not only for Babs and Addie, but also for America.

The next day they went sailing on Lake Erie. The sky was blue, and once again Addie was impressed with the enormity of the lake. George was a good sailor. Every Monday evening he and Babs participated in an evening race and brought a picnic to share with other members of their Yacht Club.

Addie was glad to stay in that night and have a simple dinner with Babs. After a delicious supper of walleye with mango salsa, freshly sliced native tomatoes, and green beans, they sat on the porch overlooking the lake.

"All right, I have collected about ten handwritings I want you to see," Babs handed Addie a large folder. "This is a guy I met at a conference named Lee Roberts. I think you were living overseas by then, so you probably never met him. He was so weird; like, totally, scary weird." Babs shook her shoulders all over when she mentioned his name. "The thing was, he wasn't that bad looking."

Addie took the letter in her hand. She remained silent. Her face lost its color. She took a deep breathe and looked at Babs. "Oh my god, when did you get this? What is the date? 1968 . . ." Adelaide looked stricken. "Babs, my business is very confidential, but recently, I got a sample of handwriting from a person I felt was very disturbed. I am almost sure this is the same handwriting, but I'd like to make a copy of it, if I may, and check it more carefully with my sample of handwriting at home. Oh my gosh, this is so unsettling."

Babs sat straight up, "You've got to be joking. Oh my god, do you think Lee would know we are in contact? How odd would that be?"

At first, I was attracted to him by his southern accent. We actually met at a conference in Denver. He followed me around the entire time. I was very flattered by all of his attention. I think he came from some small town in North Carolina. Now, it's coming back to me. He was the oldest of four children. His mother died when he was fifteen and he had to help a lot with his younger siblings.

We began keeping in touch with each other and eventually he got a job in the same town where I was living. Overtime we began living together and he became increasingly possessive. If I went out with some girlfriends he would want to know where I was going. Sometimes, he would show up at the same restaurant as if he was spying on me. It began to drive me crazy." Babs petted Sam nervously who looked as if he wanted to get up on the sofa. "No you may not get up here, no matter how scared Mummy is!"

Addie kept looking at the letter. "Perhaps it is some weird coincidence. The postmark on the letter was from Memphis, Tennessee. Oh Christ, maybe I am wrong. I will know definitely, when I get home, but usually, I am not wrong. Lee was definitely not the name he used. The name on my letter was Jake." Addie looked at Babs and took a big sip from her wine glass.

"Jake—my god, I am pretty sure that was his middle name. The only reason I know is my older sister had just had a baby when I was dating Lee. Somehow we got onto this big discussion about names and the reaction one has to a name. For example, if I say 'Sophie,' I think of someone fat. Not that I ever met a 'Sophie,' the name just sounds fat to me." Babs began to laugh hysterically.

"Gotcha. How about Gertrude? I loved that name when I was little; talk about weird! My daughter came home from school when she was in the first grade and had written 'Forsythia' on the back of her notebook! She thought Forsythia was a beautiful name." Addie was giggling.

"Well, do you think this guy is dangerous?' Babs looked intently at Addie.

Addie's expression changed once again. Her face became serious. "Yeah, I'm afraid he could be dangerous. He is very dominating. The domination goes beyond wanting to be in control; his will must prevail. He is also very detail oriented and acquisitive. This could be about things as well as people. I wonder if he has done any drugs.

"I do have a website, and I assumed that he probably found my name there. I seriously thought of sending back his letter, which was so filled with vile and inappropriate language, but then, I thought my analysis might help him. Also, as an analyst, we always tell people the content of a letter is unimportant to us. He has a 'my way or the highway' attitude, and frankly, I was frightened that he would come after me if I didn't perform the analysis. After I finished the first analysis, he sent me another sample of handwriting saying it was from his brother. My feeling was that he wanted to begin a dialogue. The second sample also had terrible vulgar language. So, I returned the letter and the check stating that his brother needed professional psychological help I was incapable of giving.

"This must be a coincidence. Certainly, there would be no reason for him to come after us. My imagination can really run wild in a situation like this. So, it is smart to try to get a grip!" Once again, Addie took a deep breath.

"When was the last time you saw Lee? Have you had any contact with him since the late sixties?" Addie sat back in her chair and took off her glasses.

"No, I haven't seen him for years. For some reason, I just kept this one letter, probably more by accident than design. Plus, the handwriting seemed so unique." Babs shook her head. "God, I practically feel afraid to take Sam out for his walk which by the way, might not be such a bad idea." Sam was beginning to pace around the room and look restless.

"Oh gosh, it would be great to get a little exercise after that delectable meal. This is a marvelous walking city." Addie stood up and stretched. "I think it would be a good idea for you to tell George about this guy. Butch will think I am anxiously over reacting, but maybe it would be prudent to be on alert. For what, I am not quite sure." Addie laughed. "Give me another glass of wine, and I will escalate this situation escalated enough to have us both on the bottom of Lake Eire by morning!"

Babs grabbed Sam's leash as they walked out the door. "Oh, I am exactly the same way. It must be a coincidence. But, I will tell you, it is so scary to look on the Internet, and plug in a name. You get loads of information about someone. After all, that is how I found you."

Addie asked, "How did you finally get Lee to leave you alone?" Babs sighed. "Oh God, it was terrible. I noticed that he began drinking heavily. The more he drank, the more possessive and domineering he became. Finally, and I don't even know how I had the courage to do this, I got a hold of his boss and we did an intervention. He was furious with me after he got out of rehab. He moved out and never forgave me."

Addie followed Babs out the door. It was a lovely summer's night. The moon was full. Its reflection danced on Lake Erie as the girls chatted away and Sam had his walk.

The next day, they visited the Erie Art Museum and saw the George Ohr exhibit. Addie was even more impressed with Ohr's work than she had expected to be. Ohr was famous for throwing pots on a wheel and then distorting them. Addie couldn't get over the thinness of the walls on the vases. With the exception of the gunmetal glazes, the colors were clear and flowing with depth.

She was anxious now to get back to Massachusetts and look at the other handwriting sample from Mr. Hunt. She also missed Butch and wanted to hear about his vacation in Iceland. Addie promised to let Babs know if the handwriting sample from Lee was the same as the one she had received from the man in Memphis . . . .

Chapter Seven

Identities Collide and Babs has a Dream

Addie hadn't been home from Lakeside more than a day when she called Babs to breathlessly report that Jake and Lee indeed appeared to be one and the same based on the handwriting samples. This news rendered Babs momentarily speechless; then suddenly they both blurted out:

"*Now* what to do?"

"Frankly, I'm not sure what to think or do," Addie said. "I'm in a quandary. What about you?"

"Wow, I frankly find the whole thing overwhelming and quite scary," Babs answered. Then, after a brief pause, she said, "Can you get a second opinion from another handwriting expert?"

"Yes definitely," said Babs. "I don't want to get paranoid about any of this, and I especially don't want to bring George into the loop if I don't have to. He's a huge worrier as it is, and learning about a kook from my past who is possibly on my trail would be too much for him to handle. In a lighter vein, she added, "He'd probably put bars on our windows, follow me wherever I went, and trade our sweet Sam in for an attack dog!"

Addie laughed and said, "Yes, I saw how protective he is of you when I was there. He obviously loves you very much"

Just then their conversation was interrupted by Babs' doorbell. "Hey Addie, sorry I'm going to have to cut this short. The little neighbor girl is here to walk Sam, and I've got to talk to her before they head out."

"No problem. Just stay in touch, and I'll do the same. And thanks again for such a wonderful time. I thought our visit was over the top!"

"Me too. Take care, Addie. Talk to you soon."

And they hung up. Each of them relieved, but with a little voice in their head asking *think maybe you better watch out?*

A week later, Babs had all but forgotten about the handwriting and was happily absorbed in preparations for her son and his family's end of summer visit. They'd be arriving in a week for seven days. This time, they would have their own apartment at a nearby lodge instead of cramming into the small Baker house. Babs felt this was a wise decision considering George had not reared any children and was less than tolerant of the "me-mine" world of toddlers. Last year, when they did stay at the house, the twins had just learned how to escape their cribs resulting in nightly chaos beyond George's endurance. Yes, she knew, the lodge will be a blessing,

In addition to getting ready for the kids, Babs had a lot of loose ends to take care of in her volunteer work. Unbeknownst to George, she recently said yes to yet another project for the hospital. Client Services recruited her to visit the medical center pretending to be lost and keep track of whether staff offered her assistance, how cordial they were, etc. She needed to finish these "rounds" and have a report to them by the end of August. Also, she had taken on editing the hospital volunteer newsletter following the untimely death of its prior editor.

These involvements gave her great satisfaction, but the pressure of getting them accomplished was beginning to prove a bit disconcerting. Just today when she went to the bank drive-thru to deposit her weekly "nanny" pay, she became impatient when the teller took forever to send the tube back with her receipt. "Good Lord," she thought, "what could the delay be? There's no one here but me."

Finally, she pressed the help button, and when the teller reappeared, Babs politely asked if there was a problem with her deposit. The teller looked puzzled then said she had sent the receipt out. Babs looked around her car and, sure enough, there it was right on the passenger seat where she had put it after apparently returning the tube to the chute and sending it back . . . But she had no recollection *whatsoever* of doing so! "Pretty scary," she said out loud as she drove away.

She wouldn't tell George about the bank because he'd just say in his I'm-five-years-younger-than-you-are tone of voice, "You know, I'm starting to worry about you." This time she might have to agree with him. But she wouldn't hesitate to tell her female friends, sure that at least one of them would say, "been there, done that!"

While Babs had concerns about her forays with forgetfulness, she was buoyed by other signs her intelligence was intact. Her most recent epiphany occurred while she was using Play Doh with her little charges. The containers were nearly impossible for anyone to open without an uncomfortable struggle and, once opened, it was a maddening challenge to remove the contents. Too thick to force out by whacking the container on a hard surface, too compacted to just pull out in a single clump by hand, so the only way was to dig it out bit by bit with your fingers. And the fingernails on those fingers would now be imbedded with whatever color you were removing.

"Aha," she suddenly thought, "Why not package the Play Doh in push up containers like the kind used for ice cream novelties?" This innovative idea pleased her immensely and she wondered who to tell or where it might lead. She wasn't sure, however how to solve the problem of the Play Doh lids. But she'd put her busy mind to work on that challenge another time.

Babs' family came and went. It was a perfect week together, especially the weather which enabled the twins to enjoy the beach every day, and the boy Max learned how to swim. The lodge apartment worked out beautifully as well, and all agreed it was the best vacation they'd ever shared.

On the heels of their departure, Babs realized she still hadn't heard from Addie: not even an e-mail. She assumed that meant there was nothing new to report about the handwriting, but she missed being in touch. After a couple of days, she brewed a cup of mid afternoon tea, plopped herself down on the sunny back deck, and called her.

"Addie, hi. It's me, Babs. Is this a good time? I've missed you!," she said, the words tumbling out of her mouth.

"This is amazing, believe it or not, I was just going to call you, Babs," Addie said. "And this is a fine time. Butch is out fishing, and I'm just putting the finishing touches on a column I write for the Manaport Weekly."

"No kidding? How'd you neglect to tell me that before? I'm impressed!" said Babs.

"Well, we have had so much else to chatter about, I guess I just forgot," Addie replied.

Babs cut to the chase. "Addie, Did you ever get the second opinion on that Jake guy's handwriting, and have you *heard* anything from him?"

"Yes and no. I mean yes," said Addie. "I got the second opinion and that's why I was just about to call you, and no, not a word from Jake. But back to the yes, the expert I contacted agreed completely that both samples were written by the same person."

"Oh dear, that is really unsettling to hear although I half expected it," Babs commented, the fear in her voice palpable. "If Lee is now Jake, he's obviously changed his name, and people don't usually do that unless they have something to hide or have done something wrong . . . . Do they?," she meekly asked.

Addie agreed but decided to make light of it by saying, "Can we change the subject for now? I'd much rather talk about the fact that Butch and I will soon be leaving for our annual trip to Scotland. Plus, I want to hear about your family's visit."

"Good idea," Babs agreed, and the two stayed on the phone for nearly an hour talking about everything: from Bab's family, to the horrors of global warming, and the war in Iraq.

"Hey, have a wonderful trip." Babs said as they were hanging up. "Oops, one more thing though, did the package to your daughter-in-law that was lost in the mail ever resurface?"

"Nope," confirmed Addie, "and I have an uneasy feeling that its disappearance is somehow tied in with Jake. Isn't that weird?"

Babs awoke suddenly in the middle of the night terrified and trembling. She knew she had been dreaming but at the same time felt the dream was real. Not wanting to wake George, and have to talk about it, she slid quietly out of her side of the bed and went into their little office to calm down and review her dream.

In my dream, I was at a volunteer recognition dinner at a conference center complex just off the interstate about 10 miles south of Lakeside. A small group of us decided to linger for an after dinner drink in the bar. It was pretty crowded, and our drink order took a while. When we were paying the bill to leave, our server took everyone's money but mine saying that my drink had been paid for by a man who just left and did not want to be identified.

Out in the parking lot I began to feel very uneasy about the anonymous drink buyer. It was a pitch black, moonless night and quite late to be driving home alone. As I got on the interstate, I made sure I was locked in and then turned on the all night oldies station.

I noticed there was very little traffic and so was startled when, a few miles down the road, a car came seemingly out of nowhere and pulled up very close behind me. I had no choice but to speed up. And when I did, the other car sped up as well getting even closer. I couldn't see through my rearview mirror into the car well enough to tell if the driver was a man, a woman, or if there was anyone else in the car. I became very frightened, especially since I was several miles from an exit where I could get off.

While I was contemplating crossing the median and going the other direction to make my getaway, the car was suddenly along side me matching and holding my speed so that we were parallel. I dared to look over and could vaguely tell that the driver was probably was a male and alone. I then sped up, and so did he. Then he passed me and cut in front of me so sharply I had to apply my brakes to avoid hitting him. Then he sped up, and I slowed down. Then he'd slow down. I changed lanes; he changed lanes. It was absolutely terrifying, but I held hope that I could escape him once I could get off on an exit. And, thankfully, one was coming up soon.

Unfortunately, he anticipated my plan because he started to pass me on the right just as I was trying to exit to the right. We nearly wrecked. I knew there wasn't another exit for 5 miles. So I got my guts up, crossed the median, and headed back to the previous exit as fast as I dared. I didn't see him coming after me and prayed he had given up.

Getting off the exit, I realized he was following me but had turned his headlights off. I had to think fast as there was no place open where I could go for help, and the area we were going through was mostly residential. I remembered an apartment complex coming up and turned in there, pulled up to the first set of buildings and just laid on my horn. The noise was deafening but absolutely nobody stirred. I kept honking the horn . . . nothing. By then the man pursuing me blocked me in so I had no way to leave. And then he got out of his car, slowly approached the driver's side of my car, and motioned me to roll down my window. I still couldn't see his face because now he had a wide brimmed hat pulled way down. But I could see his mouth, and I thought his gait was somewhat familiar.

When I wouldn't roll down my window, he went to his car and brought back one of those things AAA uses to unlock cars. I tried to stop him by grabbing the tool but ended up cutting my hand and was by then so petrified I literally couldn't move.

Finally, I heard a click from the right rear door and it swung open. I stared straight ahead, too afraid to look. Next, I felt his hot breath on my neck, and he said in a Southern draw,l husky whisper, "Why were you trying to get away from me, Babs? I was only trying to help you get home. I was worried about you . . . a pretty girl like you all by herself on the road late at night. You never know what evil lurks . . . ."

It was Lee Roberts. And then I woke up.

Babs knew she had to get a grip. The dream about Lee had knocked her for a loop. Now she found herself more distracted and forgetful than ever. It would help if she could tell Addie about her dream, but she wouldn't be back from Scotland for at least another week. George noticed how distracted Babs was much of the time lately but chalked it up to her having so many balls in the air all the time.

He'd told Babs many times he's thankful they don't have a lot of money. Because if they did, she'd be in some third world country like Oprah opening a school, or putting up funds to save the "ruff piffled" titmouse from extinction. "Oh George," she'd respond affectionately, "you are so funny sometimes."

Chapter Eight

Driven Shoots in the Boarders

It was early morning, after an all night flight, when Addie and Butch landed in Edinburgh, the capital and cultural center of Scotland. The Stubbs were particularly fond of this ancient city with its Medieval Castle which sits on a basalt rock in the old city and they had visited several times. The stone architecture, with a wide variety of styles spanning five hundred years, gives one a feeling of enormous stability. Everywhere there is a thread of intricate Celtic designs.

The taxi driver was chatty and told them about a school friend who had moved to Boston and opened up a successful bar. The Stubbs promised to look him up if they were ever near by. Addie looked out the window to catch glimpses of Scots buying their newspapers and briskly walking to work.

Their room at the Caledonia was ready upon their arrival. Constructed in 1903, the beautiful old hotel had once been the flagship lodging for the Caledonian Railway. The downstairs ballroom had previously been the station where the trains pulled in. The Stubbs chose the Caledonia for its superb location on Prince Street, opposite St. John's Church, within view of Edinburgh castle. The hotel had undergone massive renovations in 2005 and the Stubbs were delighted with their room on the second floor not too far from the dining room.

They slept for several hours to help adjust to the time change. Around noon, they rose and went for a stroll around the Queen Street area occasionally poking in shops filled with Tartans and hunting gear. Eventually they found a suitable looking pub for lunch. The Hair and Hearty Pub was located below street level with a dark interior and central bar. A group of men sat on bar stools discussing a rugby match.

Addie ordered a cider and Butch a Tennant, one of Scotland's good local beers. She then ordered a ploughman's lunch with homemade bread and a selection of cheeses. Usually she tried to keep her consumption of calorific cheese to a minimum but this week was a total holiday from every day disciplines. Butch had a plate of bangers and mash. They chatted away enjoying each other's company and observing the other patrons and their surroundings. Dusty pictures of medieval figures covered the walls along with several swords.

After lunch, they wandered back to the hotel for a nap allowing more time adjustment for their body clocks. The Stubbs, being inveterate travelers, that taking slow steps into a new time zone on day one of arrival made a huge difference in the rest of one's stay.

Scotland gets dark in January by four in the afternoon. Around seven in the evening Addie and Butch walked through the Grass Market and up Victoria Street, to a restaurant they had visited several years previously, called Howies. The restaurant had several small rooms. The menu had a moderate selection of tempting recipes boasting "Modern Scottish Cuisine."

"I am so delighted to be away from work and get a little break," Addie sipped water and looked at Butch who was studying his menu intently. "I have to confess, the handwriting of that wacko guy really put me into a dither. One's imagination can go wild. Then having Babs freaked out amplified my own feelings."

"You two girls are probably overreacting but I am glad to have this time in Scotland. It is so special to come on these driven shoots. The time will come when we're too old to participate. We have also made good friends in this area of the world we enjoy seeing."

"Hmm, have you decided what you are going to eat? Everything looks very good. I am having a hard time deciding. Let's choose different dishes so we can share."

Butch took off his glasses for a few moments. "The first decision, of utmost importance, is whether to have white or red wine."

A pretty young waitress, wearing a black scoop neck jersey with black pants and a long white apron, arrived at the table. "May I start ye off with a cocktail or some wine?" She said with a strong Scottish accent.

"What do you think, honey, white or red?" Butch looked again at Addie.

"I think I will have the salmon, so I vote for white, but I am happy doing either." She smiled back at him.

"There is a nice Lapostolle which we drink at home. Yes, we'll have this Chilean wine please." Butch looked again at the menu and declared, "Perfect. I will have the pheasant with bacon which will go nicely with the white wine." He handed the wine list to the server. When she was out of hearing range, he looked over at Addie, "Did I ever tell ya, I love ya!" He tried to imitate a Scottish accent and then roared with laughter.

They had a lovely evening of chatting and good food. Butch began with haggis stuffed into an egg roll and Addie sampled the tomato soup; they swapped samples of each other's dishes. Eating was a major pass time for the Stubbs, and the ritual of tasting and savoring each mouthful, resulted in major discussions about the seasonings and quality of the dish.

For the main course Butch had the pheasant with bacon. Giving Addie a sample, they both decided the pheasant dish she cooked at home was moister. However, Addie's main course of salmon encrusted in puff pastry, with leeks and snow peas, was outstanding in flavor and presentation. They shared a rocket salad with parmesan and laughed about the first time they were confused by rocket salad on a menu in London. With curiosity they ordered the dish only to find that in Great Britain "rocket" is synonymous with "arugula."

After dinner they wandered down the street to the Grass Market. The area had been a market for several centuries and was first mentioned in 1477 historical documents. The sight had also seen its share of executions in the seventeenth century; it seemed hard to believe with people meandering happily on Saturday night.

It was began to rain slightly, but not so hard that walking was uncomfortable. Addie liked a bit of moisture in the air, which made her naturally wavy hair curl more. Butch and Addie stepped over a wide variety of patterned cobblestones imagining all the events of the past centuries.

They stopped at the White Hart Inn on the south side of the square. The pub was alive with patrons of all ages. Many women wore tight dungarees and punk hairstyles, tattoos showing on random parts of their bodies. There was dark paneling on the walls with a bar to the left of the entrance. As the room opened, there was a fireplace shallow in design but five feet in height. Like most bars around the world on a Saturday night, there was the usual mutton-dressed-as-lamb and old men looking as if they were growing psychologically younger with each drink.

Addie and Butch found a small table in the corner. Butch ordered a Tennant and Addie ordered a Glenlivet on ice that she intended to nurse for the remainder of the evening. The pub was crowded, and before long they found themselves sharing a table with two young army officers who had just returned from Iraq.

One officer asked Butch "You know the great Scottish poet Robert Burns?" Butch smiled and nodded his head in recognition. "He used to come to this pub in 1791 and wrote one of his most famous poems sitting right here: 'Ae Fond Kiss.' If you like, I can recite it for you." Addie and Butch were enthralled. Before long, he had half the bar listening to him recite Robert Burns's poetry.

His name was Derek and he was born in Ireland. He promised the Stubbs he'd introduce them to his family in Dublin. The other young man had just been assigned a post working at Edinburgh Castle. Sadly, the Stubbs were leaving early the next morning to drive to Selkirk and could not take advantage of his offer to give them a private tour.

Around ten some local musicians arrived and the music began. There were traditional Scottish ballads as well as some familiar American pop music. It was after midnight when the Stubbs returned to the Caledonia.

The next morning, at eleven, the car and driver picked them up from the Caledonia. They drove southeast from Edinburgh into the countryside of Scotland known as the Boarders. The driver took them through the town of Galashields to an estate outside of Selkirk. As they neared Selkirk, the pastures grew in size and the terrain gave way to round, swollen hills that were still green despite the month of January.

"We have had a lot of rain this year but it hasn't been very cold up 'til now," said the driver. "How about you in Boston?"

Butch agreed, "We also have had a very mild winter. But in New England they always say, 'If you don't like the weather, don't worry, it will change in a bit.'"

"Eye," said the driver. "Our weather changes quickly here toooo." Before long they entered their friends' estate: Scotsmuir.

There were two other couples plus their hosts waiting for their entrance. Everyone arrived, within several hours of each other, in time for dinner. Robert and Carolyn Hyde-Smith, whose family had lived at Scotsmuir since 1439, were gracious hosts.

Butch had met Robert at the Wellfleet Graduate School during the late sixties. Robert's family owned a coal company and Butch had inherited an explosives manufacturing firm. When the two men discovered they shared a loved of hunting they became instant friends.

Carolyn answered the door with open arms. "We are so delighted to have you. Come in, please." She and Addie embraced.

"We are so happy to be here. Has everyone else arrived?" The Stubbs were familiar with the two other couples who were joining the shooting party. One English couple, Nigel and Amanda Winslow, were from the south of England. They always brought their well behaved Labrador retriever named Sadie. The third couple, Jane and John O'Reilly, lived in a town next to Manaport outside of Boston. Robert rushed into the hallway to greet them.

"Well this is a grand occasion to slaughter a calf and bring out the best wine. Come in. I hope your travels were as easy as could be expected. We are putting you in The Steadings. Dinner will be at seven. We have several other guests joining us. Do you want the driver to take you over?" Robert asked?

Butch responded, "That's probably the best idea. That way, we can get unpacked, clean up a bit, and then return for dinner."

"Carolyn, can I be of any help to you for dinner?" asked Addie.

"No thank you, we are quite organized, just go and get settled and be back a few minutes before seven. We have planned a light dinner for tonight, nothing fancy."

The driver drove them past the main house, through two large stone farm buildings, into a courtyard with a circle of planted grass surrounded by crushed stone. Buildings surrounded the courtyard creating an enclosed atmosphere. On the east side of the court yard was a small rental occupied by a pensioner next to a two story two bedroom apartment with: a fireplace, full bath, dining room, living room and kitchen called, "the Steadings." Butch and Addie had stayed there before and were delighted to room there again. On the south side of the courtyard, also connected to the Steadings, and constructed of stone, were offices for Robert and the farm manager. The side of a large substantial barn for farm machinery comprised the west wall.

Addie and Butch unpacked. They hung up their evening wear and flipped on the television.

"I like listening to the BBC to find out what's going on in the world from a U.K. perspective. Tony Blair is somewhat like George W. Bush with respect to the fact people do not always seem to like him much, but he keeps being re-elected. It has been my experience that the friends we have here are always well informed about politics in America. So, we better quickly bone up on hot topics in the British Isles," Addie said to Butch as she placed her sweaters in the third drawer.

"Good thinking, sweetheart, Fifteen minutes of world news will certainly make us experts on current local events. We'll be able to dazzle them for sure!" Butch roared with laughter, as did Addie. She loved his sense of humor which always had a strong grain of truth to it.

An imposing looking person in a pin stripe suit, blue shirt and red tie, sitting behind a desk began with the lead story, "Tomorrow Scotland will celebrate its three hundredth anniversary of the signing of the treaty with England. The local National Scottish Party is thinking of proposing legislation which would reverse the treaty. Now we will switch to our reporter on the street to interview some of the local Scots to get their reaction." The television screen changed to a pretty young girl with a microphone wearing a bright yellow wool overcoat.

She approached an older gentleman who was walking by.

"Excuse me, sir? What do you think of the Scottish National Party's proposal to break with England?" She held the microphone close to him.

"Oh, I think it's a grand ideeeeeeeah. What did the English everrr due for us but plunder and pillage? Needless to say, I can't use the R word on television, but the English did that some to our women as well." He smiled directly into the camera. Addie and Butch roared with laughter.

"Can you believe after three hundred years they are still talking about the same thing? Wouldn't you think they would leave it alone?" Butch was stunned. Glancing at the clock he suggested, "Why don't you take the bath first because you take longer to get tarted up a bit."

"I wouldn't argue with that statement." Addie grabbed her toilet kit and headed into the bathroom.

All of the house guests were standing in the living room when the Stubbs arrived for dinner. It was a large room, with two sofas facing each other, and a long covered stool in between them. There was a beautiful fireplace with a sitting chair rail, and a magnificent oil painting of the Scottish landscape hanging over the mantel.

Robert was very good at keeping people organized and informed. His instructions were always precise and delivered with an authoritative voice.

"Our other dinner guests this evening are Pamela and Michael Spoonsmore. Some of you have met them before. They are bringing a guest, whom I have never met, who is apparently a crack shot from the Los Angeles Police Department SWAT team. Michael met him in Arizona when he was taking shooting lessons. It should be an interesting evening."

The other American couple, Jane and John O'Reilly, had come to Scotsmuir for the first time but the Stubbs had met the Spoonsmores in previous years.

"Oh gosh, they are a lovely couple, we will be happy to see them again. If this guy is on the LAPD SWAT team he must be a terrific shot. The only difference of course is that he will be shooting pheasant instead of people," Addie piped up.

"My dear wife often has a subtle way of describing things," Butch explained.

Nigel and Amanda had visited Scotsmuir many times and were very helpful guests. Nigel leapt into the host's position of playing bartender and often took charge fixing everyone a drink before dinner and serving the wine during the meal. The Hyde-Smiths were very relaxed hosts and all the guests chipped in to help in their large L-shaped kitchen. Carolyn took advantage of one of the local caterers named Shirley, who prepared main dishes and desserts in advance.

The Spoonsmores arrived with their guest Ted Bryant. The Spoonsmores were a very handsome couple. Pamela was extremely thin and glamorous with flowing blonde hair. She wore black trousers, a black velvet top and a satin fuchsia scarf wrapped several times around her neck. Her long, dangly, red bead earrings framed the delicate features of her face. Her husband was blonde haired and blue eyed, and was an enthusiastic conversationalist. He had recently given up his law practice in Edinburgh to manage their large estate. Like many of the gentry in the Boarders, he made his money and returned to his family home to apply useful corporate skills to farming.

Carolyn walked in from the kitchen. "Robert darling, dinner is ready. Would you like to make the seating arrangements?"

"Of course sweetheart. Ladies, come with me please." Robert walked into the dining room followed by the women. The dining room table was set impeccably for eleven guests. There were heavy mats decorated with hunting scenes at each place with silver cutlery, a white wine glass carefully placed at the tip of the knife and a small butter plate above the salad fork to the left. Water glasses sat between these two benchmarks on small coasters that matched the mats. In the center of the table were two covered dishes painted with birds and of Chinese origin, four candlesticks, and two sets of nineteenth century Wedgwood salt and pepper dishes. A framed still life of cheese, bread, and a bottle of wine hung over the sideboard and a very large mirror reflecting the soft candle light hung on the other wall.

"Pamela, if you could sit here on my right, and Addie you sit on my left. Then we will skip a chair and have Amanda down on the right hand side of the table with Jane on the left and Carolyn near the kitchen. Sorry gentlemen, we will have to have two men sitting together. It is unavoidable I am afraid. Ted, why don't you sit next to Addie? Butch you sit next to Pamela, and the rest of you fill in, but try not to sit next to your wife." One and all took there assigned seats and before the end of the first course of smoked salmon, they were deeply engaged in conversation. When the second course started, each guest would turn to the dinner partner on his or her other side and talk with that guest. Alternating between courses to made each guest feel included.

Addie was looking intently at her dinner partner. "Ted, what encouraged you to become a police officer with the Los Angeles Police Department? That has got to be a very tough job?" She was trying to think of how to steer the conversation in the direction of Jake, in hopes of getting more insights into his behavior.

"Well, I am the third generation of police officers in my family. It is a challenging job. But the truth of the matter is I love it. Every day is different; every day has its own challenges and rewards. I am always meeting interesting people. Take this evening for instance, who would have thought I would be on a driven shoot in Scotland?" He smiled at Addie.

"Clearly, you are an expert. I have written hundreds of feature articles about a wide variety of subjects, and I always find that a person who is an expert in any field, no matter how minute or specialized, will always have a niche and enormous respect. I understand you are a crack shot." Addie caught a glimpse of Butch with a wry smile out of the corner of her eye. He winked at Addie. She could hear him asking Pamela how her doctorate studies were coming. Out of enormous curiosity and interest in people, Addie could usually sit at a dinner table, concentrate on the person she was speaking with, and keep up with everyone else's conversation. She and Butch loved post mortems after a dinner party as they fell asleep at the end of the evening.

"You are a writer?" Asked Ted. "That's something I often wanted to try, but never knew how to go about it. I am also very busy, so I don't know when I would have time."

"Oh gosh, being a police officer would give you a plethora of material on a daily basis. You might think of taking a writing course or keeping a journal. Writing is really like being a crack shot. I think many people consider writing a mystical talent, but it is a craft, to be practiced and used. If you are serious, get a journal with blank pages and try to write something everyday even if it is only one sentence.

Police officers have to write reports all of the time. You probably have better writing skills than you realize. I would be happy to help in any way I can. In addition to freelance writing, I am also a handwriting analyst. That is my real passion." Addie was thinking to herself, *O.K. now I am getting some place, what a great resource this man could be.* "In fact, I recently performed an analysis on a sample of handwriting which scared me to death. The person was very disturbed, violent and very dominating. Coincidentally, I visited one of my old college roommates several months ago, she showed me a sample of an old boy friend's handwritings and it turned out to be the same handwriting. I even got another opinion. Most of my work is psychological profiles for companies, but I have a liaison with a woman who worked for the Rhode Island Police Force as a Court Document Examiner. She confirmed it was the same handwriting," Addie put down her fork and stopped eating the lamb stew.

"Do you think you have met this person before?" Ted asked with straight detachment sounding as if he were in a police officer mode.

"No, not to my knowledge, he used a different name for the handwriting sample." Addie replied.

"Would anyone like some more stew before the cheese course?" Carolyn said in a slightly higher voice to capture everyone's attention.

"It was very good," Addie said standing to help clear the table. The next course she would speak with Robert on her right. Perhaps she might have the opportunity to continue her discussion with Ted tomorrow between drives.

After the cheese course with a selection of three different Scottish cheeses, a rich chocolate torte appeared on the table. It was a variable feast of flavors and generosity, too good to pass up.

As the evening ended, Robert gave marching orders for the next day. "What ladies are accompanying their husbands tomorrow on the shoot?" All of the ladies staying at Scotsmuir with the exception of Carolyn, raised their hands. "Excellent, everyone must be dressed and ready to leave by 8:30 tomorrow. Breakfast starts at 7:00 a.m. There will be fresh eggs, tea, coffee, toast, and cereal. Everyone help himself or herself, any questions? We are shooting at Addeville, the estate of Sir Thomas and Lydia Strang-Morris tomorrow."

As Addie and Butch were falling asleep, Addie asked Butch why everyone in Scotland had a hyphenated name. He chuckled and said drowsily, "I heard you working up to grilling Ted about Mr. Wacko."

Addie, Jane and Amanda were dressed in warm wool trousers with Barbour jackets, warm hats, gloves and scarves. For years, Addie thought the Scottish dress was an affectation until she realized, after following Butch on driven shoots, the development of the clothing was out of sheer necessity to cope with the weather. All the women wore the traditional British Isles' boots called Wellies. Tramping through the fields was, more often than not, a muddy experience. These three were the only ladies who accompanied their husbands.

An article of clothing called a "plus twos," made of thick tweeds or tartan cloth worn from thick Scottish cloth in game keepers weight was worn by men just two inches below the knee. The cloth was so thick that most Scots wore their coats and matching "plus twos" for the duration of their lives. The Wellies would then protect the hunters' legs from walking in the fields. On the fancier estates, all of the game keepers and beaters wore the tartan of the owners' estate.

There were going to be seven guns including Thomas who was in charge of the shoot on his property. His estate was among the largest in the Boarders with nearly 3,000 acres. The men stood in the driveway of the Strang-Morris's beautiful house and each chose a small "peg" from a small leather pouch. Each number on the peg designated the number of the shooter and the order for each shoot. As the guns moved from one location to another, each shooter would move two spaces to the right.

"We will begin to shoot on the west mount. So please be so kind as to follow me over there. The fields are quite muddy, so if we could fill each car with as many guns as possible that would cut down on the number of cars. Please no low shots or killing foxes, pick up your own shells. There will be one long whistle at the end of each drive, any questions?"

Everyone shook his or her heads in full understanding. Like all upper class Scots, Thomas had a lovely English accent. Everyone combined forces and jumped into their four-wheel vehicles. Thomas was driving Butch and Addie. He was giving information as they followed Michael to the first shoot. So far, the weather was warm. The sun was shining as they drove past a large stone ruin. Addie felt a huge wave of excitement.

"That was once a castle with a sad history. During the 16th century, the English and Scots began fighting over this area that, as you know, is called the Boarders. This war lasted for about three hundred years. The Scots hired Irish mercenary soldiers to help them fight the English. The story goes that the mercenaries retreated to this castle. The English sent an envoy to the castle and told the Irish that if they surrendered they would be saved. The Irish surrendered and the English executed them."

The first shoot was in a valley. Everyone got out of their vehicles quickly. Dramatic hills of soft, green, immaculately tamed pastures rose on either side with a thick stand of evergreens on the north hill. Sheep were grazing in the upper field quite oblivious to the men with guns and the beaters who were the group of men, sometimes women, who carried flags and twirled them as they walked with their dogs to flush out the pheasants.

Addie loved to be outdoors and walk the land. She could look south and see Selkirk in the far off distance with a slight view of the Tweed River. Thomas rushed around quickly giving orders telling everyone where to stand.

"Honey, we are number two." Butch walked to his designated spot, which had a yellow wooden stake in the field with the number 2 carefully written on top. Addie stood behind him and held his gun case. She quickly zipped up the case and pulled the strap around her body so that the case did not fall onto the ground. They were both quiet, whispering to each other when they spoke. Behind the line of shooters were the dog handlers. The dogs were silent and very well trained but wiggled with excitement, and leashed until they were ready for retrieving the dead birds. Addie and Butch could hear Beaters walking through the stand of evergreens.

"Over . . ." the one word that signified the battle cry of all driven shoots from a Beater, in a loud voice with a strong Scottish brogue. The birds were beginning to fly overhead. Butch raised his gun pointing to the sky and swung to the right following a pheasant. "Bang!" A rain of feathers fell to the ground slowly like bits of large snowflakes. A loud thud sounded. The pheasant lay dead nearby a stonewall. One of the retrievers dashed out and grabbed the bird. His dog handler motioned to the excited dog to bring the game.

Bang! Bang! Bang! Only those birds, flying directly over each shooter's head or very near were shot. There was a side to Addie which loved to see the birds continue down the valley soaring triumphantly, escaping danger.

The cock pheasants are incredibly beautiful with their brilliant green heads. Then there were the poor wounded devils flapping uncontrollably on the ground. She watched the beaters or handlers pick up a flapping bird and twist it's neck.

Ted was in the number seven peg; he shot every pheasant within his range. Addie heard one of the game keepers say to Robert "You've got a crack shot there!" Robert explained that Ted was on the SWAT team of the Los Angeles Police Department.

The shrill sound of the whistle blew when the parade of flying pheasants stopped. Instantly, the shooters broke their guns and removed their ammunition. Everyone now discussed how many birds they had shot and walked towards their cars in preparation for the next staging.

"We'll have two more shoots and then have elevenses," Thomas was very tall and thin, highly energetic, and also good at mobilizing people. He had spent many years in the British army stationed in Cypress. Clearly, he was well qualified to give orders.

The next two shoots were on the east side of the estate. The location of each shoot seemed progressively more beautiful. Large bountiful holly trees seemed over sized compared to the States, Addie thought. The cows and sheep mooed, bleated and were quite unfazed by the hunters.

After the third shoot, they broke for a cup of clear soup and sloe gin. The warm liquid and alcohol did much to warm everyone up.

"I am off on my game today," said Nigel. "I'm not going to beat myself up over it though, because it is so beautiful here I am just going to enjoy the shoot. How did you do Butch?"

"Well, I got a few good ones, missed a few good ones, the usual." Butch laughed. "Honey, have a sip of the sloe gin. You might like it." Butch handed a small stainless steel beaker to Addie.

"Oh I do think this is good. Sweetheart, I think the Humphreys actually make this themselves." Addie took another sip from Butch's beaker.

Amanda was standing near them and chimed in. "In the summer you pick the sloes and prick them. We just empty out half a gin bottle, fill it with sloes and let it set covered for about a year. Then you discard the sloes and filter the liquid. It isn't difficult, but simply requires a bit of patience." Addie felt that Amanda was very capable, the more she listened to and watched her.

"What exactly do sloes look like?" Addie asked.

"They are a small, hard berry very much like a blueberry. Do you not have them in the States?" Amanda asked.

"Not that I know of, but they could be called by another name." Addie could see Thomas waving to everyone to mount up.

They had one more shoot before lunch. It began to mist slightly and looked like heavier rain was coming. They returned to the Strang-Morris's house for lunch. Everyone entered through the back door taking their guns into the house and their Wellies off. It was perfectly acceptable to wander around in stockinged feet.

The large central hallway, which opened up to a beautiful double staircase leading upstairs was backlit by a two-story window. A large circular table sat in the entrance, covered with magazines and letters.

Everyone congregated in the spacious living room in their shooting gear. There was a large portrait over the fireplace of Sara, their hostess, sitting on a horse. She entered the room and greeted every one.

"How was the shoot? We have a full bar here, so please help yourself. You know how time sensitive these rushed lunches are between shoots," she laughed.

"Addie how nice to see you again. Please tell me what I can get you."

"It is nice to see you. I'll have a little sherry if it's handy. How has your year been?" As Sara was pouring her a glass she replied, "Oh we have had a very busy year. We are actually going to Georgia next week on a quail hunt. Apparently, you ride on horseback, dismount, and then shoot the birds. It all sounds like great fun." She laughed.

"From the looks of your portrait you will be in good shape riding from one shoot to the other." Nigel chuckled and drew attention to her portrait over the fireplace.

Lunch was served buffet style in a large dining room set for twelve. The main dish was a hearty Shepherd's Pie with sliced carrots on the side.

Thomas made an announcement, "the beaters are waiting for us at 1:30 for two more afternoon shoots. So enjoy your lunch which my dear wife has prepared, and be ready to go by that time." He held his wine glass up in celebration.

Addie was seated next to Thomas. They talked about their life histories. He told her about living in Cypress, his being in command of the British forces there, and some of the problems they encountered.

The afternoon shoots did not seem to yield as large a number of pheasants as the morning shoots, but the countryside on the west end of the estate was just as beautiful. At the end of the day they returned to the Strang-Morris's for tea. Sara had baked a dark chocolate cake with several layers of thick icing. Addie and Jane exchanged glances. Jane came over and whispered, "It would be so rude not to sample this cake when Sara has spent the afternoon creating this gorgeous sweet." She laughed and put a piece of the cake into her mouth.

When they went outside to get in their cars the beaters were waiting for them. This ritual was also part of the driven shoots. The head gamekeeper, or gillie, would shake hands with each of the gentlemen who had shot. Every man shook hands, thanked the gillie, and, in the palm of his hand, slipped him some cash. The beaters and gamekeepers were often given some of the pheasants. The head gamekeeper would know how many shots were fired and how many pheasants were killed. A count he gave to the owner.

Addie was happy to return to Scotsmuir and looked forward to a rest before the evening meal.

Before they all departed to their individual rooms Robert went over the evening's events. "Dinner will be at The Dark Horse Inn in Melrose. Please everyone, be ready to go and in the hallway by 6:45. Walter and Jacqueline Biddle-Starrs, whom some of you have met before, are joining us and will be bringing a special guest from the states. Their guest apparently is the number two guy at the U.S. post office with his wife, so please be on your best behaviors."

"Ah, shucks does that mean no dancing on the table tops?" Asked Jane.

"Only if you take your shoes off," retorted Robert with a smile. Everyone had a good laugh.

Addie and Butch walked through the courtyard back to the Steadings.

"The U.S. Post Office, did you hear that?" Addie put her arm around Butch and gave him a little squeeze.

Butch cautioned Addie in his good natured way, "Now remember honey, this man is here for a vacation. The last thing he wants to hear about is a lost package in his postal system."

"Oh, I know that, but just think of the wealth of connections between Ted, the LAPD, SWAT team policeman and the number two man at the U.S. postal system!"

Addie could barely contain herself and felt like jumping in the air with anticipation.

"Oh gosh, I thought you had forgotten about Mr. Waco," lamented Butch.

"Well of course I had, but . . . ." Addie explained.

"But, but, but . . . yeah. What?" joked Butch.

"It's good to be prepared in case there is some connection between the disappearing package in the post office and a strange person." Addie replied.

"As I've said before, I think you and Babs have active imaginations. It's probably just a coincidence that all of these events happened along the way."

"You are probably right," Addie reflected. "Oh well, we can read a little bit before dinner. It's nice to have some downtime at the end of the afternoon."

Butch looked sleepy. He was taking off his trousers and preparing to get into bed. He quickly responded, "I might even snooze at bit. This hunting is hard work."

The Inn was a classic old establishment that had been founded in 1730 and was on the National Register. The floors seemed to tilt as the group passed through the hallway into the rear dining room. Robert and Carolyn patronized the Inn often and received good attention from the family members who owned the Dark Horse.

Robert arranged the seating arrangements. To her delight, William Deluth, the number two man at the United States Post Office was seated on Addie's left, and on her right sat Iain Biddle-Star, whom she had met before. She was secretly delighted. She looked across the table at Butch seated beside the lovely Jacqueline Biddle-Stars. Addie knew Butch would enjoy speaking with her. Jacqueline was a very enthusiastic politician and a member of the local city council. Butch glanced over at Addie, smiled and, ever so slightly, raised his finger to his lips to make the silent gesture. Addie winked and blew him a kiss back.

As everyone was studying their menu, Addie engaged Iain in conversation. "Have you had a good year?" she asked with a smile.

"Oh yes, we have had a very good year. Jacqueline is up for reelection, though the district has changed so it's geographically larger. This makes campaigning more time consuming." He sipped his wine and smiled back at her.

Addie replied, "I have worked on several campaigns in the U.S. I found them fun but very exhausting, especially if you have an enlarged district.

"Well, I've planned a bicycle trip to the South of France three days after the election. So we can either celebrate or commiserate!" Iain laughed.

Addie looked at her menu, "What would you suggest I have for an appetizer? Everything looks delectable."

"It is hard to go wrong at the Dark Horse, but I am planning to start off with the smoked quail salad with chutney myself." Iain said thoughtfully.

"Oh that sounds delicious. I think I'll try that as well." They exchanged pleasantries and chatted about movies and books. Addie enjoyed Iain's very dry sense of humor.

When the waiter came around and took their orders, Addie chose to have the lamb for the main course after the smoked quail. She knew all of the food would be very well prepared.

As the first course was served, she turned towards William Deluth. "William, have you been interested in shooting for a long time?" She inquired.

"Ma'am, please call me Bill, and the answer is yes. I grew up in Idaho, and owning and operating a gun in that part of the country was as normal as learning to ride a bicycle. However, this is the first time my wife Sally and I have come to Scotland to shoot. We are very anxious to begin tomorrow. Have you been here often?"

"Bill, yes, we have. We are lucky to come every year. Or, I should say, we pray the Hyde-Smiths will keep inviting us. Everyone is wonderful and the countryside is so breathtakingly beautiful. I like to be out doors with my husband, Butch."

"So you don't shoot?" Bill asked.

"No, I have enough avocations I'm trying to master without adding another skill to the list, perhaps when I retire." Addie smiled.

"What is it you do?" asked Bill. So there it was. Here was the question she was waiting for. Here might be an opportunity to learn more about the inner workings of the U.S. Post office. Addie tried to play it cool.

"I am a handwriting analyst and work with a variety of companies to help them hire the correct person for the job as well as sort out employees who are at high risk for theft. Let's say, for example, you might have one part of the country where a lot of packages are continually missing. By looking at the handwritings of postal employees in that department, I could narrow the field for you. There is a case where a famous investment banking firm had a short fall early in the firm's history. Someone suggested to a partner, to call in a handwriting expert. The expert sifted through the handwriting samples and narrowed the suspects down to one man, who ultimately confessed." Addie knew when she was trying to get an idea across she spoke too quickly.

"Oh that's very interesting," said Bill thoughtfully. "Perhaps I'll take one of your cards. One never knows. Where do you and your husband live?" Addie was thrilled.

"We live outside of Boston, and I will bring one of my cards to the shoot tomorrow. I also have a website. Does your wife shoot?" It never does too well to look crassly commercial during these nice evenings. Butch was correct, everyone was here on a vacation and it was best to change the subject.

"Oh gosh, Sally is every bit as good a shot as I am—some days better!" Bill laughed. "That is one reason I married her. I wanted her to teach me how to shoot." Now it was Addie's time to laugh.

The rest of the evening was spent chatting with individual dinner partners. From time to time, someone would engage the entire table by telling a joke or with trying to solve the crisis in the Middle East. The experience was enjoyable.

Their routine was to shoot in the morning have a large lunch, return in the afternoon for a small nap, and dress for dinner. It was a nineteenth century existence.

There was one day for sight seeing between the four days of shooting. The group visited a glass blowing factory and several mills where tartans are made. Afterwards, they had lunch at another country inn overlooking the River Tweed, where the conversation turned to fishing. It was an eventful five days which ended all too quickly.

Addie and Butch were packed and ready for the driver to pick them up by 5:30 a.m. for their flight from Edinburgh. It had been another wonderful week in Scotland and they hoped they would be invited again next year.

It always took a few days to get sorted out after a trip. There was a lot of mail to pour through, e-mails to answer, and laundry and dry cleaning to be attended to. Addie wrote a letter to Bill Deluth in Memphis including one of her brochures, saying how much she and Butch had enjoyed meeting him and Sally. She also sent a brochure to Ted Bryant at the Los Angeles Police Department. Addie was a good sales person with great follow up.

Just as Addie was catching up on e-mails, the doorbell rang. She went downstairs and saw the Federal Express truck pulling out of the driveway. She picked up the envelope. She felt sick and, to her surprise, felt a flash of anxiety. She knew the writing. It was Jake, or what ever his name was making contact again. She apprehensively opened up the letter and began reading. There was a note written in his hand asking her to perform a vocational analysis; i.e. what type of employment would best fit his skills. Addie was afraid if she did not do the analysis, he might get so angry that he would take some revenge.

She walked upstairs to their office holding the Federal Express envelope and looked at Butch.

"Oh hi honey, who's the Fed Ex letter from?" Butch looked at her face. "Oh no, don't tell me another letter from Mr. Wacko. Maybe you should blow this guy off and not do his analysis. In fact, we are so busy why don't you just tell him you have retired." For the first time, Butch looked genuinely concerned.

"Well, I will do this one last analysis for him and turn it around quickly. I am almost afraid if I don't do it, he might come after me. Is that weird?" Addie sat down at her desk. "I even dislike having his handwriting sample in my desk. It's almost as if I feel his disturbed energy in our house." Addie shuddered.

"I have an idea, why don't we buy an airline ticket for Ted and end this whole thing!" Butch suggested.

"Oh that's a good idea!" They laughed.

"I think I will e-mail Babs and let her know, Mr. Wacko has made contact again.—oh gosh, maybe that isn't a good idea. It isn't ethically correct, for one thing. I'll call her." Addie said thoughtfully.

"He may have the phones tapped." Said Butch.

"Oh I was thinking of that," Addie said thoughtfully.

"Honey, I am kidding. You are going overboard. Do the analysis and forget about the guy. But I think you do need to draw a line in the sand here. Promise me this is the last interaction you will have with him. Promise?" Butch looked at her.

"I promise. I like the idea of telling him I've retired. What did I ever do without you?" Adelaide looked at him gratefully.

"I will protect you." He came and gave Addie a big hug. "Don't forget to tell him you're now in your late seventies and want to spend more time with your grandchildren."

Chapter Nine

Some Jarring Surprises

Babs hadn't had a good night's sleep since the dream about Lee, and George frequently expressed concern about her tired appearance and jumpiness. He also was taken aback by her tendency to snap at him now for small household misdemeanors, such as not replacing an empty paper towel roll. She still hadn't told him the reason, and was determined not to, unless at some point it became necessary. For now, she sloughed off his comments saying she felt fine; it was probably from just trying to do too much . . . as usual.

The ironic part of Bab's sleeplessness is she prided herself in how well she slept. Most of her friends complained of insomnia and having to get up to go to the bathroom at least once during the night, many of them resorted to prescription sleep aids, but not Babs. Her sleeping pill was to read for 15-20 minutes before turning off the light. Well, yes, truth be told, she also took a 5 mg. melatonin tablet about an hour before bedtime . . . if she remembered! At any rate, she had always felt blessed with good sleep and good dreams. The only ones she could call at all bad usually involved being unable to find her way somewhere, or being left out and excluded by her friends.

Before the Lee dream, Babs had loved the process of waking up from her dreams, the layers of sleep seemed to peel off her consciousness in pleasant, slow motion. If it was a particularly enjoyable dream, she could sometimes will its return and experience a continuation. This always amazed and delighted her.

But now, in the two weeks since the nightmare, it was a different story. She could get to sleep all right, usually around 10:30 p.m. but woke with a start between 2:00 and 3:00 a.m. When it first happened, she lay there, wide-eyed, for at least two hours, then fitfully slept on and off until the 6:30 alarm.

After nearly a week of this, as she lay wide awake, she suddenly remembered something Lee, now "Jake," had taught her during a time when their relationship was relatively healthy. It was a relaxation technique developed by a mind-body guru popular in the '80's, with an odd name something like Feldenkrais. Anyway, she tried it and it helped somewhat.

She would start with her toes, thinking of each one and "feeling" it with her mind. She then continued this mental exercise over her entire body ending with her head. Afterward, if she still felt wide awake, she did some deep breathing and isometrics which were also part of the Feldenkrais method Lee had taught her. How strange to feel such renewed fear and hatred for this man, and at the same time have a grain of gratitude for his earlier teachings. These unexpected kindnesses from Lee were what had kept her in his lure.

Life went on happily enough at the Bakers in spite of the dream repercussions. They were finally replacing their kitchen cabinets which meant Babs had triumphed in getting George to now work on something *above* his beloved basement. Babs wasn't lifting a finger; George and neighbor Bart Dundon were doing all the work. The old cabinets were difficult to remove as everything was nailed instead of screwed together. The new cabinets arrived unassembled and practically took up the whole downstairs while being put together. At the same time, contents of the old cupboards were piled high on tables, chairs, and seemingly everywhere in the Baker's small living and dining space even the top of Sam's crate. Things were a mess and probably would be for at least another two weeks until the base cabinets arrived from backorder. Preparing meals without any counter space was a real feat, but Babs improvised quite well and enjoyed the challenge.

Bart and George had worked together on home improvement projects since the early '90's when they built the shed in the Baker's back yard. After that, it was installing the stockade fence, followed by building a back deck off the dining area, then framing-in the first part of the basement renovations, and now the kitchen. Bart never would take any payment for his help but gladly accepted an occasional case of beer or meal out.

Bart divorced long ago and lived alone in a cottage he completely remodeled himself. He had excellent taste, and it was beautifully done. While Bart was always available for Baker projects, he rarely enlisted George for his even though George repeatedly offered. George felt bad about that, but figured it was because Bart was such a perfectionist—particularly on his own turf.

As the days sped by, Babs was increasingly eager for Addie to get back from Scotland so she could tell her about the Lee dream and learn of any developments at her end. She waited a few days past Addie's return, then called her.

"Darn," Babs muttered as she heard the answering machine at the other end. But just as she was about to hang up Addie picked up with an enthusiastic "Hi Babs!"

"Hi yourself: how'd you know it was me? I mean that it was I," she corrected herself.

"Well, because we now have caller I.D, and I'm sure you can imagine what prompted our decision . . . that weasel Jake. Hey, any problem if I call you back in about an hour? I'm trying to get a couple things in the mail. Then I'll be free as a bird, and we can catch up."

The Bakers didn't have caller I.D., but when the phone rang exactly an hour later, Babs didn't hesitate to answer, "Hi Addie." Addie was amused and impressed, saying she wouldn't have the nerve to answer like that being unsure who was really on the other end.

"Yes, well I wouldn't have the nerve to fly all over the world like you do either," Babs laughed. "How *was* Scotland? I'm dying to hear!"

"Well, it was absolutely wonderful and full of a few surprises as well. I wrote a travelogue I'll send you which describe the old world aspects of the countryside and the estates we were able to visit. And the food; unbelievable! But what I really want to tell you about now is the few surprises, plus another big one when we got home. Maybe you should sit down if you aren't already," Addie suggested.

"I'm all ears, and I'm sitting down. So fire away!" said Babs. "And when you're through, I have something a bit surprising to tell you too."

When Babs heard the first part about Addie meeting a member of the Los Angeles Police Department SWAT team; she was duly impressed; but when she learned about the U. S. Postal Service big wig; she was bowled over. What were the odds of meeting two such valuable resources at a time like this? And smart Addie had even followed up by sending a letter and her business brochure. No grass grows under that woman, Babs thought admiringly. She felt more secure and less afraid of whatever Lee might try to do after hearing about the two men of authority.

But then Addie told Babs about getting another handwriting sample from Jake, she nearly dropped the phone. It was one thing to have the dream about him, but now all of a sudden he loomed all too real again.

"Why would he send you another one? Did you respond?" Babs attempted to sound more nonchalant than she felt.

"This time he wanted a vocational analysis for determining what work a person is best suited," Addie answered. "I did do it, and mailed it off just yesterday. But I must admit I have had second thoughts. Butch made me promise this was the last time I would have anything to do with Jake. And I think that's because he feels you and I are way overreacting to the situation and need to give it a break."

"Yeh, I'll give it a break, ok, I'd like to break the guy's sick neck. I think you'll appreciate my ongoing anxiety when I tell you about the dream I had while you were gone."

"Oh, right, you mentioned you had something to report; now should *I* be sitting down?," Addie quipped.

"Yes, I think so, Addie. ok, here it goes." Babs related the dream in vivid detail, pausing only when Addie interrupted with a few audible gasps.

"Wow," said Addie, "I've got goose bumps; the kind I remember getting as a Girl Scout when we'd sit around the campfire listening to ghost stories scared out of our wits. I can only imagine what it's done to you. How are you coping?"

Babs explained her lack of sleep and the irony of getting some relief from a technique Lee had long ago taught her. Addie shook her head in disbelief and imagined the horrific dream might portend real difficulties to come. Babs admonished her to keep knowledge of the dream to herself.

"You mean you've been enduring this by yourself; you haven't even told George?" Addie exclaimed.

"Well, I haven't really had to. He does notice I seem tired, but because of his loud snoring I've been sleeping in the guest room. He isn't witness to my thrashing around, and I'm grateful not to worry him needlessly."

"Oh gad, Babs, I think you are thoughtful to spare him, but please don't be such a saint. You really should tell him," Addie advised.

"Well, I'll consider it, but you need to know we don't have the tacit understanding you obviously share with Butch, ok? Just trust me on this, Addie."

Addie was a bit taken aback by Babs' strong admonition and decided to let it go.

When their conversation ended both agreed to stay in touch regularly and *immediately* contact each other if any Jake-related matters unfolded.

Both at home and in her car, Babs was an admitted National Public Radio(NPR) and public television junkie. The radio station was her preferred current news source and general resource for in-depth reporting of worldwide events and concerns. She embraced the station's open and democratic view, and definitely fit the profile of a typical fan easily opting to listen to the end of a captivating report in lieu of being on time for a scheduled meeting or appointment. She also had paper and pen nearby in case the station referenced something she wanted to follow up on with their website, etc. In essence, she couldn't imagine living without the energizing information for as an avid listener.

Interestingly, Bab's first exposure to NPR and public television dated back to the early years of her first marriage. She and her husband became involved with the first fundraiser for Lakeside's public TV station. It was a live auction, and they were auctioneers. She remembers there were few guidelines then, and as long as people were calling in bids the auction stayed on the air. So it wasn't unusual for Babs and her husband to call it a night and drive home when the sun was coming up. Such a casual attitude would be inconceivable today.

Regardless of protocol, Babs had remained an inveterate supporter of her local station and faithfully sent her annual pledge with a slight increase each time. She was more a radio than TV fan and most regularly listened on the weekends while puttering around the house or in her car.

On a particular Saturday, while driving around doing errands, Babs caught part of a story about the Postal Service featuring Memphis, Tennessee, as the busiest package hub in the Eastern U.S. She was so struck by the location and its connection with "Jake" that she immediately pulled off the road to hear more. Unfortunately, there wasn't much more but the reporter said additional information and a video tour of the mail facility could be found on the NPR website.

As soon as she got home, Babs fired up her computer then called Addie to tell her about the post office story and suggested she check out the website as well.

"Can you do it right now, Addie? Then we could stay on the phone and watch it together." Babs asked hopefully.

"Sure can," Addie replied. "Just let me get to my office and I'll pick up the phone there. Let's get on speaker mode so we can talk while we're watching."

While she waited, Babs hoped Addie hadn't detected how nervous she was feeling. She had a strong premonition that the Memphis facility was somehow key to the whole "Jake" situation. Why would she think that, she asked herself—maybe female intuition? Oh, I'm being ridiculous, she thought. I haven't seen him in decades and probably couldn't recognize him even if he were.

The two women had time to chat briefly while waiting for the story to download, while clicking on the story icon. Addie offered that she was feeling uneasy and she wondered if Jake might not be a postal employee.

"That's uncanny, Addie. Those are my thoughts exactly," Babs said.

While they watched the video, they were awed by the facility's immense size; the equivalent of two football fields. Inside there appeared to be as many robots as people, and packages everywhere: on conveyors, on skids, on jitneys . . . . It was an organizational marvel to be sure. Following an overview, the video zeroed in on specific operations, beginning with the facility's sorting capabilities. The narrator explained the state of the art, latest technology, coupled with highly skilled labor, made their sorting the fastest and most accurate of any package facility in the U.S., including Fed Ex and UPS.

As the narration continued, the camera zoomed in on two men sorting packages as they came off a conveyor, and placing them in bins. Their hands moved so fast, they were almost a blur, but as the camera zoomed in closer something unmistakable caught Bab's eye. She gasped audibly and yelled "Addie, quick, watch the guy on the left. I'll explain."

On the left wrist of one man was a tattoo of a star, just the size and place a wristwatch would cover. Lee had the same tattoo and had always worn his watch over it. He said he hated tattoos, but got it on a dare while on a drinking binge in college.

The camera zoomed out without allowing a look at his face, but Babs did note the familiar head shape and posture. There was no beard though . . . Lee always had a beard. He'd already had one for 15 years when she met him and swore he'd never shave it off. The more his head hair receded the more determined he was to keep the facial growth. He had thought it made him look very professorial, which was true, but when he turned manic, Babs recalled, he looked nothing short of demonic.

At the same time Babs was taking all this in and thinking about Lee, she was stunned to hear Addie say, "My god, he reminds me of the Fed Ex guy who delivered Jake's latest sample. I remember the tattoo."

"What the hell's going on?" they practically shrieked in unison. They then proceeded in relatively hushed tones to discuss the improbability of such a coincidence.

The NPR video was still playing, when Addie shouted: "get a load of this!" What they heard was bigwig William Deluth would be appearing at the end of the clip to sum up the Memphis facilities current success and vision for the future.

"How extraordinary this is. Here's the man I just met in Scotland. I can't believe this!," Addie exclaimed. "Let's hear what he has to say."

As it turned out, Deluth seemed to offer more rhetoric than useful information. So Babs and Addie talked over his narration. They concluded their conversation admitting they were a bit drained and needed a break from all the Jake-driven excitement. They hung up in better spirits and both felt relieved to concentrate on other things in their lives.

Even so, a couple days after the video, Babs's growing preoccupation with Lee continued. She found herself looking around the house for any saved artifacts of their stormy relationship. George would never understand such preoccupation with the past; she was careful to do her searching when he wasn't around. She knew she'd thrown out just about everything related to Lee long ago, but thought she might have saved some of her journal entries.

Sure enough, in an unmarked file folder in the attic she found handwritten notes dating from August 1966 to October 1968: notes that reflected the thrill, deterioration and eventual demise of their relationship.

Some extracts follow:

8/13/68

Babs to Lee: "Just want to confirm the multitude and magnitude of feelings experienced while you shared your remarkable, endearing self with me last night. I am very deeply touched. All the loving things you said about us and your deepening commitment to the relationship . . . our agreement on never ending the honeymoon . . . knowing we can always feel free to tell each other anything . . . asking me to help you grow in areas where you recognize a need, and offering me the same . . . being excited about the fake fireplace and other details of our first Christmas together . . . and much, much more. As I listened last night I heard a man I am immeasurably proud of and touched by, a man whom I feel truly a part of and will enjoy giving the best of myself day after day for as long as we have. You're emotional, very devoted, very happy Babs"

9/29/66

Babs journal entry: "I have a difficult situation to face. Lee more and more obviously behaves negatively toward my actions. I sense he feels penned in and wants to get out. The ups and downs are draining, certainly for me. If the love is there, it's becoming increasingly buried beneath a mire of uncertainty. Any discussions result in an impasse."

10/14/66

Babs to Lee: "I fully agree you need to have your own place and hope that happens within a month. I realize we can't meet each other's needs right now and I am asking you to consider something which would help me through this transition. Would you be willing to talk with the counselor I've been seeing, either over the phone or in person, to have some feedback from you about me if—you were comfortable in providing that kind of participation to help her in the process of helping me? It was my suggestion to her and she agreed it would be a plus, if you were comfortable in providing that kind of participation. I would like to help you in any way I can, so please don't hesitate to ask. I'm happy I was able to help you find a job you're growing to like so much after so many bad experiences. And I'm glad the company realizes how fortunate they are to have you. Bottom line: I see you regaining the feeling of success and challenge you've wanted to recapture for so long. So, onward and upward to you, sweetheart. Wish the same for me as I work on my growing up; phase 999! I love you."

12/2/66

Babs to Lee: "So . . . it's not you, and I know that. And I am sorry I have been such a trial. I am frightened by what has been happening to me emotionally and functionally, Lee, and hope you value our relationship enough to stick with me while I conquer it. Thanks for listening, soul mate."

New Years Eve 1967

Babs journal entry: "Lee was drunk and asleep at 10:30 so I'm doing this one solo. 1967 has been a year of frequent turmoil, confusion and uncertainty, yet a good one when viewed as a learning curve. I've learned much about myself and my own self deception, what makes Lee tick, how to accept a child's absence, that I can only count on myself, that life cannot be enjoyed when taken too seriously, that everyone doesn't have to like me, that I am entirely too hard on myself, that Presque Isle is music for my soul, and more . . ."

6/27/68

Babs journal entry: "I am angry, disgusted, disappointed and gaining strength by the minute to STOP thinking so much about Lee and more about ME. It's time, and I'm ready. I will no longer be manipulated and jerked around by such a weak, immature person . . . even though I love him very much. Respect is waning, and the love will too in time, unless there are drastic changes. Alcoholism with a character disorder has become my description of this enigmatic person I hardly know anymore. I've come a long distance quickly from the me who insisted we were fine and all was surmountable. Who was I kidding? This is a bad union at best, and I'm ready to bolt.

9/3/68

Babs to Lee: "Please hear me. I am so glad there will be time and geography between us for a couple days. The reality of 'us' has become unbearable to me. I'd rather be alone than in a situation that promotes such wariness, mistrust and creeping destruction. As Babs I'm strong, purposeful, positive and giving. As Babs with you I'm unsure of my validity almost daily. It's time to stop such game playing and move forward."

The preceding was about all Babs could handle, and when she stopped reading, she felt both relieved and disturbed. Babs relieved anew that she got out of her relationship with Lee when she did. However, disturbed that she felt he was now looming out there as a renewed menace. She was distressed at herself for thinking about him so much, just like the old days she had overcome. What would he do? Would he appear in her life again?

Chapter Ten

More Write Information

It was early in the morning when Addie climbed the three flights of stairs to her office. The space worked well. It was high and quiet. Addie always felt centered and ready to concentrate when she entered the room.

She was looking forward that day to finishing her analysis of Abraham Lincoln. What was that unique quality he possessed which enabled him to cope with so much adversity? Addie loved being a handwriting analyst. There were no handwritings exactly alike. People can share characteristics, but personalities and the combination of traits are so individual. *People are like snow flakes,* Addie thought as she took a pen out of a terra cotta honey jar from New Zealand that she had rescued from her kitchen; an item too beautiful and practical to be thrown away.

She sat at her desk and looked at the four page green work sheet she had almost completed. First, she had measured one hundred strokes of Lincoln's handwriting. He was deeply emotional and action oriented. She poured over the small sized text which she enlarged on the copy machine. Addie would take the original size of Abraham Lincoln's text into account, but, for now, she wanted to scrutinize other characteristics and could only do so when the copy was enlarged. The relatively small text of Lincoln's copy indicated he had great powers of concentration.

Butch came into the office and turned on his computer. Even though he had sold his company, he was on five other boards which still required some close attention. He checked his e-mail daily.

"Hey Babe, what are you up to?" He looked over at Addie.

"I'm looking for those unique combination of characteristics which made Abraham Lincoln one of the greatest presidents of the United States." Addie peered over her reading glasses and smiled back.

"He wasn't in office very long, 1861 to 1865. Without old Abe, the United States would have been a different place. Luckily for the country, he felt that succession was illegal, and—even though he hated war—he felt that was his only option. What have you come up with?" Butch was looking at his computer screen.

Addie paused from her work. "Gosh, he was only in office for four years. I guess in my mind's eye, he was so important that his time in office should have been longer."

"Well, if it hadn't been for John Wilkes Booth, he would have served his full second term." Butch reminded her. "One thing that has always impressed me about America is, after the Civil War, the South capitulated. They did not keep on fighting or go into the hills. Lincoln tried very hard along with General Grant to create an atmosphere of reconciliation. Lincoln made a famous speech, in which he insisted upon, 'malice towards none: with charity for all'."

Addie looked at Butch approvingly. "Honey, I am so impressed you can remember that speech verbatim."

"Hey Babe, stick with me." He smiled and gave her a confident, coy, funny expression which always sent Addie into gales of laughter.

They both worked quietly for the next hour; lost in concentration. Butch continued to check his e-mails and reply to them with rapid hunt and peck typing style. Addie continued pouring diligently over Lincoln's handwriting.

"Well, don't keep me in suspense, what have you come up with?" Butch turned to Addie.

"Oh my gosh, I think maybe I found Lincoln's one characteristic which made him so strong. Yup, maybe this is it." By this time, Addie had changed seats from her desk and was sitting in front of her computer typing her report. "Look at the formation of Lincoln's 'd.'" She moved closer to Butch so he could see the text. "Do you see how low the stem of the letter d is formed? This is the sign of an independent thinker; so few people in the general population have that characteristic. This shows someone who believes so deeply that what they think is correct that they don't care about someone else's opinion. The independent thinker listens to others, is polite, but in his or her heart doesn't really care what others think."

"There has got to be more to it than that." Butch suggested.

"You are correct," Continued Addie. "I will give you the complete analysis to read, but essentially Lincoln had a first rate mind. He exhibited all combinations of thinking patterns. He was first and foremost an analytical thinker. He liked to sort and sift through information. Analytical thinkers have keen reasoning ability. See how pointed and jagged the tip of the first letter 'm' in the word Abraham is?" She showed the sample of writing to Butch again. "But then notice, the second formation of the letter 'm' in his name is more rounded than in his last m. That is the sign of a cumulative thinker. Cumulative thinkers—Thomas Jefferson and Thomas Edison are two prime examples—are slower to analyze information and want to see all of the facts before they make a decision. Lincoln must have thought, pondered, and probably agonized over every verdict. However, by the time he got there, he was convinced he was right. Lincoln was very investigative and worked hard at getting to the original root of any situation so that he could base his decisions upon accurate facts.

"Look at these well balanced 'f's, this indicates that he was as good at organizing ideas as well as carrying them out. Once again, not all people have that ability. Many politicians are good at organizing ideas but not implementing them. Lincoln was very honest and straightforward. That doesn't surprise us; we would have expected that wouldn't we?" Addie glanced at Butch.

"Oh my god, hands down, absolutely!" Butch responded.

"Are you teasing me?" Addie laughed and continued. "Lincoln was verbal and found communicating by words easy, but he was also very diplomatic. See these 't' bars that are long? He led others with enthusiasm. He also liked to talk and argue.

"Well, that is typical for lawyers, isn't it?" Addie paused. "One thing I realize when looking at this handwriting, as opposed to the handwriting of Lee Roberts, that Wacko guy I got that disturbing sample from, is the combination of traits, that Roberts is so dominating. Interestingly enough, Lincoln never was. See the way Lincoln dots his 'i's, they are small and right over the stem. That indicates Lincoln is good at detail and very loyal. Now look at Robert's letter 'i'," Addie picked up another sample of handwriting in front of her computer and showed it to Butch, "see how thick and almost bludgeoning that example is. The 'i' dot is almost like a club. A person who would not hesitate to use force; it is a 'my way or the highway' sort of mentality."

"You need balance." Butch said.

"Exactly, you need balance; and you, sweetheart, are loaded with it. Well, I think I really learned something today. It is as much the combination and integration of characteristics that make up a successful personality as it is the individual traits. There are leaders and CEO's who may be dominating, but if they combine this with other traits such as restraint, or diplomacy that attribute is more evenhanded. General Eisenhower demonstrated some characteristics of domination, but he was also cautious. So that helped to balance that attribute."

Butch glanced at the clock, which said 1:00 p.m. He started to collect the trash from the wastepaper basket, "Honey, you just keep working on your important study and I will continue doing the housework. You know, I'll make lunch and unload the dishwasher."

Addie glanced at the clock. "Oh my gosh, I didn't realize how late it had gotten. I have some good homemade soup and freshly baked home made bread for your lunch today."

The phone rang on line two. Addie picked it up. "Adelaide Stubbs, Handwriting Analyst."

"Ma'am, I hope I haven't disturbed your lunch, but this is Bill Deluth. We met in Scotland." His voice was deep and firm.

"Of course I remember you, Bill. How are you?" Addie motioned to Butch with her right hand pointing to the phone that this was someone special.

"I am very well. But we have been having some problems with our Memphis operation, and I'd like to send you three handwriting samples for analysis."

"I would be delighted. Can you overnight them?" Addie was thrilled to hear from Deluth.

"Well, I felt that was going to be your answer. So I already took the liberty of sending them to you. They should be arriving today."

"I will have to ask you to please sign a confidentiality statement saying that this information is private and for your eyes only." Addie instructed.

"That will be no problem, my fax number is on my stationery. Just call my secretary Mary before you send the fax, and she will bring it directly to me." Bill replied.

Addie added, "thank you very much for thinking of me. I'll be back in touch as soon as I have the results. Usually, what I like to do is e-mail the analysis for quick results, follow it up with a phone call, and answer any questions. You will also be receiving a bound hard copy through the postal service."

"I would appreciate that. How is Butch? Say, that was a wonderful time we all had together in Scotland, wasn't it?" Bill sounded a little more relaxed, now that the business discussion was completed.

"Butch is as great as ever, thank you." Addie smiled over at Butch. "Those trips to Scotland are just the best. We love going. I hope we can all get together some time in the near future. Please send my best to Sally."

"I certainly will do that. Thank you for helping us with this problem." they hung up.

As Butch and Addie descended the stairs to the kitchen, they heard the front doorbell ring. Butch glanced outside the window. "Looks like the Federal Express truck."

He went to the front door. "Honey, it's for you, and you need to sign for it." Addie said hello to the driver and signed the electronic scanner. "This is from Bill Deluth." Addie quickly tore the envelope open and examined the contents. There were three samples of handwriting all right. She glanced at them quickly. The third one looked frighteningly familiar. She shuttered. There it was: another example of Lee Robert's handwriting. *Does this pose an ethical problem*, she thought.

"You look like you've just seen a ghost," Butch looked at her. "Oh no, let me guess, one of the handwritings is from Mr. Waco. Lee what's his name?"

"How did you guess? It looks like it. I'll double check it with the original sample. This guy must work for the post office. How weird is this? It's all too strange that a person I never met sends me a sample of his handwriting as a result of my website, then it turns out that he had a relationship with my old roommate, and now he works for the post office." Addie looked somewhat distraught.

"You know what they say, 'truth is stranger than fiction.'" Butch retorted. "Let's eat I'm starved."

They headed into the kitchen, where Addie took out the soup from the refrigerator and began preparing a sandwich for Butch and a salad for herself. "Sweetheart, help me here. You have had a lot of business experience. Is this a conflict of interest? My analysis of Roberts is confidential, but if he is a criminal . . .

Well, what do you think I should do? How can I protect myself legally?" Addie looked at Butch, who was whipping up a glass of chocolate milk to have with his lunch.

"First, you want to verify that this is the same handwriting you received earlier, and then you want to disclose that information to Bill. Would you just mail Deluth a copy of the sample analysis you have already done for Hunt?" Asked Butch.

"No, certainly not, I performed two analyses for Mr. Hunt, or whomever: one was a self-analysis, and the other was a vocational analysis. These were very confidential. The report I will write for Deluth will be pointing out characteristics for an employer. So I totally understand what you are saying. I will just disclose everything, and let Bill interpret the information for himself. Man, this is just so weird, it gives me the creeps." Addie shuddered.

Chapter Eleven

The Plot Thickens

Ever since National Public Radio cameras invaded his space and caught him on tape at work, Jake had felt pretty wary. Even so, his in-house thefts continued to escalate. He now diverted at least a package a day and had developed a keen sense for what to steal, as though he could see through the package to the contents.

In cahoots with his pal Stan, the two were accumulating considerable financial gain. In just a couple months, between Jake's and Stan's postal stash, they had fenced over $250,000 worth of "lost" merchandise. Both found their criminal activity exhilarating and very addictive.

Meanwhile, Jake's supervisor and others, diligently involved in trying to unravel the mystery of so many missing packages in Jake's section, *appeared* to be dead-ended at every turn. Jake delighted in their struggle, yet did feel a growing general unease he decided to share with Stan.

In their favorite booth for scheming, at the neighborhood deli, Jake impatiently waited for Stan to arrive. He did his usual finger tapping to pass the time. When Stan showed up, Jake immediately noticed a change in his usually laid back demeanor.

As Stan slid his big bulk into the booth, he barely whispered, "hey, Jake, something's going on, but I can't tell you here. I don't think we should even be seen together. Can I drop by your place tonight? We really need to talk."

Jake was taken aback by Stan's urgent tone, "Yeh, sure."

"I'll wait until dark, and I'll drive my girlfriend's car instead of my truck," Stan whispered back.

The deli was busy, but the short stay of the two men did not go unnoticed by their regular waitress Rosie.

Walking home from the deli, Jake tried to imagine what could have happened. When he talked with Stan the day before, everything was fine, and their lunch today was supposed to be just a pleasant brainstorming session about their growing "business."

It got dark around six o'clock in early February, but it was now nearly seven, and still no Stan. Jake paced, wondering whether to try calling him. He decided against using his home phone, or even his cell phone, until he knew what was going on. His sense of dread increased the later it became with no sign of Stan.

Finally, around 10:00, after too much coffee, too many cigarettes and a couple of joints, Jake decided to drive to a pay phone. Every move he made now was though he was being watched. Which, of course, he knew was ridiculous . . . or was it?

He pulled up to the first phone he could locate, about 3 miles away, and was grateful to find it in working order. As he dialed Stan's number, he kept the booth door slightly ajar so the overhead light wouldn't go on. This way, any passerby who noticed the phone booth was occupied wouldn't be able to make out any details of the person inside.

A woman answered on the first ring sounding somewhat breathless and upset. "I'm trying to reach Stan. Do I have the right number?" Jake asked.

"Who IS this?," demanded the woman.

Jake wasn't sure what to tell her. Jake didn't who knows how trustworthy Stan's wife was or what she knew.

He finally said, "this is a business associate of his, and we were supposed to get together tonight at 6:00. But he never showed up"

"You're damn right he never showed up, 'cuz at about that time the stupid asshole was being hauled off in handcuffs. So, whoever *you* are, and if your business had anything to do with his business, you might want to decide you never heard of Stan, "if you know what I mean," the woman advised harshly.

Jake said nothing and hung up the phone in slow motion, as though measured movement would ensure his safety. He needed to be able to think about what had just happened. Mentally he felt like a blank slate, and physically he was numb.

He managed to get into his car and drive home, his mind still a blank. He opened a Pepsi and flipped on the TV more out of habit than intent. He surfed the channels aimlessly for a few minutes, and muttered to himself nonsensically that female news anchors were whores and the co-anchors were their pimps and no wonder we never get the straight scoop on the news.

ll:00 p.m. it's time for the news, he thought. The sudden realization was his jolt back to reality from the shock at the phone booth. Maybe there will be something about Stan on the news . . .

Sure enough it was headline news on all three Memphis stations. Jake zeroed in on the station he considered most credible, and, after a commercial, the lead story began: "A seven month undercover investigation of theft at local postal facility leads to one arrest." Following that introduction, video footage showed Stan Farrell, with head down, flanked by two officers being led from his home to a squad car. The accompanying narrative detailed the who, what, why, where and when of the bust. Farrell was an employee at the facility and alleged mastermind of the scheme. The investigation is continuing as authorities suspect Farrell did not operate alone. *Mastermind my eye*, thought Stan, *that idiot couldn't find his way out of a paper bag if it hadn't been for me.*

Jake's reaction was hair trigger and violent. He had never wanted a drink so badly in his life, but there was none at hand. So he threw the remote across the room hitting a mirror, which shattered, sending small shimmering chards onto the otherwise lackluster carpet. He then karate-kicked the television, knocking it off its already precarious perch and onto an array of plants. Dirt flew everywhere, along with stems, blooms, and pots.

As suddenly as he had erupted, he stopped. Seeing the physical damage he had inflicted startled him. He hadn't lost control like that in years. In a flash of clarity, he understood. He was scared shitless! And mad at Stan for getting caught, and paranoid the cops would now be on his tail. Hell, he was probably already under surveillance and hadn't realized it.

Time to get out of Dodge, he thought. He already knew the how, but where? No stranger to skipping town, Jake already had Plan B figured out in terms of getting away and not leaving a trail, if and when, the need arose.

Two months earlier he had filled out a change of address form for a package addressee he thought would be a good fit for a new persona. Jake had intercepted Allan Stewart's package initially, for being insured, having "fragile" stamped all over it, and being an unusual size and shape: it turned out to be a violin, this Stewart guy had purchased on Ebay to add to his extensive collection. Replacement value $125,000; purchase price, $75,000, according to the papers enclosed.

As Stewart's mail and packages started arriving at Jake's address, he was able to build his needed arsenal of bank and credit card statements, new checks, tax information and other data. He kept them in a safety deposit box, separate from other safety deposit boxes he maintained at several banks. It didn't take long to learn that Al was single, 55, well educated, and wealthy as hell-lived the life of a gentleman farmer in Virginia, outside Charlottesville.

With adrenalin pumping, Jake emptied his various bank accounts, safety deposit boxes, packed a carry-on bag, threw anything perishable in his apartment into a dumpster, bought a plane ticket under his new alias, and was in the air less than 24 hours after seeing Stan on the news: a manic episode in full swing.

Jake's biggest concern was that, under interrogation, Stan would implicate him in the fencing operation. Plea bargains were attractive to felons, and Jake could imagine Stan opting for one if it could reduce his sentence. *Whoa, Al,* he said to himself, practicing his new name, *aren't you jumping the gun a bit. Relax, the guy has been arrested, not convicted, and if we covered our tracks well, they may have to throw the whole thing out for lack of evidence.*

After calming himself down for a while, Jake was able to relax a little and enjoy the flight. It was early evening with clear skies and out his window he could see the brilliant sun setting. In two hours he'd be in Pittsburgh with an hour layover before the final leg of his trip . . . to Lakeside.

Yes, Lakeside. Why not? He could look up Babs and wreak a little havoc in her world until he decided what to do more permanently. Thanks to Al, he now had a passport so could easily leave the country if need be. In the meantime, Babs would provide the diversion he badly needed.

Al's plane was on time. He immediately went outside the terminal for a long overdue cigarette. It was so cold he couldn't tell his breath from the smoke as he exhaled. Al hadn't felt the bite of this kind of cold in years and was ill prepared. He'd need a heavier coat and warmer gloves for this visit. That's for sure.

After his smoke, Al re-entered the terminal and went to the Budget car rental desk where he signed out a front wheel drive hybrid the clerk assured him this was a good choice for getting around in all the snow and ice. What the clerk didn't know was that Al wanted the hybrid for its virtual silence. *You can't hear them coming or going; great for stalking prissy old bitches,* he mused to himself.

"I don't imagine you get much weather like this in Virginia, do you Mr. Stewart?," asked the clerk. Just as the clerk asked the question, Al realized he was about to sign "Jacob Proctor" instead of "Allan Stewart" on the rental contract. *Phew, that was close,* Al thought. *I've got to be more careful with this name stuff.*

When he checked into his motel, a mere five minutes from the airport, he signed his new name with relative ease. The motel had no restaurant, and he was hungry, so he asked for a recommendation *with* smoking. "Sorry, as of February first, there's no smoking in any public places in Lakeside," the clerk said apologetically.

Al ended up going to a nearby drive-thru for some burgers and back to his room where he could eat, watch TV, and smoke to his heart's content. By the time he ate it was after 10:00, and he suddenly felt bone tired after all the tension of the last two days. He was out like a light, but not until he took a minute to scoop the phone book out of the nightstand drawer and see if there was a listing for Barbara or George Baker. Indeed there was; actually, it just said: B.Baker, 228 Bayview Drive, 459-5253.

When the phone rang, Babs was playing ball on the stairs with Sam to tire him out. The weather had been too rough even for a lab to be out for very long. There was a lot of canine, as well as human, cabin fever at the Baker's these days.

"I hope it's George," she said to the dog as she grabbed the phone, and it was. He and his brother Ed were on their annual bonding trip for a week. They'd left that morning and were headed for Atlantic City, New Jersey. Ed had driven up the night before from his home in Charlottesville, VA, where he had moved following his retirement 10 years ago. He loved to drive and wasn't the least daunted by any distance or weather conditions. His cars were generally big, luxurious, and comfortable so George always enjoyed the ride.

After a couple days of gambling in Atlantic City, the two would probably head down to Stone Harbor where they had spent many summers growing up, then on to Cape May for a fabulous seafood dinner and overnight. After that, if they weren't sick of each other, they'd probably go down to Washington to soak up some history. George shuddered at the cost of accommodations there, but Ed always had "ins" or deals that made their overall travel costs reasonable.

"Hi, dear," Babs said. "I take it you got there ok?"

"Absolutely, everything went great. We're staying at the Borgata. Let me give you the phone number before I forget. Cell phones don't work too well inside the hotel for some reason; probably because of interference from all that "ching" in the slots," he joked.

Babs took down the number then they chatted about odds and ends including the weather, what was in the mail for him, that Ed had left his nose hair clippers behind, that Sam was driving her crazy, etc. Before hanging up, and after each of them saying I love you, George chimed in with his predictable reminders of "don't forget to lock up and pull the shades before you go to bed, make sure the flashlight next to the bed works, etc.

"George, we're fine," she countered. "Sam will watch out for me, and, remember, I was on my own for a long time before I hooked up with you," she said gently.

"I know hon. Sleep tight I'll call you again tomorrow. Ed sends love too. Bye now."

George's phone call to Babs came at around 5:30 p.m., just a few hours before Al Stewart's plane landed in Lakeside . . .

Al woke around 3 a.m. with an urgent need to go to the bathroom. He felt foggy and disoriented as he fumbled for the light. For a moment he'd forgotten where and who he was. But once in the bathroom, clarity returned, and he was now wide awake. Awake enough to want to begin working on Babs.

He fished his cell phone out of his coat and dialed her number. A sleepy voice answered on the third ring, "Hello, Bakers." Al didn't speak but breathed heavily into the mouthpiece several times and hung up.

Chapter Twelve

Three Samples in Question

Addie took out three manila file folders and three green four-page work sheets from her desk. She carefully wrote the name of the three specimens of handwriting Bill Deluth had sent her: Jake Proctor, Stan Farrell, and Mark Soderberg. She took each of the samples and made copies; then she enlarged each copy of handwriting.

She glanced at the handwriting of Jake Proctor quickly and noticed the marks over the 'i' dots were thick and bludgeoned denoting domination. Addie decided to put this handwriting aside and complete the analyses of the two other candidates first. All three handwritings had different slants; Addie was delighted to have the variety.

Carefully, she took out her ruler and measured one hundred strokes writing each word onto the tabulation sheet for determining slant. After counting all the strokes, Addie colored the perspectograph, that measured the writer's emotional pre-disposition.

The slant of Farrell was very far to the left the majority of the time. This may have indicated an extremely emotionally removed individual, a person who did not show his true feelings. What feelings he did have were for himself but not for others. He had little self-awareness of his own actions. Farrell was probably deeply hurt in his childhood. Addie surmised that he had a very close relationship with his mother. The writer that slants backwards is often self-possessed and motivated solely by his or her own self-interests. Farrell was intelligent with comprehensive thinking patterns and a keen imagination in the realm of ideas. Under the section of the analysis which indicated fears, Farrell showed he was very jealous and prone to worrying. He was very dominating and extremely stubborn the kind of stubbornness that makes a person immovable.

Farrell was also highly acquisitive, liking to acquire not only things, but ideas. He scored poor marks under the components of integrity. In regard to social traits, Farrell did not like to be alone. Addie noted that he had excellent manual dexterity. That characteristic makes sense, she thought, if someone is handling packages and dealing with machinery, which probably breaks down from time to time.

She stretched before doing the next analysis. It took her about three to four hours to prepare a good report. She liked to write up her analysis, and then go back and edit her findings the next day, or later in the afternoon after some exercise.

Scientifically, using the exact same careful procedure, she analyzed on the handwriting sample of Mark Soderberg. Addie's method had always been to objectively perform each handwriting analysis that was sent to her. She tried very hard to mentally report only those characteristics that she saw in each person's handwritings; and if she did editorialize, or give an opinion, she made sure she specified that she was giving an editorial comment at the end of each report.

Soderberg's handwriting indicated he was a person who was driven more by logic than emotion. Like Farrell, he did not like working on his own. He had good investigative thinking patterns and the ability to be decisive. Soderberg was highly intuitive but also exemplified a person whose thinking could become confused at times. His deep pen pressure indicated a passionate nature but a person who did not show his feelings. He had little imagination and tended to be pessimistic. Addie felt this man did not have the characteristics to steal but wanted to be as professional as possible with her report. She was dealing with three people's lives and those of their families. She would never give her opinions, only her clinical analysis. Soderberg demonstrated high marks on integrity, and, although he might be brutally frank, he also exemplified a person loyal to others and his own ideals. *No*, thought Addie, *this is not the man.*

She went into the kitchen to make herself a cup of tea. She wrapped her hands around the mug to warm them and watched the steam vaporize. Thoughtfully, she started a dialogue in her head; *people's handwritings do change with age, medication, drugs and alcohol. All handwriting is brain writing and reflective of what is going on inside a person's head.* She remembered looking at two samples of handwritings of President Kennedy. One handwriting sample from when he was a teenager at Choate. He was a high, but practical, goal setter and very diplomatic. By the time he was president he had become less practical in setting goals and more visionary; his goals were far off in the distant future. His strong trait of diplomacy had waned. Perhaps he did not need it any more.

Addie knew she could not postpone looking at Jake's handwriting much longer. When someone changes their identity, clearly they have something to hide.

She wondered how Babs was doing. Addie felt conflicted. Her work for the post office was confidential, but, if Jake's handwriting demonstrated that he was becoming more dangerous, she felt it might be important to contact her dear friend. She had first analyzed Jake's handwriting about seven months ago, and it had not been an analysis for an employer, which this report would be.

Addie slipped a slice of lemon and teaspoon of honey into her tea mug then headed back to the office. Once again, she took a sample of Jake's handwriting and enlarged it on the copier. With her ruler, she measured every upward stroke until she had charted one hundred. Jake was highly emotional and overly responsive. These characteristics can be advantageous for a fighter pilot, but usually personalities like this must be highly trained and disciplined. The majority of the slant was to the far right, but ten percent of the slant was in the opposite direction heading to the left. This indicated an individual who is prepossessed and thinks only of himself. This pattern of reversed slants indicates a person who has a fractured personality. What makes this individual happy one day will not make this individual happy the next day. It is a complicated dynamic. Addie was concerned that some of the wavy lines could indicate drug use. The pen pressure in the handwriting was heavy, indicating a passionate person. However, the characteristics accompanying a conservative person who likes to conform to society were not present. Jake was a real loner and paranoid. He trusted no one. Addie examined Jake's mental processes. He was very bright with a highly analytical mind, which is investigative. He is a person who wanted to find the underlying cause of a problem. He was extremely good at detail. Interestingly enough, his handwriting indicated he is an independent thinker. That is a rare characteristic for someone who is working in a highly regimented organization like the Post Office. Clearly, he must hate his job, thought Addie. Jake scored high on imagination. He would have the ability to create new ideas and methods of operation. Like Farrell, Jake is very acquisitive.

The blunt marks over the 'i's, indicating a dominating nature, really scared Addie. The strokes were heavier and thicker than his previous handwriting samples from her files. He is becoming more violent, she thought. He is also extremely vain, a person who feels superior to others. He is highly sexual, but suffered from sexual frustration, which probably stemmed from some early childhood experiences. Not surprisingly, Jake is also very stubborn. There is a wavy baseline, which could mean a certain versatility, but due to other negative characteristics, Addie interpreted this as Jake's volatile emotional nature. Like Farrell and Soderberg, Jake also showed good manual dexterity and precision. Addie surmised that he would be good at fixing machinery and a good athlete.

Addie typed up all three reports. She knew Bill Deluth was very anxious to get them. She needed to clear her head before proofing. So she persuaded Butch to take an afternoon walk.

They drove to the beach. It was a bit cold but the winter air was refreshing. Both Butch and Addie tried to get an hour of exercise every day.

"Butch I am very worried about this last handwriting sample from Jake." Addie turned the collar up on her coat. The sun sparkled on the ocean while flocks of black and white mergansers, bobbed up and down near the shore.

"Well, we have an alarm system. The guy lives in Memphis which is some consolation, although, admittedly he must have a driver's license. He really wouldn't have any reason to come after you, would he?" Butch asked, putting his arm around Addie as they walked down the beach.

"Do you remember the second Federal Express package I got from this guy? It was delivered by a man who had a tattoo. I remember it because it was in a star shape right underneath his watch. I remember noticing it. He also was not driving a Federal Express truck, which I realize is not that unusual. I actually called the company a few days ago and asked them if their drivers ever made deliveries not in Fed Ex trucks, which the representative said was entirely possible.

"But Babs called me and said she thought she had seen this guy, Jake, or whatever he is calling himself these days on a Public Broadcasting Network story about the post office in Memphis.

"But you may be right. I am overreacting; unless he knew that I was analyzing his handwriting for the Post Office. I always operate as a sub-contractor. So the information is confidential and only for Bill Deluth.

"But, I'm nervous about Babs, and her safety. I told you Jake's handwriting was the same as her old friends, didn't I?" Addie looked at Butch. She was always impressed with his good looks even though she had looked at him a thousand times. She took a deep breath and enjoyed the smell of the ocean air.

"What! This wacko is someone Babs knew? I'm not sure I really understood that. Does he know you two know each other? When did you discover this? Maybe you did tell me, but it just did'nt sink in. Does George know about this guy?" Now Butch did look alarmed. Addie felt somewhat relieved that he was finally tuning in to the seriousness of the situation.

"I am not sure whether or not Babs has told George. She had a pretty uncomfortable relationship with that guy Lee before George arrived on the scene. And this Jake Proctor's handwriting matches that of both Babs's Lee Roberts and "Mr. Wacko," Jake Hunt." Addie loved walking on the beach.

"Uncomfortable, like how? Tell me more. And what do you mean they *all* match?" Butch looked at her.

"Well, I guess they had a love affair and at first Babs was very attracted to him. He is a Southerner and interested in history, which is one of her favorite subjects. She thought he was attractive and really fell head over heals for him. She said she even fantasized about them getting married. Well . . . all young women fantasize about getting married to someone they are attracted to so that part is not all that significant.

But then she said he became very possessive. Every time she had dinner with a girlfriend, he would show up at the restaurant to make sure she was actually having dinner with whom she had said she was with. He became increasingly needy and almost could not let her out of his sight. By that time they had moved in together.

She noticed that he was drinking a lot. Finally she organized an intervention with his brother and boss. He did go for treatment, but never ever forgave her. Shortly after that Lee left Lakeside and returned to the South.

When Babs and I had our visit, she pulled out handwriting samples for me to analyze. I had just done the analysis of a guy named Mr. Hunt, and there was the *same* handwriting sample. You do remember that incident when I received handwriting with the perverted language? I sent copies of the handwriting to Barbara Brattle, the consultant I used for court document work, verifying that the writer was the same."

They had walked almost the length of the beach and really had not looked up at Darby Island.

"Yes, of course honey, I do remember that. What are you going to tell Deluth?"

Butch stopped now and looked at her; clearly, he too was beginning to worry.

"I will disclose everything, including my prior connection with Mr. Hunt who it turns out is not named Mr. Hunt at all. When you perform a handwriting analysis, as you know, you give the characteristics of a person without trying to make any value judgments—or at least this was very much my training. The employer then can take the information and make his own conclusions. I e-mail the report and then discuss the findings. If the person who has hired me asks my opinion, I give it to them.

I think after I have talked with Deluth, I will call Babs and just see how she is doing. My work with the post office is confidential, but I want to make sure that she is all right. Certainly, she would have told me if Lee had contacted her."

"Well, I am glad you told me about this. I don't think I realized all the potential ramifications, sweetheart. I'm sorry if I haven't been more supportive." Butch gave Addie a little hug.

"Don't be silly. You are always supportive. But now, I think we just should be cautious about who comes up our driveway, and phone calls that are hang ups . . . All those little signs they have in the movies."

They finished their walk and chatted about seeing an opera on video that night.

Addie felt greatly refreshed from her walk. Exercise always helps put everything in perspective. She also felt happy about the fact that Butch really had tuned in to what had been happening with Jake and Babs.

Back in her office, Addie went over all three of the handwriting analyses. She improved some of the language and tightened up the text in all the reports. She then e-mailed the information to Bill Deluth with a message that she would call him at 10 a.m. to go over any questions he may have. Addie felt relieved. Her completed assignment would wait until tomorrow. She tried to discipline herself not to think about the stressful situation.

At 10:00 the next morning, Addie settled in front of her computer, telephone, and a hard copy of each analysis. She dialed Bill Deluth's number and spoke with his secretary who connected her with Bill.

"Well good morning. Thank you so much for getting this information to me so quickly. I can see that there is quite a lot to this handwriting. I have been going over the reports." Bill Deluth had a steady reassuring tone of voice.

"Good morning, Bill. I am calling to thank you for giving me this opportunity and to see if you have any questions. Firstly, I think I had better disclose several very bizarre coincidences. Do you have a few minutes, or am I interrupting something?" Addie asked.

"I do have a few questions. You are my number one priority today so take as much time as you need." Bill responded.

Addie continued. "About seven or eight months ago, I received a handwriting sample from Mr. Hunt with a Memphis, Tennessee address. I have a website, called Handwriting-Traits.com, so I assumed that the individual found my services there. Truthfully, I was delighted someone saw the site. The contents of the letter were perverted and disgusting, but because I tell my customers, I do not pay any attention to the text and just analyze the formations of the letters, I decided to proceed. What was ironic, was earlier that day, I had gone to the post office in Manaport, to lodge a written complaint because I had sent a package to my daughter-in-law in San Francisco, Priority Mail that never arrived. About a month or so later, I went to Lakeside, Pennsylvania, on Lake Erie, to visit my old college roommate Babs Baker. She had saved quite a few letters from various people and one was an old boy friend who she felt had a very unusual personality. The old boyfriend's letter, was the same handwriting I had analyzed a month before for Mr. Hunt. But, of course, you know him as Jake Proctor and Babs knows him as Lee Roberts. Just to confirm my analysis, I sent two copies of the handwritings to a court document examiner by the name of Barbara Brattle who has worked for the Connecticut Police Department. She confirmed that the same person wrote the handwriting samples from Mr. Lee and Mr. Hunt. And I can tell you these both match Proctor." Addie stopped talking to listen to Bill's reaction.

"Did the post office ever find the package or reimburse you for the postage?" asked Bill. Addie could hear the seriousness in his voice.

"No to both questions. But now that I have disclosed that information, let me tell you the highly systematized and scientific process of each analysis. I measure 100 strokes in a handwriting sample and plot the findings of the handwriting slant onto a chart. This gives me the Emotional Predisposition, which is the most important factor of a person's make up. You may notice that Farrell, Soderberg and Proctor all have handwritings that slant in different directions." Addie paused to get Bill's reaction.

"Good Lord, my handwriting also slants to the right, but I am not sure that I want to show you anything I have written." Bill chuckled.

"Oh don't worry. If I told you President Eisenhower's handwriting had a far right handed slant would you feel better?" Addie laughed.

"I believe that I would." Bill answered.

"People with handwritings, which slant to the right are the drivers of society. They are usually the ones who force action and extend themselves to others. Eisenhower, for example, was very empathetic and caring about his men. This characteristic made him a good general.

Now clearly, handwriting analysis is not that simple. There are other strong mitigating qualities, which make huge differences. Proctor's handwriting is a good case in point. He has that drive but he is also acquisitive and duplicitous. So, you have an individual who is action-oriented, likes to acquire things and measures low on the integrity chart. This is an editorial comment, if you will allow me to make one; people with this profile like to acquire things for the sport of it. You will also notice under the second heading in the report, entitled Mental Processes, that Proctor is very bright—exceptionally bright. He is a loner, however, and does not necessarily like to work with other people.

His co-worker Stan Farrell also has similar characteristics but is not a loner and likes to be around people. Farrell is also very bright, but he is someone who will always think of himself first. Soderberg's handwriting slant's vertically. He is driven more by logic than emotion. He has high marks on integrity even though he may not be the most diplomatic guy on the block. All three candidates show good finger dexterity and excellent spatial relationship capabilities." Addie tended to talk very quickly when she was excited and she felt her blood pressure going up.

"What do you think about Mark Soderberg?" Bill asked.

"Well . . . I try very hard to just present the evidence and let you do further investigating. Soderberg does not like to work alone. Even though he does not *show* much emotion, he does feel things deeply. See how heavy the pen pressure is. Soderberg has high marks on integrity. He does not have a joyful personality or a light touch. But if you are asking my opinion, based on the findings and characteristics, I would start interviewing Farrell and Proctor first. Soderberg may also have seen some behavior in the other colleagues he is uncomfortable about, but that is really where on-site investigation takes over. Good police officers are excellent at studying body language and using techniques to make people give more information than they wanted in an interview. Proctor has a very large ego. He probably feels greatly superior to anyone he works with." Addie slowed her speech down a bit.

She and Bill continued to chat and go over some other parts of the analysis for the next five minutes. "If you have any other questions or would like me to talk with someone else, please don't hesitate to call me." Addie told Bill.

"Thank you very much Addie, you have been most helpful. Needless to say, this is highly confidential material and it is very important that you don't discuss this with anyone. Send my best to Butch." Bill was getting ready to sign off.

"I certainly will do that Bill. Please don't hesitate to call me any time. My office is in our house, so I am easily reachable in the evenings or on the weekends."

"I'll stay in touch. Thanks again." Bill hung up the phone.

Addie sat motionless for a few seconds listening to the dial tone. Jake and Stan could easily have worked together she thought, but one would really have to use her information and complete a further investigation. It sure did not look good.

Butch walked into their office and turned on his computer.

"How did it go?" He asked.

"I would like to think it went very well," responded Addie. "Of course, you never know. Bill sent his best to you. He really is a nice guy. Bill also reminded me that this investigation was highly confidential, which is a given. I do think that two out of the three handwriting samples are by people who could be capable of committing crimes," said Addie thoughtfully.

"I wonder how Babs is doing. I might give her a call to find out how things are going. Just a, 'hi, how are you, want to hear your voice,' kind of phone call. I guess they just had some big snowstorm. I wonder if they do any cross-country skiing."

Chapter Thirteen

Things Heat Up In Wintry Lakeside

It was now a week since Al had "officially" become Al and left Memphis. Except for the bitter cold and lack of sunshine, he liked Lakeside. It wasn't too big; it wasn't too small, and it was easy to navigate. The people were friendly, but not too friendly, and he found them very helpful in suggesting restaurants, shopping, things to do, etc. As far as anyone knew, he was in Lakeside doing market development consulting work for a franchise interested in the area. The day after his arrival, he'd headed to a Kinko's to have business cards made backing up this fake profession.

Also, the day after his arrival, he began in earnest to stalk Babs. Hearing her voice again was all he needed to bolster his resolve. He'd never really stalked a woman before but had fed a morbid fascination for such activity. The tabloids were full of instances of celebrity stalking, and he always read such accounts with relish.

He wanted to know Babs's every move. He'd watch her, he'd follow her, but she'd never suspect a thing. After he knew her daily routine well enough, he'd form a plan to start his reign of terror. He didn't necessarily want to hurt her physically, just destroy her psychologically.

Early evening on the day after his arrival, Al sat in his car a half a block south of Babs's house. A local street map, available at his motel, made it easy to find her address. Although the rental car had a lot of bells and whistles, it didn't boast a GPS system. Before he parked, Al drove around the neighborhood a bit. He wanted to see how and where cars were parked so he could follow suit and not be conspicuous. Cars seemed to be everywhere in every which way. Few of the homes had garages and many of the driveways were no longer than one car length.

It was now dark. Al had a clear view of the Baker house which was ablaze with light, but all the shades were drawn. They were opaque though, so movement could be detected if someone were to pass by a window. Al noted two vehicles at the residence: a late model red Ford pick-up in front of the house, and a royal blue PT Cruiser in the driveway.

The house itself came as a surprise. It was a small two-story asphalt shingle structure, not at all what Al would have figured for Babs with her hoity-toity background and breeding. She'd gone away to boarding school. His roots were far more humble, and he had always carried bitterness about not being "to the manor born."

Even though the house was modest, Al had to admit it looked very cared for. There was even a section of the proverbial picket fence on one side. It looked as though the back yard was fenced in sections; stockade and chain link from what he could tell.

Al sat there for a good hour, and decided he wasn't going to see any activity worth sticking around for that night. Then he noticed an outside light go on in the back yard, and could see something moving about. He soon realized the Bakers had a dog. *Must be going out for the last pee of the day*, Al thought. He couldn't tell what kind of dog, or how big, but he did wonder if it was a barker and if it was mean or friendly.

Back in his room, Al felt restless. He checked the TV listings; nothing appealed to him. He thought of his daughter and wondered if he dare call her. He thought of a lot of things in no particular order but with increasing intensity. He became agitated and longed for a joint. He couldn't bring any pot with him through airport security, and he had no contacts to score any in Lakeside, but he decided to find one. He knew the best place would be a bar, and he'd noticed Lakeside had one on just about every corner. A stiff drink would taste good too, but he didn't dare. He'd managed to stay away from the stuff this long and couldn't afford to blow it now.

Not two minutes from his motel, he pulled into the Mario's Tavern parking lot. It was the middle of the week and the place looked packed. *A good sign*, he thought to himself. Another good sign was seeing some dudes milling around a car even though it was too cold to be outside socializing. Al parked nearby, grabbed his keys, leaving the car unlocked, and walked casually toward the group of men.

"Hey guys, what's up?" Al said, "I'm new around here and lookin' to score some weed 'wondering if you can help me?"

"You a cop?" asked the largest and meanest looking of the loitering foursome.

"Hell, no," Al answered and showed the guy his business card.

Everyone relaxed, introduced themselves and exchanged harmless conversation.

Ten minutes later and $300 lighter, Al headed back to the motel with an ounce of pot and a cell phone number for any future needs. He suddenly remembered he didn't have any papers to roll a joint and so stopped first at a convenience store. He also stacked up on cigarettes, Diet Pepsi, and the latest tabloids. It'd be fun to get high and read about two-headed babies, the male dog who had puppies and stuff like that. Maybe there'd even be some news about celebrity stalking to give him ideas about his Babs project.

Back in his room, he found the weed was high quality and very potent. After only a few tokes he was buzzin' with thoughts of how to proceed in his role as bitch stalker the next day.

The next morning, not having checked the weather forecast he was surprised to see there had been quite an overnight snowfall. At least six inches, he guessed. Now, not only did he need a warmer coat, but he also needed some kind of boots. It was only nine o'clock, and he guessed the nearby discount store didn't open until ten. He figured he could shower, grab a quick breakfast, be there when they opened, and leave the rest of the day to work on Babs. Al was *very* eager to work on Babs. If pot was his opiate, she was now his stimulant.

Al was in such a hurry to get his purchases out of the way, he neglected to stop at an ATM for cash before heading to the store. While at the check-out with boots and coat in hand, and a long line of shoppers behind him, he quickly decided to pay with one of his new "Al" credit cards. This glitch in his carefully laid fugitive plans made him nervous. His antsy demeanor was noted by the clerk, and she made a mental note to remember this guy.

As he drove toward Babs' neighborhood, Al was impressed with the road conditions; plowing was well underway, and driving was very manageable. However, because of plowing, however, he had a bit of a challenge parking near Babs's house this time. Where it had been clear, there were now piles of snow along the sides of her street. He lucked out when he saw a perfect little indent he could pull in and remain almost hidden but with the view he needed to watch her house.

What he first noticed was the truck was plowed-in and obviously hadn't moved an inch since the day before. He assumed that George used the truck. So could it be that he wasn't home, that he was away somewhere? The next thing he noticed was the PT Cruiser was gone.

Al had started a log recording his stalking, noting the date, time, and any activity. It made him think of bird watching. He even had the binoculars. *Now,* he wondered, *how long would he have to wait for this particular little birdie to appear?*

While he waited, the sky cleared, and the sun came out. He saw people walking their dogs, UPS making a delivery, some guy using his snow blower, and other normal neighborhood activity. After about 45 minutes, through his rearview mirror, he noticed a PT Cruiser coming down the street. A royal blue one—had to be Babs. He desperately hoped she didn't notice his car or him in it. He didn't dare look as her car passed by. Instead, he held up a paper and pretended read. "Whew," he sighed, as the car went by.

The Cruiser pulled into the driveway, but it was a full two minutes before anyone emerged. Al remembered Babs was a public radio junkie, and figured she was riveted to some story she couldn't bear to miss.

Finally, there she was, an older Babs, a slightly heavier Babs, but Babs all the same; the same blonde hair, the preppy clothing. Her eyeglasses were the only real surprise. 'Used to be she'd never go anywhere without popping in her contacts lenses.

Al watched her open the back of the car and remove several shopping bags, then disappear into the enclosed front porch. A second later she reappeared to collect the mail from the mailbox attached to the house. As she did so, she looked up the street in Al's direction. A woman and her dog were walking towards her direction. Babs yelled, "hi" to them and commented on the wonderful, overdue sunshine. Al rolled the driver side window halfway down so he could clearly hear the women's conversation.

The woman enthusiastically agreed, then asked "When will George be back?"

"Not 'til Sunday," Babs said. "Enjoy your walk I plan to get out with Sam a little later" then she turned to go back into the house.

Al couldn't believe his luck in finding out George was away and wouldn't be back for four more days! He decided to wait another hour, at most, to see if Babs emerged with Sam whom he now assumed was the dog he'd seen in the backyard. If they didn't show, he'd leave. Too many people were coming out of the woodwork to walk their dogs or stroll in the sunshine.

Not fifteen minutes after making his decision, Al saw Babs head out with Sam in tow. Fortunately, she was walking the other direction and wouldn't pass his car. The dog was large, probably at least 80 pounds, and appeared to be a purebred yellow lab. *Never met a lab I didn't like or who didn't like me*, Al thought, relieved. In fact, he once owned one, a black male. Even though the dog was good-natured, his strength proved disastrous for one of his girlfriends who was in the dog's path when he was chasing something. She ended up with a broken leg. He remembered reaming her out for not getting out of the dog's way of the dog and breaking up with her after her leg cast came off.

For the next two days, Al drove through Babs' neighborhood every couple of hours from early morning to late afternoon, but her car was never there. He decided she must have a part-time job somewhere. But what about the dog, maybe a neighbor let him out during the day, or maybe Sam went with her? Al was frustrated with lurking around in vain.

It was no better in the evening. He'd go back after dark, and she'd be home by then, but there was absolutely no activity. Nobody came over. She never left. And he noticed all the lights were out by ten p.m., usually earlier.

He didn't want to start his reign of terror until the day before George was due back. But in the meantime, he needed more stimulation. The next day he'd follow her.

He arrived on her street the next morning by 7 a.m.: lights were on at Bab's, and her car was there. At precisely 7:50 a.m., out she came, carrying what looked like a lunch tote, purse, and a larger tote. Al waited until she backed out, then followed a safe distance behind. He almost lost her at a traffic light but managed to catch up. Her destination was a beautiful home in an upscale neighborhood next to a public park. He noticed assorted children's play equipment in the yard and some Easter decorations on the front door.

About 10 minutes after Babs entered the house, an SUV backed out the driveway, followed by a van. A female was driving the SUV; a male was driving the van. "Babs must be their sitter," Al guessed. He decided she'd probably be there all day, and didn't want to stick around. Instead, he'd get stoned and take a drive around the peninsula which was 13 miles of natural beaches, wood trails, and a brand new environmental center. Then he'd go for lunch at a German deli that had been highly recommended by the motel receptionist. After that, maybe a movie matinee, or better yet, an adult movie venue, he was horny as hell.

The deli was in an attractive strip plaza near the peninsula. Al got there a little before noon to find it already crowded and patrons waiting. The interior was jammed with tables for most occupancy of limited space. He didn't relish sitting in the midst of the congestion, but was hopeful for a table on the perimeter toward the back. He was soon in luck and quickly claimed the spot before anyone else had the same idea.

The place smelled marvelous, and he could see from other's selections and the deli case nearby that the food was top quality. There was also a bakery section, and he already imagined getting some pastries to go. While he waited for a menu, he started thumbing through the *Lakeside Morning News*, which he found to be a surprisingly good read.

When his order came, he took his time savoring the pastrami and assorted cheeses piled high on thick slices of rye bread dripping with mustard and mayo. He couldn't really read while maneuvering the huge sandwich and instead enjoyed some people watching. He could see beyond the sea of people out to the sidewalk as well. A flash of blue caught his eye, and he saw that a car similar to Babs's was pulling in front of the deli to park. *Now calm down,* he said to himself. *It's a popular car and color so there are probably lots of them in town. Also, you know she's at that house taking care of kids,* he told himself half convincingly.

Jesus Christ, it was Babs, out of her car now and heading right for the deli, and with another woman. What the f—, Al thought.

The two women entered and immediately headed for the bakery counter. Al was temporarily immobilized by their appearance but quickly collected his wits and made sure to hold his newspaper in such a way his face was hidden from their view. He was antsy to pay his bill and leave but knew he'd best sit tight until the *pastry princesses* were well on their way.

The chance encounter really shook him up. Al finally left the deli, he feeling more vulnerable and less in control of himself than he had for a long time. If she'd seen and recognized him the jig was up, wasn't it? He'd no longer be able to proceed with his plan to taunt and terrorize her. The thrill of the chase would be gone. He might as well be holed up in his motel room and think about where to go next.

Babs couldn't put her finger on it, but admitted to her friend a sense of uneasiness the last few days. "Maybe it's because George is away," she offered. "But somehow something is amiss, and I don't feel safe," she added." This was what the two women talked about when they left the deli, not knowing that ominous Al was trying to be invisible just a stone's throw from where they were standing.

When they said goodbye after lunch, Bab's friend made her promise to call her any time if she felt frightened or just needed to talk. Babs promised, then the two hugged and went their separate ways.

Al was shaken by running into Babs at the deli that he decided to re-think his approach. Lakeside was proving to be a small big town, and he didn't want to risk revealing himself needlessly. He'd now think long and hard about how to scare the shit out of her without being detected. Tomorrow: Saturday was the day he planned to start.

Before dawn, and after the morning paper was delivered to her door, Al stealthily crept up Bab's front steps and placed a special surprise in the rolled up newspaper. It was no longer alive, but it was sure to scare her plenty.

Chapter Fourteen

Murderers, Stalkers, and Sexual Deviants

"How did you sleep, sweetheart?" Butch rolled over and gave Addie a good morning kiss.

"Not very well. I keep thinking about Babs and worrying. I just have this uneasy feeling about Mr. Waco. It's one of those intuitive-female-sixth-sense sort of feelings I get from time to time." Addie looked at Butch, surrounded by bed sheets.

"Oh those 'from time to time feelings is it?'" Mused Butch.

"Yeah, 'those from time to time feelings.'" Addie joined in the laughter. "I am actually quite psychic. For example, once I was really thinking about my dear old Mum. I went to the phone to call her, and she was on the other line before I even started to dial her number. It was incredible. I also had that experience with another old room mate named Marcy—you remember her—she roomed with Babs and me our last year of college in Boston."

"I do remember her—I remember all of you cute girls. Well, why don't you call Babs and see how she is doing? I do think as your legal advisor you should not reveal that you have been doing any work for the United States Post Office however." Butch sat up in bed. He was on his side holding his head with his left elbow in a crooked fashion.

"I totally agree. I will just give her a call and see how she is doing. Sort of a 'hi babe, what's new . . . any weirdos lurking around frightening you to death?' Just joking. We call each other from time to time as well as communicating by frequent e-mails. So, that is nothing unusual. Mm . . . What is today? Saturday, she wouldn't be working. I'll give her a call after breakfast. I know that she and George are early risers. I could not call all of my friends early in the morning, but I can call the Bakers. It's interesting how you get to know the habits of your friends, isn't it?"

"What do you want for breakfast?" Butch was moving towards the bathroom. He was usually the first one downstairs to pick up the two newspapers the Stubbs read every morning: *The Boston Globe* and *The Wall Street Journal.*

"It's Saturday. I could be talked into bacon and eggs," said Addie.

"How about baked eggs?" Butch smiled back at her.

"Your famous baked eggs, would you really make those for me? Would ya, huh, huh? Gosh now I know you love me!" Addie sat straight up in bed, grabbed a pillow, and affectionately threw it at Butch.

"Hello, the Baker residence." Addie heard Babs's voice and was delighted she was at home.

"Hey Babe, how are you doing? It is your old friend Addie. I felt like talking to you and hope this is a good time for a bit of catching up."

"Oh, this is a great time. George is in Atlantic City with his brother for their annual bonding trip and our adorable little dog Sam and I are holding down the fort. How have you been? It is so nice to hear your voice. I'm just sitting here having a cup of coffee and thinking about the rest of my day." Babs took another sip of hot steaming brew.

"What have you been up to? Did you ever tell George very much about Jake? I mean Lee." Addie decided to cut right to the chase. She thought this was a good opportunity to bring up the subject without George in the house. "I know you can talk freely with George away."

"It is so weird you brought this up. No, I never really talked to him about it. Why, do you know something I don't, that I should?" Babs sounded very concerned.

Addie felt uncomfortable, but decided to avoid the question. "We are going to Palm Beach on Monday and I am giving a short lecture about my analyses of the American presidents. I noticed that there is another lecture

being given by someone about 'Murderers, Stalkers, and Sexual Deviants!'"
She began to laugh.

Babs howled with laughter. "'Murderers, Stalkers, and Sexual Deviants!'
You have got to be kidding! It sounds fascinating. I wish that I could go
with you. Please take notes and e-mail me after the lecture. Is this open to
the public or just to other professional handwritings analysts?"

"This lecture is just for people in the industry. We often get together
and give papers to each other so we get some feedback before giving the
information to the outside world. It is interesting, sometimes painful. Most
handwriting analysts do not mind disagreeing with each other, and I always
learn something. Palm Beach is a beautiful area. So there will probably be
a fun group. Sometimes they book these meetings in Ohio because it is
in the central part of the country. Now however, the executive committee
has started to get smart and hold the meetings in locations that are more
desirable. It will be fun to get a little sun. How's your weather up there?"

"We just had a big snow storm, a bit of a freak in Lakeside this time of
the year. To get back to a more important topic, I have been thinking of
telling George a little more about my relationship with Lee. It seems sort
of uncomfortable though. You really think I should?" The tone of Babs's
voice was thoughtful.

"Well, look at it this way. You were involved with Lee before you
even met George. It is not like being sixteen, for god sakes. When you get
married at this age, it is a given we all had a past. I know this sounds weird,
but I told Butch about the letter and the coincidence of the handwritings
being the same. I think he finally understands how nervous I feel from time
to time about this situation. I notice that he is careful to ask someone on
the phone who is calling if he doesn't recognize their voice. He also takes a
good look at who is coming up our driveway. I may be over protective of
you, but I just think it is prudent to clue in your husband. You could cook
George a good dinner and make an evening out of it. You know . . . tell
him, 'there is no one I love more than you, but there is something I want
you to know about.' Just think of how complicated it would be if you ran
into Lee, and then had to explain things to George. When does he get back
from Atlantic City?"

"Oh, in a few days. He and his brother like to gamble, then they usually
go to Stone Harbor on Cape May where they spent summers as boys, and
then onto Washington, D.C. George is a big history buff like me. He and his
brother can talk for hours about the Civil War and World War II." Babs had
a very distinctive cadence to her voice Addie loved to listen to her. She was

melodious. "Oh my gosh, I just thought of something. The phone rang last night at about 3:00 a.m. No one answered when I said 'hello,' and then there was some heavy breathing. Jesus, now I am feeling a little freaked out. Luckily, I have Sam here. He is a good watchdog and has good hearing. It is amazing I didn't think about it until now." Babs looked out the window as she spoke.

"You are kidding. God, that is a bit scary when you are alone. Do you have some good neighbors that are close by? You do, don't you? Why don't you call one of them and find out if anyone else in your neighborhood has been bothered? It's nice to just alert everyone, don't you think? Do you have anyone you could call in the middle of the night? Would you ever consider calling the police?" Addie asked.

"Now you are totally freaking me out. It was just one phone call. But I must admit that the more I talk about it, the creepier it feels," admitted Babs.

"Do you have a good friend you can call and tell about the phone call? It only happened once." Addie suggested.

"Well, I do have a lot of good friends I could call, so maybe I will. That way when I am missing, George will know to ask the police to trace all the incoming calls to the house." They both roared with laughter.

"I am going to give you my cell phone number. After the lecture about 'Murderers, Stalkers and Sexual Deviants' I will try to give you a call and see if I learned anything you should know. In the meantime, just mention the phone call to some of your neighbors; it really can't do any harm. Who knows? It probably is nothing, but it could be a robber watching the whole neighborhood." Addie cajoled Babs a bit.

"True—why don't you throw in a terrorist attacker while you are at it?" Babs shot back.

"I was thinking along those lines. Everything you read about police investigations tells you nothing can compare with the information the police and the FBI discover from talking to people in the neighborhood." Addie read a lot and loved to try to back up her remarks with factual data. "It was great to talk with you. Please promise me you'll be careful. Call some friends. I will call you in a couple of days from Florida. My cell phone number is (879) 322-5497. Call me if anything unusual happens."

"Thanks a lot for calling. I will be careful; it's very comforting to have a dog. Sam is still a puppy, but he is very protective of me and certainly is a good watch dog," Babs reassured Addie.

The opulent lobby at the Ritz Hotel in West Palm Beach had floor to ceiling mirrors and three elaborate glass chandeliers. The gold, gray, and silver wallpaper with butterflies and flowers evoked a Chinese theme. Large alabaster bowls of fresh chrysanthemums and a variety of tropical shells sat on a myriad of coffee tables. Well-dressed patrons chatted with each other or read newspapers. Large green palm trees flanked the long French doors leading to the pool and ocean beyond.

Addie and Butch sat outside for lunch despite a strong breeze.

"This is a real role reversal; usually I am the one accompanying you on a business trip. How does it feel to be a kept man?" Addie looked at Butch and smiled.

"Oh it's tough work, but I think I could get used to it!" Butch smiled "Would you like some wine with lunch, sweetheart?"

"I think I better stick with ice tea, but I certainly will join you after I have made my speech at dinner this evening." Addie smiled at the waitress who brought them menus.

"What time are you on?" Butch asked

"I am the first speaker, thank goodness. Then, I can relax. I must admit I'm a bit nervous. Usually when I give a lecture, it is to people who know nothing about handwriting analysis. But this is the first time I have spoken before a group of experts. It will be interesting to get their reactions. I hope I won't have any trouble with my Power Point demonstration."

"I can help you if you get into trouble," Butch offered.

"I know you can, honey. That's why I love you so much," Addie looked deeply into Butch's blue eyes.

"Well, I think I may have a glass of wine. Yes, this being a kept man could grow on me." Butch laughed. They ordered salads and chatted through a relaxing lunch overlooking the pool and ocean. The breeze created small white caps on the ocean.

There were about seventy-five handwriting experts attending the conference from all over the United States. The conference room filled up quickly and Addie was delighted that things were going as planned. Butch was sitting beside her and glanced at the program, "Hey, look at this. There is a retired prison warden giving a lecture analyzing the handwritings of 'Murders, Stalkers, and Sexual Deviants.'" Butch roared with laughter. "I didn't think this conference was going to be as exciting as this."

"Boy, am I glad my analysis of the American Presidents is coming first. I'd loose the group's interest for sure after that juicy subject." Addie took a deep breath. She knew from experience when she started to speak she would be fine, but now she had butterflies in her stomach.

Craig Meyers, President of the Handwriting Experts of America, gave the welcoming remarks and introduced Addie. She choose six American Presidents to discuss with visual images of their handwritings: George Washington, Abraham Lincoln, Ulysses S. Grant, Franklin D. Roosevelt, John F. Kennedy and Richard Nixon. What was of great interest to her, and her main thesis, was that Americans choose presidents based more on the conditions of the time than consistently looking for the same leadership characteristics.

She considered George Washington to be the quintessential American. His characteristics are that of a strong, entrepreneurial personality, showing tremendous drive and great self-determination. He was, in fact, the very essence of what Addie considered the prototype of an American personality.

Abraham Lincoln had tremendous passion and empathy for humanity. He was a cumulative thinker and tended to absorb information in building block fashion. One of his major characteristics was patience.

Many historians did not consider Grant a good President. However, he was an excellent general demonstrating great drive and determination on the battlefield.

Franklin Roosevelt was highly intuitive and looked at the big picture; he was conceptual in his thinking; once again the correct man for the times.

John F. Kennedy was a visionary and it is easy to look at his handwriting and see how he was able to give the world his remarkable, uplifting speeches.

Richard Nixon's handwriting was interesting from the perspective of showing how his self-confidence diminished during the Watergate scandal. Nixon's handwriting demonstrates a fast change in attitude.

Addie's speech seemed to be well received with some good questions at the end, which she felt she answered competently. She sat down and felt so relieved that it was over. She could actually hear her heart pounding and realized she was having an adrenalin rush.

"Good job, sweetheart," Butch whispered. "Now for the porno lecture," Addie laughed and felt much better for doing so.

Craig Myers then introduced Dr. Myron Hinkle. Hinkle had spent his entire career in the Criminal Justice Department and then became a handwriting expert in his retirement. He began by telling the audience he had spent his career in the United States prison system, and why he had become interested in handwriting analysis. He had wanted to see whether or not it was possible to forecast a person's behavior before they became a criminal. He admitted that there was no conclusive evidence, as such, but he did certainly see a pattern of handwriting behavior with criminals.

Hinkle's findings were coupled with other data from the prison systems and not as exclusively based on handwriting samples as Addie would have liked. Nevertheless, the information was interesting. He began by showing the handwritings of serial murderers.

Dr. Hinkle had a deep baritone voice and presented his information well, "There is a wide range of characteristics that seem to be present among murderers. Most however, exhibit a heavy blunt mark over the letter *i*. One might say that about many of the heads of major American corporations, as well." Everyone in the audience began to laugh. "People have been trying to figure out why since time began, some members of every population lose their ability to reason and control of their emotions to the point of rage. The Romans had theories about murderers and felt they were possessed by demons. Some English scientists felt a full moon heightened madness and there was a physiological explanation between body types and criminals. One theory evolved suggesting a person bearing a tattoo was more likely to be a criminal than people not wearing tattoos because the practice harkened humans back to a more primitive time in our evolution.

Theories will continue, but one thing that is true is more men commit murder than women. Women comprise 51% of the population but comprise only 10% of the murderers. Congratulations women, though this is not a mark of achievement for those of you who believe in Women's Liberation and equality." Once again, the audience laughed.

"During the 1990's, lawyers tried to use the diagnosis of Postpartum Depression as a reason for infanticide. I am not a doctor, I am a handwriting analyst and criminologist so I do not care to comment on that aspect of American legislation. We do have here a sample of a women who killed her four children." Dr. Hinkle flashed a handwriting sample on the screen. Addie, of course, along with every other handwriting expert sitting in the room, mentally made her own observation.

Dr. Hinkle continued his talk, "What we have here is a variety of slants within the same context of one writer, giving us a fractured personality. What makes this woman happy one day does not make her happy the next day. She is a loner and cannot relate easily to other people."

Addie felt uncomfortable. Viewing criminal handwritings made her queasy. She always prayed to God to let only good people into her life.

Usually she succeeded. Luckily Dr. Hinkle finished talking about murderers and went on to a discussion about stalkers.

"My god, this is freaking me out. I am going to need to take a fishing trip after this," Butch leaned over and whispered in Addie's ear. Addie began to laugh.

"You are not the only one. Can you imagine spending your entire career with this segment of the population?"

Dr. Hinkle continued, "According to a recent study, one in twelve women will be stalked sometime during their life without even knowing it. Stalkers are usually very meticulous about their victims and keep elaborate notes. There is so much information available on the internet today that a smart stalker can find out what type of car his victim is driving, her license number, and where she shops.

Celebrity stalking is highly publicized and there are any number of cases in which the victims end up murdered. The stalker becomes obsessed with his victim and in his twisted mind does not want anyone else to have his victim if he cannot have her. A stalker is acquisitive and highly possessive. On the grand scheme of things, they tend to be brighter than many other types of criminals. One celebrity stalker said he wanted to rape, torture, and cause pain to his victim."

As Dr. Hinkle pointed out, "Stalking is 'psychological terrorism.' The legislation, which has evolved from this form of terrorism, is described as 'someone who willfully, maliciously, and repeatedly follows or harasses another victim and who makes a credible threat with the intent to place the victim or victim's immediate family in fear for their safety. There must be at least two incidents of this crime and a pattern of intent to continue the behavior must be established for a person to be convicted."

Addie could not help but think about Babs. She and Butch were usually together now that he was retired, but Babs was still working and George was away. Oh gosh, Lee's handwriting showed a domineering personality, which was very acquisitive—he liked to hold on to things for the sake of holding on to them. Could he actually have the capability of becoming a stalker? *I must not let my imagination run away with me. Lee certainly was very bright with a cunning mind.* Addie could visually remember his handwriting—those very deep pointed tips to his 'm's and plunging heavy lines downwards indicating a very investigative mind. He was also persistent, so persistent. Addie also thought, looking at someone's handwriting like Lee's, that if he had applied himself in a more noble direction he could have become a contributing member of society.

"Oh great," whispered Butch. Now the part I have been waiting for: sexual deviants! I hope those characteristics don't show up in my handwriting."

Dr. Hinkle did have quite a good sense of humor, "and now the part of the lecture you have all been waiting for: sexual deviants." Once again the audience laughed. "The letters 's' and 'p' are almost always associated with sexual and athletic abilities. Interestingly enough, an exaggerated letter p within the context of a word can also mean a highly argumentative personality."

Oh Christ, thought Addie, *Lee's 'p's were so exaggerated! This confirms my suspicion that he could be dangerous.*

Dr. Hinkle showed five examples of handwriting samples. The first example was the handwriting of a man that had raped his mother. The second example was a brother who had raped his sisters. The propensity towards domination was not that uncommon unfortunately.

However, the sample that really undid Butch was the example of handwriting of a man who raped prostitutes and then surgically removed their eyeballs. Butch leaned over and nudged Addie, "Where do they find these people? I mean this is just amazing." He could only cope with his reaction by laughing.

"Quiet. They find these people in the state penitentiaries where they belong," Addie whispered back to Butch who also couldn't help but laugh a bit as well. The information was so horrifying.

Dr. Hinkle continued: "Sexually abnormal behavior begins early in childhood. Most of the abusers have been abused themselves, especially in the case of pedophiles. Violence, which is so often accompanied with this behavior, becomes more dramatic with each repetitive action. Prostitutes are at greater risk of being abused, being on the fringes of society. No one cares about them and they often don't have family members who know where they are.

The recidivism rate of abuse for sexual predators is very high and most of the drugs do not seem to work very successfully. Once a sexual predator is out of the prison system he, or in rare cases, she, will often not take the drugs because it dulls the individual's libido." Dr. Hinkle paused and took a sip of water.

He concluded his remarks and took a few questions. Most of the questions related to the formation of certain letters. One questioner wanted to know how Dr. Hinkle had concluded his theory regarding the letter "p" in relation to sexual deviation.

There are several schools of thought in studying handwriting analysis in America as well as England and France. Europeans cannot get a top job without having their handwriting analyzed.

The audience was ready for a break. There was a cocktail party before dinner and everyone mingled. Many people were very nice and approached Addie with further questions about her work on the American presidents. Butch was sociable and an asset in a situation like this making light conversation with many of the other guests.

The dinner was in the main dining room. The food was quite good; a salad for a first course, a fillet mignon with mushroom sauce, new boiled potatoes, peas and an ice cream cake for dessert. It was about nine o'clock when the dinner finished. Craig Meyers gave some closing remarks and went over the schedule of lectures to be given the following morning.

"Let's get a night cap," Butch said to Addie after dinner. "I need to recover from that information."

"You are on." They sat in the bar and Butch ordered a port with Addie following suit.

"Well, how did you like the lecture?" Addie asked Butch.

"When Dr. Hinkle showed the handwriting of the man who surgically removed the prostitutes' eyeballs after raping them, I was totally riveted!" Butch was laughing.

"God, wasn't that over the top? I knew if I looked at you, I would start laughing." Addie said. "It is so painful, so horrifying, so terrifying that we laugh as a coping mechanism to deal with the heinous nature of the crime.

I am going to call Babs tomorrow; I know it's too late to call her tonight. She is an early bird, and I do want to tell her about some of the findings. God, I wonder if she has heard anything from Mr. Waco since we last talked.

I am also curious about you-know-who's investigation. I did let him know in an e-mail where I was going to be if he needed to get in touch with me." Addie lowered her voice. "I never like to mention names when I am in an airport, bar, or public place. You just never know who could be listening." She leaned close to Butch.

"You are so correct. There could be an eyeball deviant masquerading as a waiter," Butch chimed back.

"Well, I am glad my speech is over, and I can thoroughly enjoy the rest of the speakers. It will be interesting to compare the analysis of the top fortune five hundred company presidents with some of the handwritings we saw today." Addie took another sip of her port.

"The handwritings may be frighteningly similar." Butch motioned to the waiter to bring the bill.

"Well, sadly, criminals can often have characteristics which would help them make an honest living, but their energy is misdirected. That is certainly true of the criminals convicted for fraudulent crimes." Addie finished her glass of port and stood up. "Bed is going to feel very good tonight. Let's get up early and take a walk on the beach before breakfast. It would be good to get some exercise before sitting in the lecture hall for the day."

"Sounds like a great idea to me. I will set the alarm for 7:00, breakfast at 8:15—don't you think?" Butch asked.

"I want to call Babs before the conference starts tomorrow."

Butch and Addie followed their plan. They rose early and walked on the beach. It was still breezy and the surf was still formidable. There were washed up jelly fish, soccer balls, bottles, and a potpourri of caste off items from boats. Servants were raking the seaweed from the beach in front of some of the large houses along the shore.

"As much as I enjoy coming to Florida, I am not a Florida person and would never want to live here. These houses must cost a fortune. Think of the maintenance and taxes of being right on the beach." Addie looked at Butch who put his arm around her.

"I totally agree with you. This coast is too exposed to the Atlantic and often windy. Most of these houses seem to have swimming pools in addition to the beach. I wonder how many people actually put their feet in the sand? Yup, face it, we are New Englanders.

Also, if you want to come to Florida, just stay in a hotel where someone will make your bed and clean your room. Then you never have to worry about hurricanes or increasing taxes." Butch always had a clear way of looking at things, and Addie loved that about him. He had been a very good businessman during his career.

Addie showered and quickly dressed. She put on a blue linen skirt with a blue and white short-sleeved silk blouse and low sling back heals. She reached into her bag, got Babs's home number, then dialed. She could hear the phone ring, but there was no pick up. Addie left a message.

"Hi Babs, it's me Addie. 'Just thought I would touch base. The lecture series is very interesting. I will be in meetings all day and my cell phone will be off, but I will try to catch up with you around 5:00 tonight. You have my cell phone number, so you can leave a message. Hope the snow has melted.'"

Chapter Fifteen

The Canary and the Casino

It was just before dawn when Bab's piercing scream broke the early morning silence. Al had parked nearby, out of view, to witness her reaction but knew he better leave the area quickly now that her scream and Sam's barking were sounding an alarm something was amiss in the neighborhood.

Driving away, he felt very satisfied with his vicious prank and relished its effect on Babs. Would she have nightmares? Would she be afraid to get the newspaper? It was only a dead bird, but discovering one in your morning paper could be unnerving, Al mused.

As he drove along, he also wondered if Babs would ever "get" the significance of his avian choice: a canary. Did she ever see the Godfather movies? If so, she might understand. A "canary that sings," synonymous with a snitch or stoolie, is a *dead* canary in mob culture. Maybe when she tells her dear George about what happened, he'll help her figure it out.

When Babs screamed, she flung the bird and newspaper violently against the porch floor. Then, still trembling all over, she hurried into the house to quiet Sam. Once he was settled, she sat down at the dining room table, rested her head on her arms and fell apart. She became so congested from crying, she finally had to get got up for some tissues. Slowly she began to shift gears emotionally and pull herself together enough to assess the current event that had left her filled with dread.

Who would do such a thing? Why? Certainly not the adult delivery people, they were the most reliable and courteous carriers George and Babs had ever had. It used to be everyone had a paper boy, a kid who got a chance to earn some money and gain a sense of responsibility at an early age. George had been a paper boy, and she believed that experience helped shape his strong work ethic.

Ruling out the paper deliverers, Babs thought about the neighbors and neighboring area. Except for a few rental properties, there was little turnover of residents. Any teenagers they knew were good kids like the little gal who walked Sam and the trio of adolescent entrepreneurs who started a "handy boy" business. Why they were so honest and honorable, they told a client they couldn't accept "that much" for the work they did and insisted on returning $10 of the $40 they received. Now, where do you find kids like that nowadays? Babs reflected.

The only possibility she could come up with was perhaps someone transient from a nearby motel. Rumor had it many parolees, drug pushers, stayed there. Babs hated to profile, but she did believe all the unsavory looking types who suddenly appeared in the neighborhood came from there, to walk down to the beach in nice weather. But this was winter and the weather was dreadful. Babs was back to square one with her mental sleuthing.

She decided to take Sam for a brisk walk and continue her thinking. But first, she had to get dressed. It was only 7:30 on a Friday morning but late enough that nosy Norm, would be outside in a flash to greet her for an "intelligence chat" if he had heard her earlier screams. Although he could be extremely annoying, he was a great watchdog for the neighborhood, making just about everything his business. Over the years, Babs and George wisely opted to tell him little.

While getting dressed, Babs realized she'd have to get rid of the bird before letting Sam out on the porch; the newspaper too. It was still lying right where she'd thrown it. She dreaded touching any of it, especially the hapless canary. How had it died? Cruelly? Humanely? Should she keep it as evidence?

Yes, she decided; who knows what could happen next? With new courage, resolve, *and* rubber gloves, Babs managed to scoop up the bird, wrap it in aluminum foil, shove it in a baggie, and put it in the basement freezer.

Her fear had changed to determination because she convinced herself the incident was a random act and not directed specifically at her or George. Believing this freed her up emotionally, and she found herself practically skipping along in her boots when she and Sam finally got outside. They intentionally headed in the opposite direction of nosy Norm's, though she'd find out soon enough if he'd heard or seen anything.

As they walked, Babs thought about her recent conversation with Addie when Addie threw the fear of God into her after hearing about the three a.m., heavy breathing phone call she'd had. "That was random too," Babs now convinced herself. She figured it was probably a bunch of kids having a sleep over and looking for mischief. Heck, I used to do it myself, she thought. We didn't do heavy breathing, but we did say things like "Is your refrigerator running? Well, you better go catch it." Then we'd quickly hang up and roll on the floor laughing.

She spent the rest of their walk reminiscing about childhood pranks and laughed out loud remembering when she and her friend Amy put bobby pins up their noses to make themselves sneeze. When they'd sneezed enough to be completely stopped up, they were able to convince their mothers they were coming down with colds and couldn't possibly go to school.

By the time they arrived home, Babs was buoyant and turned her thoughts to George's return the next day. He would be calling that evening en route, and she couldn't wait to hear his voice. She saw no need to tell him about the silly bird.

Even though Babs told Addie she planned to reveal more to George about her relationship with Lee, she decided that would remain on hold too. As much as she loved and enjoyed Addie, she began to feel the woman overreacting a bit.

"You *what?*" Babs shouted into the phone at George. "You're kidding me, aren't you?" she continued. "*How* much? Tell me again, and I'll try to believe you," she added more quietly.

Without interrupting, Babs listened, while George confirmed that he had won $2,200 on a poker slot while waiting for Ed to check them out of the hotel that morning.

She was incredulous and very happy for him. The last time he'd won anything that she could recall, was a free audio logy exam at a Health and Aging Expo.

"Hurry home honey, so I can help you spend it," she teased.

"Don't worry, I will and you can," he shot back. "Now that Lakeside has its own casino, we'll go there and win some more! Hey, I've done all the talking. What's new at your end since yesterday? Anything exciting?" George asked.

Babs assured him "no, nothing exciting," except that Sam had found George's favorite sheepskin slippers and given them a whole new look. "I don't think L.L. Bean's replacement guarantee applies to canine damage, do you?" she joked.

They chatted a little longer, then Babs could hear antsy Ed in the background, waiting to get going.

"Ok, babe, Ed and I are off like dirty shirts for some drinks and grub, and guess who's paying? Love you. Look for us mid-afternoon tomorrow. Bye . . ."

"Love you too, sweetie. And Sam says the same. Bye . . ."

No sooner did Babs hang up than the phone rang. Caller ID showed it was Addie. *Oh dear,* thought Babs, *she left a message earlier today, and I never called her back. I just didn't want to get into any discussion about Lee or find myself telling her about the bird,"* she rationalized.

"Addie, hi," she said brightly. "Sorry I didn't call you back."

"Hi, Babs. That's ok. Is this a good time?" asked Addie.

"Sure is. I'm having a glass of wine, my dinner is in the microwave ready to zap, Sam's napping, and I just got off the phone with George. So all's well, and you?" asked Babs.

"I couldn't be better myself, and I'm so pumped from this conference I can hardly stand it. Butch actually referred to me as 'behaving deliriously '. I *do* get excited about handwriting; we all know that about me!"

Babs didn't want to add fuel to the flame and cleverly switched gears by letting Addie know their chat might be interrupted by a call waiting beep. Normally she ignored them, but explained this would be an important call from her son concerning a vacation they were trying to put together in July.

And just as Babs finished telling Addie about George's big casino win, there was the hoped for beep.

"Well, I just got beeped, Addie; thanks for understanding I need to take the call. George gets back tomorrow. After we have a few days to adjust to each other, I'll give you a call," she laughed.

'That's fine; talk with you soon."

And they hung up.

Babs was relieved to have the interruption and always delighted in talking with her son. He, his wife, and their four-year old twins were hard to keep up with. They were a typically busy, striving young family with a lot on their plates day to day. Fortunately, mom and dad recently changed their dual retail careers for more manageable schedules, and were enjoying the benefits of more family-centered time with less stress.

Babs was especially happy that for they would be blending families for a summer vacation, for the first time. This would happen in Sea Isle, New Jersey, for a week in July. It turned out to be the same week George's mom and uncles would be nearby for their annual visit to Stone Harbor. His mom had never seen Babs's grandchildren and was ecstatic it would finally happen.

George was thrilled too, as he had spent the majority of every summer of his youth on these shores with his parents, assorted cousins, aunts, uncles and grandparents. Their family had a house, which unfortunately had been sold long before any nostalgic progeny had a chance to claim it.

After the second phone call, Babs welcomed an early bedtime and slept better than she had in ages. Having enjoyed a good rest, she woke early and was eager to take Sam for a morning walk. After that, she'd get things in order for George's return. This meant a lot of straightening up and putting away. He was a neat freak, she wasn't, and she'd learned to respect the difference.

When she took Sam out, she noticed nosy Norm was out and about. Sure enough, as soon as she and Sam approached, Norm made the dreaded inquiry, "I thought I heard you scream early yesterday morning and then Sam barking his head off; everything all right?" he asked.

"Yes, everything's fine, Norm. I'm squeamish about critters showing up where they don't belong and found one on the porch that freaked me out. That's all. Thanks for your concern though."

Al completely fed up with the weather in Lakeside, wouldn't stick around another minute if he didn't have the pleasure of terrorizing Babs. He'd stayed away from her house since that morning, and it was now early evening. He hoped she'd had a horrible day and was scared out of her prissy wits. He wondered if she told George about the bird. Probably not, he decided she'd wait until he got home.

How long will I wait and what will I do next? he speculated. While smoking a joint, he conjured a number of scenarios, none quite terrible enough. He finally decided to lay low until George returned and then concentrate his efforts on scaring both of them. "Terror for Two" he gleefully dubbed the project. He would again set up surveillance near the house, hope to catch them leaving, and then he would follow. After a week away, surely George would want to take his little lady out somewhere?

When George and Ed arrived, Babs and Sam were at the door waiting. It was a warm welcome all around with hugs, kisses and plenty of licks from the dog. Babs had finished cleaning up the house just in the nick of time, and had even managed, putting on some make up and giving a quick manicure to herself. The men looked forward to a home cooked meal and a quiet evening if that was all right with Babs. They were tired and just wanted to relax.

"Sounds like a plan to me," said Babs. "We're having a chicken casserole, brown rice, tossed salad and rolls; and no dessert, unless you beg, because it looks as though you both came back with some excess baggage."

"Hey, that's not fair," said George. "You know this shirt always makes me look heavy."

"Mine does too," Ed chimed in.

"Whatever," Babs responded, flashing a huge grin and shrugging her shoulders. "Dinner will be at 7:00. Until then, how about a game of Scrabble?"

George dreaded these requests and would usually decline, but with Ed there, he knew he couldn't. Ed didn't really want to play either but never let on.

"Sure hon, we'd love to," George managed to say. "On one condition, though. We can have the TV on for college basketball. Ed has a big bet riding on UVA."

"Fine, and speaking of big bets, where's your casino stash?" asked Babs.

George whipped out his wallet and showed her the check, which was somewhat less than $2200 since the IRS had its share.

Babs won the Scrabble game, Ed's team won the basketball game, the dinner was excellent, dessert was not an issue, and everyone decided to call it a night at 9:30. Ed wanted to get on the road early, and Babs had an early morning volunteer commitment.

Before falling asleep, George and Babs made plans to go to the new casino the next evening. Babs was amazed that he wanted to go there on a Saturday. It would be so crowded. George hated crowds. He assured her he was more "crowd proof" since hitting the casinos with Ed.

"So that was George", Al muttered to himself as he watched from his car up the block from the Baker's. George had come out of the house and was headed toward his truck. *Big guy,* Al thought. *A helluva lot bigger than me.* It was already dark so he couldn't make out any details of George; it was enough for now just to note his formidable size.

George got in the truck, started it up, then got out and went back into the house. When he didn't come back out after five minutes, Al figured he was warming the vehicle up to go somewhere . . . with Babs. Sure enough, not a minute later, out they both came, into the truck they climbed, and off they went. "I'm in luck," Al mused as he followed from a safe distance. It was 6:00 p.m.

Following them proved tricky in the dark, and they were taking an unfamiliar route. It was undoubtedly a series of short cuts. Finally, they turned onto Interstate 79 South, and from there the going was easy: I-79 to I-90 East, then right off the State Street exit for about a quarter mile where the Bakers turned left into Lakeside Downs. The monolithic structure appeared out of place in the rural setting. Around its perimeter was a parking lot that seemed to stretch for miles, and it was packed. Al noticed the Bakers were opting for valet parking, but he didn't dare. He slowly drove around the various sections, and, after a few minutes, found a spot. He wondered what his chances were of finding the Bakers once he got inside. The place was huge.

Babs had never been to a casino and could barely contain her excitement. As they went in, they noticed several uniformed greeters flanking the entrance. One of them looked familiar to Babs and turned out to be an old friend she hadn't seen in decades. Dominic. Dominic Bruno. He recognized her too. After she introduced George, Dominic asked if this was their first visit, and would they like him to show them around?

Answering yes on all counts, Babs and George followed their amiable guide who deftly helped them snake through the crowd on the tour of the facility. He pointed out the restroom locations, various restaurant venues, the multiple cashier stations, a number of bars, and then casually mentioned there were over 2,000 slot machines for their gambling pleasure! There were slots for every pocket book, from penny machines on up to $100 a crack. Gaming tables and horse racing were in the plans for Phase II in 2008.

Both George and Babs had read all about the new casino but weren't prepared for its size, especially the noise. There was a constant din of computerized sound from the machines. Babs figured the cacophony was intentional; somehow geared by the gaming gurus to get more of the patron's money. It was maddening, but became less noticeable as the evening wore on.

They decided to start out together on the nickel slots, but it was hard to find two available machines next to each other. Instead of waiting, they went to one of the little bars and ordered drinks; Babs a wine and George a beer. Heading back to the nickel machines with their drinks, they were just in time to get two adjacent slots. "OK, here we go," they said simultaneously as they each surrendered a $20 bill.

Babs watched George out of the corner of her eye to see what he did. She really didn't understand all the button choices. Was there skill involved? She surely hoped not! In trying to see what George was doing, Babs realized how dimly lit the place was. That's intentional psychology too, she was sure. Oh well, she'd just pretend she knew what she was doing and not worry about it.

George apparently was doing well with his $20 investment judging from his frequent "go get 'ems" and "atta boy" remarks. Babs had no idea how she was doing and asked George to help her decipher the different flashing icons and numbers. "Geez, honey, you've already doubled your money," he declared.

"You're kidding?" Babs said. "Show me how you know that."

George patiently explained how the game worked, and Babs was thrilled with her beginner's luck. "I'm going to keep going and see if my luck continues," she exclaimed.

"Atta girl," George said, "and I will too."

As they played on, the casino was gradually filling to capacity, and all the slot machines were taken except a few of the $100. The place was becoming very crowded and congested to the point where people trying to walk through the aisles were bumping into people sitting at the machines. It was happening to Babs and George, but they didn't mind because they were having too much fun. The jostling seemed all in the spirit of the casino experience, and if they did get bumped, the bumper usually said, "Oh I'm sorry" or "Excuse me."

Babs, however, was about to have a different experience.

Whoever bumped her this time said, "How did you like the canary, bitch?"

Chapter Sixteen

Unexpected Visitors

Butch and Addie had returned from Florida and were sitting at the breakfast table reading their newspapers. Mousetrap was about to make his usual pounce on the breakfast table. A somewhat shocking display of bad manners, but Addie and Butch had tolerated this poor behavior in Mousetrap the cat for so long—they considered it part of their normal breakfast routine. Usually, Mousetrap sat down immediately on one of the newspapers after licking the remains of Addie's oatmeal dish.

"What do you have on the boards today, my love?" Addie asked Butch who began every day working on Sudoku.

"I have a meeting with Mayflower Health Care at noon. I'll probably leave around eleven and be back by 3:30 or so. How about you?" Butch looked over the top of his glasses.

"I have a lot of letters to write and I'll catch up on my e-mails. There is always a lot to do. However, I must say I thoroughly enjoyed our time in Palm Beach and the handwriting conference." Addie took a sip of her tea.

"Oh, you did a great job, honey. I also enjoyed the lecture about 'Murderers, Stalkers and Sexual Deviants." Butch could not mention the name of the lecture without laughing.

"You are so funny. That title would sell out any house, I am surprised Dr. Hinkle hasn't been on the Jerry Springer show," Addie added. "I did find it interesting. The one thing you have to be careful of is showing the public at large a little bit about handwriting analysis because then they feel they know a lot about the subject. The results can be disastrous. It is a little like asking a doctor if a stomachache means you have appendicitis. It can mean you have appendicitis, but a stomachache does not *always* mean appendicitis. It is the same principle in handwriting analysis. A lot depends on the accompanying characteristics.

Anyhoo . . . . I think I will defrost a lovely elk steak from the freezer for dinner tonight. Could I persuade you to forgo more intellectual pursuits this evening, and slum it a bit watching a movie by the fire? I feel a little bit like goofing off, our lives have been so serious." Addie looked at Butch with a smile.

"I would be delighted to celebrate the spoils of my hunt by an open fire with you, my dear," Butch smiled back. "We have several movies to choose from but let's wait until this evening before making such a momentous decision." Butch picked up the newspaper, pulling it from under Mousetrap who had fallen asleep on the kitchen table.

Addie was sitting at her computer, sipping her cup of tea. Butch had gone to Boston and she was enjoying the solitude of the house. She leafed through half a dozen business cards she had collected at the conference and put them in alphabetical order. She would answer each one systematically, add the names and addresses to her contact list, then send them a note with a copy of her brochure. Addie liked following-up and writing notes. She enjoyed the connection of people to people and felt a strong network of relationships was every bit as valuable as money in the bank.

Rarely did she hear a car drive up her driveway when she was in her office upstairs in the attic, so she was very surprised to hear the doorbell ring. She quickly ran downstairs expecting the Fed Ex man with a package that needed a signature. However, to her surprise, she found two large men smartly dressed in business attire.

"How do you do, M'am. My name is John Longworth and this is my partner Mike Addelborough. We are from the Federal Bureau of Investigation and would like to ask you a few questions." John Longworth stared straight at her.

Addie was stunned.

"Oh my Gosh, well come in. Or is this the part in the movies where one usually asks to see some identification?" She blurted out.

"Absolutely, it is smart to be cautious," said John pulling out a badge and showing it to her. Mike followed suit. Addie looked at the badges and then back at the men.

"Do come in, please. Would you like a cup of tea? I was just about to refresh my own cup. Please follow me." Addie led them into the sunny kitchen.

"I would like a cup of tea, thank you," said Mike.

"None for me, thank you Ma'am." Addie flicked the switch on her electric teapot.

"Do you like lemon or milk?" She looked at Mike.

"Just plain is fine, thank you." He answered.

"Earl Grey, English Breakfast, Jasmin, Imperial Keemun, Tung Tin Oolong, or Hu-Kwa?" Addie inquired.

"Tung Tin Oolong would be a treat M'am thank you." Mike looked surprised and delighted.

"A very good choice of a special tea; certainly one which deserves a pot." Addie took an old Rose Medallion teapot, that had belonged to her grandmother, off the shelf and rinsed it with hot water. Next, she filled a small tea ball with the smoky tea and dropped it in the pot slowly adding the hot water from the electric kettle. After it had steeped for several minutes, she placed the teapot and three small cups on a tray. She glanced at John and smiled. "Just in case your change your mind."

"Come gentlemen; let us sit in the living room. It is not every day I have a visit from the FBI." They smiled and followed her into a room with a fireplace.

"Where did your develop your affection for Chinese teas, Mike?" Addie began pouring the tea.

"I was in Vietnam in the Navy, before being hired by the FBI. We had R & R in Hong Kong, where I developed a taste for Chinese teas." Mike took the cup from Addie.

Addie looked at him. "Good for you. We are rapidly running out of congressmen and presidents who have served in the armed forces let alone a war." Addie turned to John. "John, are you sure you wouldn't change your mind and try some Tung Tin Oolong?"

"Well, perhaps a little, just to try." John gave in to Addie's prodding and she was delighted.

"Now that we are prepared for a meaningful discussion, do tell me why you are here." Addie looked at both the men.

"We are doing an investigation and it is our understanding that you have performed several handwriting analyses for Mr. Deluth, from the U.S. Postal Service. We have read all of the reports, but we want to know more about this Jake fellow."

"Certainly, I will be happy to help you in any way I can. Well, as you know, I have never met any of the three people whose handwriting I analyzed for the post office. Ironically, I sent a package to my daughter-in-law in San Francisco that never arrived; I presume it was stolen. The package contained a beautiful green glass necklace I bought in Venice, if that happens to turn up anyplace."

"When was that?" asked John.

"It was May 23rd. I remember specifically because my daughter-in-law's birthday is the 27th of May, and I wanted her to get the package on her birthday. I sent it Priority and stupidly did not insure the package, thinking that this is America and the postal system is safe and reliable." Addie continued.

At that moment, the phone rang. "Sorry for this interruption, let me just see who is calling." Addie stood up and looked at the caller identification. It was Bill Deluth. Addie, picked up the phone. "Hi Bill, I think I have two friends of yours sitting here."

"I wanted to call you and tell you that there would be two FBI agents coming to see you. I guess they beat me to the punch." Bill's voice had a slight chuckle to it.

"I am glad you called. Thank you very much for checking in." Addie was greatly relieved. She didn't honestly know how much she should communicate with the agents and also wanted to make sure that these men were who they said they were.

"Speak with them freely. You have my permission to tell them everything." Bill added.

"I will send you an e-mail and be in touch." Addie smiled. "We are having a nice cup of tea and are about to get down to business."

"Excellent." Bill hung up the phone.

Addie returned her attention to the FBI agents. "O.K. I have never met any of the three suspects from the Post Office. What is very interesting however, is Jake Proctor's handwriting sample looked familiar to me. I knew I had seen his handwriting previously. I have a website, which generates some business: although most of my work is with Fortune Five

Hundred Companies. Well, I had received a handwriting sample from a highly disturbed individual named Hunt. The subject matter of the sample contained terrible language, so much so, that I contemplated not doing the analysis at all.

However, as a handwriting analyst, we always tell our clients that we do not pay attention to the content of the handwriting as much as actual strokes. This was close to the same time that my package failed to arrive at its destination." Addie continued. John and Mike had small note pads and were writing.

"You realize, of course," said Addie "I am going to want to see both of your handwritings before you leave today." They laughed. "Seriously, I keep a sample notebook of handwritings of people from different walks of life. It helps me understand what characteristics make up a good FBI agent, or musician, or plumber."

"That is very interesting, but tell us more about Jake," John said, focusing on the real issue of their visit.

"I will be happy to show you that analysis as well. He is very bright and has highly analytical thinking patterns, but is also very dominating and a sexual deviant. Now, when I say dominant, I mean an abnormal desire to have his own way. He can not tolerate anyone who disagrees with him or gets in his way.

"Here, however, is the interesting part of the story, which I did disclose to Bill Deluth, and perhaps he shared with you as well. When I was in college in Boston, Boston University to be exact, I had a roommate whose maiden name was Babs Lutz. She is now married to George Baker and lives in Lakeside, Pennsylvania. Before she met George, she had an unfortunate relationship with a man named Lee Roberts. She was very attracted to him at first, but then he became very possessive. According to Babs, the experience was very frightening. They even lived together for a short time. She realized he had a serious drinking problem and when she organized an intervention, he never forgave her. Lee ultimately moved back to the South where he came from.

"Well, I know I sound as if I am rambling, but I am trying to give you some background. After years of going our own ways, Babs and I have reconnected our friendship and decided to get together for a visit. Butch, my husband, went to Iceland on a fishing trip at the end of the summer, so I went to visit Babs. She hauled out some samples of handwritings she found interesting and asked me to analyze them . . . You know the usual, what do you think about this person or that person, etc. It is a bit of an occupational hazard.

"To my astonishment, one of the letters she showed me was similar to the sample I had just completed on this Hunt fellow, and I was quite shaken. I work with another handwriting analyst, who is a court document examiner, so I sent her the two copies of handwritings. She analyzes the verification of handwriting samples, but I do the psychological profiles, so it is a nice working relationship. She confirmed that the two samples of handwritings of Lee Roberts and Jake P. Hunt were in fact the same person."

Addie stopped to catch her breath.

"When was the last time you spoke with Babs?" asked Mike.

"Oh Gosh, just a few days ago." Addie replied.

"Had she heard anything from this ex-boyfriend, or seen him lately?" John inquired.

"Not to my knowledge. However, her husband had just been away, and she said she had gotten a strange phone call in the middle of the night with a hang up. When I visited her, I did break my professional ethics a bit and told her to be careful of this guy. I suggested she might want to discuss with George her previous relationship with Lee, but I am not sure she did." Addie was beginning to feel concerned.

"Is her husband still out of town?" Mike asked another question.

"No, he's back. I think he went to Atlantic City with his brother. Something they do every year. Do you think I should call her?" Addie inquired.

"No, please don't. In fact, we can not force you to keep our conversation confidential, but we strongly urge you to keep silent so our talk will not compromise the investigation." John suggested firmly.

"Are either of you married?" Addie looked at both of them.

"Well, both of us are married, and, of course, you can tell your husband. But it is very important for us to keep all the information about this investigation confidential for very obvious reasons." John put his teacup down. "Thank you, I enjoyed the tea."

"Would you like to have Babs's address and the earlier samples of handwritings from Lee or Jake, or whatever he is calling himself today? They might be helpful to you. I am anxious to assist you in any way I possibly can. Also, if I do find out something more what is the best way to contact you?" Addie asked.

"Here are our cards. You can e-mail us or call us on our cell phones."

"Could I possibly persuade you to give me a small sample of your handwriting before you leave?" Addie pleaded. Mike and John glanced at each other.

"Sure, just a quick one." Mike quickly scribbled something down and handed it to her.

"Hmm, very interesting. You have a good imagination. I think you could be a writer; might be a fun thing to pursue when you retire. You certainly would have a lot of experience to draw from."

"That's very interesting that you say that, I actually have always wanted to write. Thanks, thanks a lot. I will keep that in mind." Mike smiled and looked very pleased.

"Please John, how about a sample from you as well?" Addie laughed and looked at the other FBI agent. He wrote a few words on the notebook she handed him.

"Hm . . . very mysterious. You love intrigue. Well, how could you not being in this business? You are both very good at detail and like to focus on small facts. Come on, I'll show you my office and get you Bab's address and the other two samples." Addie led the men upstairs. She made copies of the samples in her files, and she gave them Babs's address. Addie enjoyed their visit and wondered what it must be like to be an FBI agent. What kind of person actually goes into that type of work? She took the agent's handwriting samples and carefully put them into her large scrapbook, writing the heading FBI Agents.

Butch came home around 4:00. He had stopped at a German sausage factory on the way out of Boston and bought some knockwurst, one of his Saturday lunchtime favorites. He bounded into the house with a white package under his arm and a big grin.

"Hi Honey, I'm home," he called out. Addie got up from her desk and went to greet him with a big hug and a kiss.

"I am so glad to see you." She gave him a big hug. "How was your meeting? I see you visited the German sausage factory, terrific."

"Oh, it was great, thanks. We got a lot done. They made me head of the compensation committee." Butch placed the package of knockwurst down on the counter.

"Excellent. I think you deserve to be head of every committee. You have a lot to bring to the company." Addie adored this man, but more than loving him, she felt that he had such good sense and perspective on all problem solving issues.

"How was your day?" Butch took off his coat.

"How was my day? How was my day, you ask? I was visited by two FBI agents!" Addie said.

"Are you kidding? My gosh, what did they want? Was it something to do with Mr. Wacko, or the post office scandal?" Butch was giving Addie his fullest attention.

"Right on. It was about Mr. Wacko, the post office investigation, and those missing packages. I am worried about Babs, but the FBI agent insisted that I not contact her. So . . . guess I will do something I rarely do, and follow orders. At first, I think they didn't even want me to tell you that they had been here. Then I asked both of them if they were married. So of course, they got the message. I wish they had told me more about the investigation, but I didn't feel it was appropriate to ask them." Addie was delighted with the attention from the officers. "You know, I think it would be advisable for you to have the FBI agents names, e-mails and cell phone numbers in case I turn up missing." Addie said in earnest. They looked at each other and burst out laughing.

"This is a bit scary, I must admit. We are also quite isolated up here. Gosh, will they tell you when the investigation is closed? I wonder if you will have to testify, did you ever think of that?" Butch opened the refrigerator door, took out a bottle of milk, and poured himself a glass.

"Sweetheart, I am sorry. Would you like a cup of tea? I am forgetting my manners." Addie said.

"No thanks. Well, I am glad you told me about this situation. You probably will have to testify at some point.?" Butch finished his milk.

"No, I hadn't thought of that which scares me even more. Well I will just have to cross that bridge when I come to it." Addie reflected.

"I am going to get out of these city clothes, then go up to the office and check my e-mails." Butch rinsed his glass and put it in the dishwasher.

"I'll give you the information for the agents. It is on my desk. I'm afraid to e-mail you any pertinent data. What if Mr. Wacko has hacked into my computer?" Addie looked at Butch, and once again they began to laugh.

"Well, you have never met this guy, have you?" Butch asked Addie.

"No, not that I know of. But remember there was a Fed Ex guy who came to the door and had a tattoo partially under his watch? I noticed it immediately. Babs told me that her old boyfriend had the same tattoo in the same place. That might have been him. After what we learned in Florida about criminals using the Internet, and the statistic that one out of nine women is stalked without her knowledge, I just thought it would be prudent to be a little more cautious." Addie suggested a bit defensively.

"I totally agree. Come upstairs and give me the agents' names and numbers, right now while we are talking about it." Butch moved towards the stairs.

"Great idea. Did I tell you Bill Deluth called to say the FBI agents were going to visit me, when they were already here?" Addie followed Butch. "Bill is such a nice guy. I hope we see the Deluth's after all of this is over. I am really worried about Babs, luckily George has returned from Atlantic City. So, she will not be alone."

Chapter Seventeen

Strange Incidents Escalate

As soon as he asked her how she liked the canary, Al immediately vanished into the casino crowd and headed for the exit. He would have loved to have seen Babs's reaction, but his vivid imagination would have to suffice. What would she do? Would she tell George? What would *he* do? But, Al didn't really give a rat's ass what they did. He was already way ahead of them, savoring his next move.

While watching their house over the past week, Al had developed a feel for the neighborhood and was especially attracted to an apparently unoccupied Tudor. It was across the street from where he usually kept surveillance and kitty-corner to the Bakers. With all the snow, there were no tire tracks in the driveway, and at night just a couple of the same lights were always on. The home was twice as large as any other on the street, and Al wondered if, at one time, it had been an inn. Whoever lived there now was probably a snowbird, basking in the sun down in Florida.

The property was at least an acre deep and well hidden from view by a towering Privet hedge. Between the hedge and the house was a sizable pond, now frozen over and partially snow covered. There were also several screened in porches at ground level, adding to Al's feeling that the place was once a guest venue. Regardless of what it was, he had a growing desire to check it out and somehow use it to advance his "Terror for Two" activities.

Did someone really say what she thought they said: "How'd you like the canary, bitch?" Even in the noisy casino, she was sure that's what she heard from over her left shoulder. As she whipped her head around, all she could see in the dim lighting was the congestion of people; no one looked familiar; no one looked suspicious. Babs then looked over at George who was completely absorbed in his gambling and apparently oblivious to what had just happened.

Am I going crazy? Did it really happen? Babs wondered. She wasn't ready to deal with it and especially didn't want to alarm George. So she managed to feign a normal demeanor for the next half hour while they both continued to gamble. They each had made modest, but respectable, gains and wanted to quit while they were ahead. After they saw the cashier and headed out, reality hit Babs like a ton of bricks; and she broke into a cold sweat. With her arm linked in George's, she pulled him quickly aside, told him she suddenly felt nauseous, and thought she might have to throw up. George noticed there was a restroom nearby and managed to get her there . . . just in time. She was horribly pale when she came out, and George wanted her to sit down, but there wasn't a seat to be had.

"Once I get some fresh air, I should be fine," Babs assured him.

They waited outside while the valet service got their car, and in those few minutes, George was happy to see the color return to Babs' cheeks.

"Was it something you ate?" George asked.

"I don't know," she lamely answered. "Maybe the crowding got to me. It was a little too close for comfort in there. But I feel OK now, so please don't worry."

"But I do worry about you; you're my wife, and I love you, you know."

"I know honey, thanks."

They were quiet on the ride home. Babs was grateful for the cover of darkness. She didn't want George to notice the waves of fear that intermittently came over her. One minute she was fine; there was no dead canary, and no one had asked her how she liked it. Minutes later it was all real, and the attendant fear was manifested physically. Cold sweat first, next vomiting, and now the waves of awareness that left her feeling drained and limp. If she had to name what she was experiencing, she would call them "emotional seizures."

Sam greeted Babs and George with lavish licks and tail wags. Babs welcomed the diversion of letting him out, giving him a few treats, then playing "tennis ball" in the living room. This game involved kicking the ball, Sam retrieving it, bringing it back, and dropping it to be kicked again, retrieved again, and brought back again. Lately, Sam added pushing the ball under something where he couldn't retrieve it and the human would have to. Usually this annoyance ended play pretty quickly, but tonight Babs was loving it—anything to get her mind off the dead canary and the ensuing canary inquiry at the casino.

Satisfied that Babs seemed fully recovered and was enjoying her time with Sam, George proffered a few yawns, reminded her to lock up, and headed for bed.

Neither of them had checked for phone messages when they got home, but Babs thought of it now and was relieved to find there were none.

If she could just manage a good night's sleep, she'd be able start the new day fresh and ready to think rationally about the mysterious events that plagued her. Toward that end, she bypassed her usual melatonin tablet and took a much stronger sleep aid.

The pill did its magic, and she didn't hear a thing until Sam's 6:15 a.m. whine/whimper alarm. She and George played a game of "I don't hear him" most days to see who would get up first to let him out. Since today was Sunday, they played the game longer than usual. Finally, Babs relented. Her mind was starting to race and she hoped she could slow it down with some physical activity.

So up she got, let Sam out, fed him, gave him a rawhide, let him out again, and by then, a brilliant sun was rising and the sky was cloudless. The change to milder, sunny weather was supposed to stick around for a couple days, and Babs was delighted.

She yelled up to George, in case he didn't already smell it, coffee was ready and *she* was ready for a break from Sam. There was a grumble in response, but she knew he'd soon appear. They were both morning people, dog or no dog. For the last years of his career, George had worked the six to three shift and was used to getting up as early as 5 a.m. Babs just got up early regardless.

Sunday was the one day they ate breakfast together, and it was always enjoyable. The menu invariably included juice, milk, bacon, toast, fresh fruit, and a choice of either scrambled or "daddy style" eggs which were soft boiled. On very rare occasions there were pancakes or grits. Babs personally hated grits, remembering them as a lumpy staple when she attended boarding school in her teens.

While they ate, they thumbed through the Sunday paper and competed to find the "six differences" in the cartoon section. It was an important ritual to both of them and one of the simple pleasures of their marriage.

With breakfast out of the way, Babs was restless to keep busy and announced to George, if he would handle dishes, she would take Sam for a walk. This would give her much needed alone time to sort out the canary incident and what to do.

OK, she said to herself as she and Sam headed down the street at a fast clip. Sam seemed to enjoy the accelerated pace, and Babs needed it to nudge her brain into some constructive cognitive action.

OK" she said again, out loud this time. *I find a dead canary in our newspaper. The perpetrator happens to see me at the casino and uses the chance encounter to continue the harassment. Wait a minute, why am I saying the instead of his or her harassment? Because,* she now recalled, *the voice at the casino was very high pitched, raspy and most probably disguised. Hmmm.* It then occurred to her that perhaps the encounter at the casino wasn't chance but was planned, and she and George had been followed there.

She stopped in her tracks with that thought and felt the cold sweat and nausea of last night hitting her again full force. The sudden change of pace startled Sam, but he seemed to sense something serious and that Babs needed his full canine cooperation.

After a few minutes, her latest "emotional seizure" ended, and she and Sam headed home at a greatly reduced, more gingerly pace.

As they ambled along, she resumed her "ok" mental preface, and decided out loud she would begin her efforts to solve the canary caper by calling the couple who deliver their newspaper and also her cleaning woman. They might have noticed something or someone unusual that would tie in. What she really wanted to do, though, was call Addie and spill the beans because in her deepest heart she now felt Lee was somehow mixed up in all this.

I just can't call Addie, not now, she thought. *But if and when I do, I'll also tell George all that's happened.* This decision gave her some relief from the tremendous guilt she felt over keeping things from him.

George was puttering in the basement when they got home. Actually, he was varnishing the swim platform for their boat. Granted, this was February, and the boat platform wouldn't be used for another four months. Anything boat oriented was always a priority for George, even though their new kitchen counter top was to be installed soon, and George still hadn't finished the base cabinets. "Oh well," Babs would sigh to herself, "we wisely learn to pick our battles." Bab's priorities often stumped George as well, so that evened out the playing field a bit.

Seeing that his project would keep him down below at least until lunch, Babs was able to make her two phone calls undetected. When she reached the newspaper couple, they were gracious but no help at all. No, they'd seen nothing unusual; heck they could hardly see anything at that hour, especially when customers neglected to keep their outside lights on. "You Bakers are really our best customers; lights always on and you always return the plastic sleeves and rubber bands. We appreciate the tips too," they chimed.

When she reached her cleaning woman Dottie Putnam, it was a different story. Dottie drove a 20-year old car that was always on its last leg, but remained road worthy "out of spite" she'd say. She longed for a new car and made a point of knowing which had the best MPG ratings, safety features, and so on, so she'd be ready when dear old "rugalator" finally bit the dust.

As it turned out, one of the cars she particularly liked was parked just up the street from the Bakers last Tuesday when she cleaned. "It was one of those hybrids, you know?" Dottie said to Babs. "It was parked across from the Ward's, and there was someone sitting in the driver's seat reading the newspaper. I couldn't really see anything but an arm holding up the paper. The car was gone when I left at 2:00. I did think it kind of odd parked there like that," she offered.

"Why do you say that?" asked Babs.

"Well," replied Dottie, "in all the time I've cleaned for you and the Wards I've never seen a car parked there, let alone with someone just sitting in it on a bitter cold day. The Wards won't be back for another month you know. As it is, I don't like being in that cavernous house by myself while they're gone, and now what if someone's casing the joint?" she said with an uncharacteristic note of alarm in her voice.

Babs asked the color of the car and a few other details, then made light of the whole inquisition and changed the subject. She and Dottie had been friends since childhood and always had plenty to yap about. It was a good thing Babs was usually at her nanny job when Dottie cleaned because nothing would get done if they were there together.

Dottie was a real marvel. She had contracted polio when she was six months old, and to this day, used her crutches better than many of us use our legs. Her laugh was infectious, her humor wonderfully mischievous, her faith unshakable, and her friendship invaluable. *Lucky me to have Dottie in my life,* Babs thought happily after they hung up.

The more Babs pondered Dottie's car observation, the more she felt it had a connection. She called Dottie back and casually asked her to let her know if she saw the car again when she came to clean in two days. "You bet I will," Dottie assured her. "And if it is, you can be sure I'll find out what it's doing there!"

"When do you go to the Ward's again? Babs asked.

"Cathy wants me there Thursday to let in some electrician for a wiring estimate, and while I wait for him I'm to polish brass and silver," Dottie answered.

Shortly after Babs got off the phone with Dottie, George "surfaced" with one of his "I'm hungry as a bear" looks.

"How about come back in a half hour, and I'll have tomato soup and grilled cheese ready. Sound good?" asked Babs.

"Don't forget the pickles and chips," he responded.

"Oooh, you sure do press your luck sometimes, Mr. Baker," she teased back.

While fixing lunch, it became clear to Babs that she would call Addie after all. Hearing Dottie's uneasiness over the car brought her own discomfort to a new, fresh level. She always figured Dottie as virtually unflappable. Now she wondered what Dottie would think if she knew about Lee and half of what had been happening.

With lunch out of the way and George off on some errands, Babs grabbed the opportunity to call, praying as she dialed that Addie was home.

She was, and she answered virtually on the first ring.

"Oh Addie, I'm so glad you're there. I really need to talk to you," Babs blurted anxiously.

"What's the matter, Babs?," she asked

Babs told her everything from the canary in the newspaper, to the parked car, and her growing feeling that Lee was somehow involved. And no, she still hadn't said a word to George, but her fear, and the tension of holding everything in, was causing her anxiety attacks or "emotional seizures" as she chose to call them.

Addie listened without saying a word, letting Babs go on and on, and when she stopped, there was silence.

"Addie," Babs said, "are you still there?"

"Oh, of course I am, Babs. I'm just listening and stunned. I wish I had a magic wand to wave it all away. The dead bird and the person at the casino are connected for sure. That car sounds very suspicious to me like someone was spying on you. There aren't any other points of interest in your neighborhood like a pond to draw someone there." Addie's voice showed her concern.

"I know you've been hesitant, but please, please do tell George about all this. He can handle it. He cares deeply about your well-being and deserves to know. Promise me you'll tell him?" pressed Addie.

"I promise," said Babs with conviction.

Chapter Eighteen

The FBI Follows Up

John Longworth sat at his desk at the Boston FBI office. He and his partner, Mike Addelborough, were tracking computerized records for Jake Proctor.

"This seems interesting," John turned to Mike who was sitting at his desk in the same office writing the report of their visit with Addie Stubbs. John continued, "Jake Proctor was charging his gas and a few meals up until March 13th, but then all of the charges on his credit card seem to have stopped. There is no record of him charging anything beyond that date."

Mike looked up at John. "Has he paid his rent for March?"

"Good question. Let me call the Memphis office and see if they can get hold of his bank statements and interview the landlord." John picked up the phone and began dialing Tennessee. "How are you coming with the report on the Adelaide Stubbs interview? I am getting hungry."

"Oh great," said Mike. "What a funny lady."

"I can't believe you did that gig with the Chinese tea-god, I have been your partner for ten years, and I didn't know you liked Chinese tea! Maybe we should go to Chinatown for lunch?" John kidded Mike.

"Would you like to eat at the Silver Dragon? It's a Thai restaurant closer, and not to mention cheaper." Mike offered.

"Sounds good." John answered, phone in his hand waiting for the Memphis office to pick up. "Hello, this is John Longworth, calling from the Boston office. Yah, that's right, is this Sandra? Well how are you darlin'? You have the loveliest sounding voice in the entire FBI network." John broke out into gales of laughter. "Well, I certainly hope to get to Tennessee soon. Will you have dinner with me when I come?" more gales of laughter. "Is Jed Thomas there?" There was a slight delay . . . "Jed, hi, this is John Longworth, from the Boston office. We haven't been able to find any traces of Jake Proctor since February 23rd. Have you been out to see his landlord? Mind if I put you on speaker phone, so my partner Mike can hear your answer?"

Jed continued. "Hi Mike, how are you?

Mike responded, "fine thanks."

Jed continued: "We are already ten jumps ahead of you. We went out to Proctor's apartment and then interviewed his property owner who does not live on the premises. The guy said that Jake seemed pretty quiet and kept to himself. He paid his rent on time and actually prepaid his March rent—said he was going on vacation. We would like to do a search of his apartment, but so far the Bureau doesn't feel they have enough information to issue a warrant. We did locate the roommate of his old girlfriend Daisy Marshall, here in Memphis. The roommate said Proctor became violent when Daisy wanted to break up with him. He beat her up a couple of times, but she never filed charges. Daisy had been in the slammer for a cocaine addiction so was not a friend of our outstanding law enforcement personnel, if you get my drift. Her roommate said Daisy left and went back to Mobile, Alabama, to her mother's house to get rid of him. What have you found out on your end?"

"Well, this is quite interesting. We just interviewed a handwriting analyst by the name of Addie Stubbs who had done an analysis of Proctor's handwriting for the Postal Service. Mrs. Stubbs had recognized Proctor's handwriting. Apparently, he had sent her a sample some time in the summer, under the name of Jake P. Hunt, for an analysis. She has a website, so she didn't think much about it until she was visiting an old college friend in Lakeside, Pennsylvania and saw the same handwriting, yet again.

Her old friend had dated Proctor it seems, only then he was known as Roberts. It was about forty years ago. According to Stubbs, the woman in Lakeside, named Babs Baker, had a similar experience. Baker, whose maiden name was Lutz, said Roberts had a drinking problem and became very possessive. She engineered an intervention, which finished their relationship. When this guy finished rehab, he returned to the South.

There was no mention of violence, but sometimes people don't share that type of information with each other. You realize that Jake Proctor's middle name is Lee and Lee Robert's middle name is Jake? Sounds like the guy likes aliases. We'll call the Pittsburgh office and send someone up to speak with Baker." John said thoughtfully.

"We just had some dealings in upstate Pennsylvania, and worked with an agent named Miles Dell, from the Pittsburgh office. He is a good man. See if you can get him to visit Baker. Miles was fast and thorough when we asked him to do some work. Hopefully, he will be in the queue for rotations," Jed remarked. "The Mobile office is already trying to track down Daisy to see if she has heard anything from Jake lately." Jed finished up.

"Thanks Jed. Now, here is the important question, is Sandra as cute as she sounds on the phone?" John asked.

"All one hundred and seventy-five pounds of her!"

Despite the heavy rain, Miles Dell and his partner Bill Light headed for Lakeside from the FBI office in Pittsburgh.

"Have you heard the weather report?" Miles asked.

"Yeah, it looks like we could have a big storm coming our way tomorrow." Bill said turning the radio dial to the weather station.

"Oh, that's our luck. We always seem to get these assignments upstate when the weather is bad." Miles retorted.

"It's called being the younger members of the FBI team. Send out the little kids to do the jobs furthest away from the office," Bill glanced at his watch which read 1:00 p.m. "We should be in Lakeside by 3:30, maybe 4:00 given the weather conditions. We might have to spend the night depending on what we find out from the Baker woman."

"In the meantime, we can listen to a little ghetto rap to get into the brain of the criminals." They both laughed. Bill knew that Miles was a great lover of opera and his fiancée played the violin.

"Have you listened to the lyrics of some rap music? It's amazing there isn't more crime, instead of less. Ah well, they are defending their right to freedom of speech," Miles mused. "Would you object to a little *La Bohème*?" Miles flipped a compact disk into the CD player.

"How are the plans coming for your wedding?" asked Bill.

"Really well, Sara has found her dress. Her parents are into a big splashy affair, which I could do without, but Sara is their only daughter and her Mom wants to do it up right." Miles turned towards Bill.

"Yeah, I know what you mean. We had a big wedding. For women, getting married is like receiving a Masters," Bill mused thoughtfully.

"What do you think the chances are of Proctor being in Lakeside?" asked Miles.

"I would say about seventy-five to one that he won't be there. Who in their right mind would want to leave warm Memphis, Tennessee and drive north to Lake Erie, at this with weather like this? The guy would to be crazy." Bill took a deep breath, "of course he is crazy, which is why we're trying to find him."

"Did you read the handwriting report?" asked Miles.

"I did. I can't decide whether I think there is any validity to handwriting analysis. I'm somewhat skeptical. However, having said that, my wife Ginny saw an add in the newspaper, and we responded. We both sent letters to this handwriting expert; I was amazed at how accurate the results were."

It was around four in the afternoon when Miles and Bill drove into the driveway of 228 Bayview Drive. Daylight was beginning to fade, and the lights were on at the Baker's house. They rang the doorbell and heard a dog barking.

"Hope he isn't a biter," Miles remarked to Bill.

Babs opened the door and looked very startled to see two men formally dressed, in heavy coats, standing on her front door step.

"How do you do? Are you Mrs. Baker?" Miles led with the question.

"Well, yes I am. Who are you?" Babs looked surprised.

"We work for the FBI and would like to come in and ask you some questions about Jake Proctor." Miles and Bill took their badges out of their coat pockets and showed them to Babs.

"Certainly, come in. It's so cold," said Babs. Sam was barking loudly and jumping. "He is just a puppy and very excitable," Babs said apologetically.

Miles held out his hand for Sam to smell. Slowly, the dog began to settle down. "That's a good dog. Well, you have a great watchdog here. He is doing just exactly what dogs are supposed to do."

"Come in please. Would you like something to drink? I just made a pot of decaf coffee."

"That would be great, it's a long way from Pittsburgh." Bill answered politely.

"Milk or sugar?" asked Babs.

"Milk for me and sugar for Miles," answered Bill.

"Well, I can see why you two are partners," laughed Babs.

"Mrs. Baker, when was the last time you saw Lee Roberts?" Miles asked.

"Gosh," Babs answered, "probably forty years ago." She began to feel sick. She could feel her mouth go dry and the palms of her hands get sweaty. She was amazed at how frightened she felt.

"Mrs. Baker, if you could just try to remember everything about Roberts and your relationship with him. We realize forty years is a long time, but any little bit of information might be helpful. For example, where did you meet him?"

Miles was gentle and kind. The sound of his voice was not authoritarian.

"Oh you are so right, forty years is a long time ago. I was on my first conference for my company in Denver, Colorado. I was pretty excited and feeling very grown up, but horribly naïve about the ways of the world and, especially, men." They all chuckled and Babs continued. "There was this nice looking guy in my first seminar. He had a heavy Southern accent. He struck up a conversation and was very friendly, giving me a lot of attention. He followed me around for the three days of the conference, and then we began a long distance romance. He said he was just in the process of getting divorced from a horrible woman. I was so innocent, I believed him. He applied for a transfer from his company to Lakeside. We were very happy in the beginning, and eventually lived together for a while. When you are young and single, it seems perfectly natural to develop relationships easily.

We had a lot in common, or that is what it seemed like, at the time. He loved history and so do I. He knew a lot about the Civil War, which he called 'The War of Northern Aggression.' In fact, he loved that there was General Robert E. Lee and he was Lee J. Roberts. He might even have claimed to be a descendant, now that I think about it. The longer we lived together, the more possessive he became. If I went out with a girl friend, he would suddenly drop by the restaurant as if he were checking my story. Then I slowly realized that he had a terrible drinking problem, so I organized an intervention. After he finished rehab, he left Lakeside, and returned to the South. I never heard from him again, thank god."

"Mrs. Baker, did Lee Roberts ever psychically harm you?" Bill asked.

Babs looked so sad, Bill felt instantly sorry for her. He could see how painful his question had been. He found it hard to be an FBI agent and deal with other peoples complicated emotions. Bill was a great study of body language. He watched Babs cross her arms and look out the window. There was a long silence.

"I was coming back from an early movie with two old friends. It was when my relationship with Lee was beginning to go sour." Babs hesitated a bit. "I was returning to the house, as I mentioned. I had put the key in the front door, and he came up behind me without saying a word. As I put my key in the door, Lee grabbed me from behind and pushed his way in the front door. I was terrified," Babs stopped and began to cry slightly. Years of pent up emotions came welling forward. She had not realized how much she was keeping that incident pent up inside her for the last forty years. "He forced himself on me and was began to hit me. Thank god, my friend came back to the house because she had left a book she needed for work in my car. She could see we were having a fight. She threatened to call the police if he didn't leave." Babs broke down into sobs.

"I am so sorry. I think I just pushed this awful experience back into the recesses of my mind." Babs stood up and took a box of Kleenex out of a drawer. "That is when I knew I had to get him into some treatment program. He returned the next day apologizing profusely, saying how much he loved me, and that he just didn't know what had gotten in to him. He was really sorry, it was his intense love for me that made him possessive."

"Mrs. Baker, did you ever notify the police?" Bill asked. "Please take your time. I am so sorry we have to ask you these questions."

"No, I didn't call the police. It was the late sixties, and we had been living together. I was embarrassed about the entire situation and didn't think the police would be sympathetic. Times were different then. We didn't have the education we do today regarding women's rights the protections the law offers."

"I totally understand, Mrs. Baker. I have a little girl, so I am very glad of the changes, I certainly hear what you are saying." Bill tried to console her.

"Please take your time. Can I get you a little more coffee?" Miles inquired.

"Oh gosh, that would be great. It is in the kitchen." Babs replied. Miles walked into the kitchen and poured another cup of coffee. He glanced outside, saw the fenced in yard, and took note of the other houses in the neighborhood.

"Mrs. Baker, do you know a handwriting analyst named, Adelaide Stubbs?" Miles brought the full cup of coffee back to Babs who was regaining some self-control.

"Addie? Yes, I do. She was an old college roommate of mine. We both went to Boston University. She was here in the summer for a visit. I gave her some handwriting samples to analyze. I had a few old letters from Lee I had forgotten I'd even kept. When Addie looked at the handwriting, she looked upset. She said she had seen that handwriting before. She has a website and felt that the contact had been generated by her Internet site. Apparently, she had done an analysis of his handwriting earlier in the year. We were both totally freaked out. After a few glasses of wine, we decided Lee would come after both of us! I don't know how he would have known that Addie and I knew each other. It all became too weird." Babs took a sip of her coffee. "Thanks for getting me another cup of coffee. I really appreciate it."

"Mrs. Baker, Jake Proctor, who you knew as Lee Roberts has been working for the U.S. Postal Service in Memphis, Tennessee. We have reason to believe he may have been involved in a series of mail frauds." Bill offered up the information.

"That is amazing. I was watching a show about the U.S. Postal Service on public television and I thought I saw someone who looked like Lee. So that *was* him." Babs sat straight up in her chair.

"He had some vacation time coming, but has not shown up to work for the past two weeks. We have reason to believe he has left town. Is there anything out of the ordinary, which has happened to you lately, just the littlest deviation from your routine that you can think of?" Miles asked Babs gently, trying not to alarm her.

"Oh gosh, well yes. You may think I am crazy, but I must admit I have been thinking about Lee a lot lately. My husband, by the way, doesn't know anything about him. George went on his annual trip to Atlantic City with his brother a week ago.

"When he was gone, I did receive a phone call in the middle of the night. No one responded, but there was heavy breathing." Babs paused. "I hung up."

"Do you recall the exact hour?" asked Miles who had been scribbling notes on his small pad of paper.

"Oh gosh, it must have been around three or four in the morning. The other thing that happened, which was really weird—I found a dead canary wrapped up in my morning newspaper." Babs was feeling sick. Her mouth went dry again and she took another sip of coffee. "I was pretty freaked out about the canary and asked a few neighbors if they had seen anything weird happening. When I called my cleaning lady, she said she had seen a car parked down the road a little ways. She also cleans for some people named Ward who are away during the winter months. Their house is the big white Tudor at the end of the street with the high hedge around it."

Miles asked: "When does your cleaning lady come to clean, and what is her name?"

"Her name is Dottie Putnam and she comes on Tuesdays." Babs continued, "now I am really beginning to feel afraid. I also had a very strange experience last Saturday night. After George came home, he was very anxious to go to our new casino. He had won several thousand dollars in Atlantic City and was feeling lucky. Well, I was game, forgive the pun. I was sitting at a slot machine when someone jostled me and said: 'how did you like the canary, Bitch?' I was shell-shocked. But before I could get a good look around, no one was there. I must admit I felt faint and very uneasy." Babs began to look very worried.

"Mrs. Baker, I don't want to alarm you, but I do think you might be in some danger. Would you mind if we put your house under surveillance? Here is my cell phone number and e-mail address. I want you to call us if anything else unusual happens. We will probably also talk to your cleaning lady. How would you feel about a wire tap on your phone?" Miles asked.

"Gosh, this is all so overwhelming. I am going to have to discuss this with my husband. Can I call you sometime tomorrow?" Babs asked.

"Of course you can. Please feel free to call me any time, the hour is not important," Miles said. Both he and Bill were closing their note pads. "The chances are we will be hanging around Lakeside for a few days before going back to Pittsburgh."

"Do you really think he is here?" Babs asked apprehensively.

"We just don't know, Mrs. Baker, but your safety is very important to us. You are working aren't you?"

"Yes, I am a nanny for the Bedford family, and I work there four days a week from Tuesday through Friday. Their address is 25 Homestead Circle. I really don't want to tell them about this if I don't have to . . . for obvious reasons," Babs pleaded.

"We certainly understand, Mrs. Baker. I don't think it will be necessary at this time." Bill added. Both he and Miles were on their feet getting ready to leave.

"Thank you for coming. I was beginning to feel a little crazy thinking these signs meant nothing, and yet I also felt terrified on another level, if that makes any sense at all," Babs blurted out.

"It makes perfect sense, Mrs. Baker. You are obviously a strong, capable woman, not easily rattled and in control of your life and your emotions. Please remember, do call us if you think anything is out of the ordinary. We really are here for your protection." Miles handed her his card. "We can not tell you what to do. However, due to privacy issues and for the sake of this investigation, we would prefer you not mention this conversation to anyone." Miles shook her hand.

Babs, nodded her head in agreement. "I understand."

Miles and Bill got into the car. "What do you say, we visit the cleaning lady? She must be home now," Bill said looking at his watch. "Might be worth spending the night here instead of going back to Pittsburgh, I'll call Ronda, at the office, and see if she can make some reservations."

"Sounds like a good plan. Sara's playing in a concert in Philadelphia. I am glad I don't have to make that dreaded call that I wouldn't be coming home. Does your wife hate you being away so much?" Miles asked Bill.

"It was worse before we had our kids. Now she has so much to do with three little babies there are times I think she likes *not* having to cook me supper. She is a good sport about it. She did know what she was getting into when she married me," Bill answered dialing his home number on his cell phone.

"Hi honey, we are going to stay in Lakeside tonight. I'll call you later." He turned to Miles, "She must be picking up Jason from preschool. I got the answering machine. I'll call the office and have them book a hotel reservation. Damn it, tomorrow is supposed to be that big rain storm." Bill dialed the office and spoke to Rhonda, the secretary. She was very efficient and booked a room at the Blue Moon Motel while Bill was on the line.

Miles was looking at a map of Lakeside. "Here is the cleaning lady's address. Looks like we will have to drive to the other side of town." It took them about twenty minutes to get to the multi-family where Dottie Putnam lived.

"Mrs. Putnam, I am Miles Dell and this is special agent Bill Light. We would like to ask you some questions." They showed her their badges.

"Land sakes, what is this all about? Have I done something wrong?" Asked Dottie somewhat startled. "Come in. I was just preparing dinner for my husband. He works for the railroad, and will be home in an hour." Dottie opened the door wider.

"Mrs. Putnam this won't take very long," said Miles as they entered a spotlessly clean apartment.

"Please sit down," said Dottie. She was now more curious than frightened.

"Tell me what is going on. Has there been a murder?"

"No, nothing as dramatic as that." Bill offered. "Mrs. Putnam you work for a Mrs. Baker, do you not?" He continued.

"Yes, she's is a neat lady. I have known her all my life. You couldn't ask for a nicer human being, got a nice husband, too. She finally got it right, you know what I mean? That first guy she married was a doozie. Does this have anything to do with him? I always knew he was a bad apple." Dottie was sitting in her easy chair.

"No, it has nothing to do with her ex-husband. We are looking for an old friend of Babs who might be in the area. There is a limit to what we really can tell you for investigative purposes. I do hope you understand, Mrs. Putnam." Miles chimed in. "You mentioned to Mrs. Baker that you had seen a car sitting near her house with someone sitting in it last week. Do you remember what kind of car it was or what color?" Miles had his notebook out and was prepared to write any information down.

"Oh dear, my car is always on its last legs, so I am constantly trying to decide what kind of new car to buy. Haven't quite saved up enough money yet, but I am getting there. The car that was up the street from the Bakers looked like one of those hybrids. My husband and I thought it would be great to have at least one car that was good on gas. He has a truck, which he loves. I wouldn't be able to get him to give that one up.

"Let me think about the color. It must have been a dark color because I like blues and greens. I would have remembered if it was a pretty color like that. So no, I am guessing it was dark. Maybe black? I noticed it because, in all the times I have been cleaning for Babs, well of course, I call her Babs—having known her all my life it would be hard for me to call her Mrs. Baker, now, wouldn't it? As I was saying, in all the times I have been cleaning Babs's house, I never saw anyone parked in that one spot right opposite the Ward's house. I clean their house too. There was this guy sitting in the car reading a newspaper. It was gone when I left the house. I didn't think that much about it at the time.

"Do you think there will be a robbery in the neighborhood and that strange man was staking out some houses?" Dottie asked excitedly.

"We have no idea. It certainly is not against the law to sit in a parked car no matter how ridiculous it seems to any of us. Mrs. Putnam I am going to give you my card. If you happen to see this car again, can you please call us?" Miles handed her his card.

"Should I try to get the license number? That is usually what they do in the movies." Dottie was now thoroughly enjoying the adventure and her possibly helpful involvement.

"I think it would be better to just give us a call, Mrs. Putnam. With the exception of your husband, we would greatly appreciate it if you did not mention this to anyone else. I am sure you can understand our reasons." Bill looked straight into Dottie's eyes.

"Oh officers, you have my word. Although I have to tell you, now I feel a bit nervous about going to clean in that area. I am supposed to let an electrician into the Ward's house on Thursday. I also planned to clean some of the brass and silver that day. They will be away for another month. It is a big house and I don't much like being there by myself as it is. If it weren't for the electrician I might skip a week or wait until my husband could come with me on a weekend."

"Mrs. Putnam you have been very helpful. You have my card. Don't hesitate to use it. You can call me twenty-four hours a day." Miles stood and stretched out his hand to Mrs. Putnam.

"That goes for me as well, Mrs. Putnam," said Bill, handing her his card.

Addie was sitting at her computer about to write up an analysis for one of her favorite New York clients. As usual, she had a large pot of tea by her side and Butch was sitting at his computer answering his e-mails.

"Gosh, you type so quickly." Addie looked at Butch.

"I know, I should have been a secretary," mused Butch. The phone rang and Butch looked at the identification screen on their telephone. "Hmm. Don't recognize this number, and it is on your line." He handed the phone to Addie.

"Adelaide Stubbs, may I help you?" she answered.

"Mrs. Stubbs this is John Longworth, calling from the Boston FBI office."

"Good morning John, do you mind if I put you on speaker phone? My husband is sitting right here; he is aware of this situation. I felt it was important to tell him about this for safety reasons. I do want him to hear what you have to say." Addie pushed the button on her cordless phone, so that Butch could hear their conversation.

"No, certainly not, Mrs. Stubbs. We were just following up and wanted to know if you have heard anything from Jake Proctor." John inquired.

"Well, no I have not. I did call Babs Baker, my friend in Lakeside, Pennsylvania, who had known him a long time ago, and she said she had some weird things happening to her but thought they were just coincidences. I did not mention anything about our conversations as you had requested. Do you think you should contact her?" Addie asked sounding concerned. It was hard for Addie not to want to solve everyone else's problems as well as her own.

"We are having someone from our Pittsburgh office contact her as we speak. Mr. Proctor has not come back from his vacation, and we have reason to believe that he is not in Memphis any more. Please let us know if you hear from him, or have anything out of the ordinary happen to you." John cautioned.

"Officer, we are going to go to Bar Harbor, Maine, next week to pick up a boat and will be out of the house for the next five days. I will take my cell phone; you have the number. The service is sketchy up there, but let me give you my husband's e-mail address. He will take his laptop. We will be stopping at Marinas along the coast so communication will not be impossible, just somewhat unreliable." Addie felt concerned.

"Mrs. Stubbs what is the name of your new boat?" John was mentally thinking he could track them down by the Coast Guard if need be.

"It will be called the *Bluefish.*" Addie responded.

"Sounds like you have a fisherman in your family," John said light heartedly. He could hear a man's voice laughing in the background; John also loved to fish.

Butch chimed in: "how did you guess?" Now it was his turn to laugh.

"What kind of boat did you get?" John asked with curiosity.

"A Sea Martin Motor Yacht. Addie loves to be on the water, and we both like to fish. We're looking forward to some cruising up and down the coast. We'll have to get you out on the boat sometime."

"You won't have to extend that invitation twice," John replied. "Stay in touch, you have our cell phones and know how to reach us."

"John, I am worried about my friend, Babs. Should I call her?" Addie asked with concern.

"She is already being visited by our agents from the Pittsburgh office, but we would prefer you not contact her at this time for obvious reasons." John instructed.

"That is a bit of a tough order for me, but certainly I will defer to your judgment. It goes against my, 'when-in-crisis: act' mode." Addie replied.

"I certainly understand your concerns, but please trust me Mrs. Stubbs. We have been doing this for a long time." John's voice had an authoritarian tone.

"I certainly understand." Addie complied.

"Have a safe journey." John signed off.

Addie hung up the phone and looked at Butch. "God damn, this is freaking me out. I think I might take my jewelry and silver to the safe deposit box."

"Good idea. We also have a lot of guns around here, but they are locked up. Not that it would take anything to break those locks." Butch pitched in.

"I wonder, should we notify our local police we are going away?" asked Addie.

"No honey, we have the alarm which we will set; things are insured. This guy doesn't have any reason to come after you. I'm more concerned about Babs. Besides, who would want to come to New England and upstate Pennsylvania in this kind of weather? He is probably sitting on some tropical island. I,m just hoping we won't have a major storm when we bring the boat down. We are getting the boat very early in the season, but I can't wait any longer!" Butch said.

"If the weather looks bad, lets put into port please." Addie pleaded.

"We certainly will. The boat has heat, and we can take our time coming down the coast. The Sea Martins are very seaworthy boats, and we are good, sensible yachtsmen." Butch was very reassuring.

"Honey, you are right. We might be safer on the high seas than at home. Gosh, I hope they catch this guy. He is really crazy."

Chapter Nineteen

A Crafty Carpenter?

After the FBI agents left and George came home from happy hour with "the boys," Babs asked him to fix them both a drink while she got out some cheese and crackers. This was an unusual request as it was nearing their 7:00 p.m. dinner time, and she rarely encouraged George to have another drink, especially if he'd already had a few.

"I thought we'd just order out tonight, all right with you dear?" Babs asked as she arranged slices of smoked Gouda and water biscuits on a little tray. "Fine by me, as long as we have it delivered," George answered sweetly. He sensed Babs had something she wanted to talk about, and he further sensed the subject matter would be disturbing.

"And George, before we go in the living room, will you please put Sam in his crate? I don't want him to bother us."

With this added request, George was now sure something was up.

Two drinks and a pizza and antipasto delivery later, Babs had poured out to George the details of her past with Lee and all related events leading up to the present. He managed to sit quietly and listen, patting her hand at intervals and getting her some tissues when the tears came.

She appreciated his being so tender hearted, concerned, and not the least bit judgmental, as she rattled on and on in verbal disarray. George could be a son of a gun, but when push came to shove he was the strong one: 'the take charge person.' Babs remembered when each of her parents died, it was George who saw to the details, offered comfort, and made sure everyone was ok.

It was getting late and they were both drained, but they took the time to get a tablet and jot down a few notes about what had been happening with a "to do" list for the next day:

1. Call FBI agents Dell and Light to ok surveillance and a wire tap on the phone.
2. Do not communicate with Addie or Dottie for the time being.
3. Make sure respective cell phones are on 24/7, and carried at all times.
4. Start locking front porch door and coming in house with back door key. Get extra back door keys made.
5. Say "I love you" more often.

"I work tomorrow honey, so you'll need to make the FBI call and get the key made. I can't tell you how much I look forward to the distraction of the children to take my mind off all this crap that's been happening," Babs sighed.

"You got it, babe. And, if Lee's really here, we'll find the creep sooner or later. Meanwhile, you've got the protection of the FBI and should be able to rest a whole lot easier," George offered in an effort to reassure her.

The meteorologist predicted a big snow storm the next day. Despite the poor weather report, Al wanted to continue with his plans. He knew he'd have to act fast though. He'd already taken care of turning in the hybrid for a different car. Two weeks was long enough to be seen in it, especially when he now suspected authorities were probably looking for him, or rather for Jake.

Just a couple days ago he'd noticed two men in dark overcoats exiting the Baker's around 5:00 p.m. Although he couldn't really see them very well due to the snowy conditions, they looked official. He did sense however they weren't anyone the Baker's knew. Did Mormon's or Jehovah's Witnesses make house calls at that time of day? He didn't think so. How about insurance salesmen? That could be. Or . . . *detectives? Damn,* he thought, *this cat's going to have to be a whole lot more careful about how he goes about catching his mouse!*

Al's replacement car had tinted windows but nothing else to distinguish it from every other boxy, late model, neutral colored sedan. In fact, there were two just like it in Bab's neighborhood. *That's good,* he thought.

As luck would have it, Al's plan proceeded better than he could have imagined over the next two days. He already knew who lived there; he'd gone to the town hall and found their names in the city directory: Gail and Glenn Ward. He also knew they were away because he'd been checking their mailbox: consistently empty. To minimize detection, he was going to park the car on the next street over and enter the property from the back.

The day he planned to enter the empty house, he drove by the front of the house and noticed a car in the driveway; a car he was sure he'd seen somewhere before. There was also some kind of service van alongside the car, but he couldn't make out what the sign on its side panel said.

Hmmm, Al pondered out loud as he drove past, *this could be my lucky day, but I gotta figure out a reason to show my face and be let in the house by whoever's there.*

Twenty minutes and a trip to a dollar store later, his manic persona in high gear, Al returned to the property, pulled in the driveway, and parked behind the service van. He could now see it belonged to an electrician. *That even sweetens the deal,* he thought. "Can I pull this off? You bet your sweet ass I can!" he exclaimed while banging the steering wheel with the palm of his hand for emphasis. Retractable tape measure, clip board and tablet in hand, Al nonchalantly headed toward the open garage which looked like the appropriate entrance to try.

A cheerful looking older woman on crutches answered his knock.

"May I help you?" she asked sweetly.

"Why yes ma'am," Al responded politely. "I'm a friend of the Wards, and Glenn sent me here on a secret mission as a surprise for Gail when they get back. I do custom cabinetry, and she's been wanting a window seat in one of the rooms facing out to the pond. Glenn wanted me to decide where it would work best. I've already lined up a seamstress to do the cushion. Right now I just need to pinpoint a location and get some measurements. Would that be ok?"

"Most certainly, Mr . . . . Uh, what was your name?" the woman asked.

"Oh, I'm sorry," Al responded. "Pete, Pete Jordan. And yours? Glenn neglected to tell me who would be here. Just that today was a good day to come," he convincingly lied.

"I'm Dottie. I clean for the Wards and help out with odds and ends while they're away. Do come in, Mr. Jordan," she said brightly.

Al suddenly realized why the car outside was familiar. Not many old relics like that one around. He was sure he'd seen it at the Baker's. *Dottie must clean for them too,* he thought, more than pleased by the coincidence.

As he followed Dottie into the house, he saw whom he figured was the electrician fiddling on the wall along the garage entryway hall with what appeared to be security system equipment. Al nodded as he passed by, and the man nodded back.

When A. and Dottie got into the first room of the house, a spacious living room, Al risked asking if there was a problem with the security system.

"Actually, no," Dottie answered, "just a routine check-up." The Wards get a little nervous about possible break-ins when they're away." Following a brief pause, she added, "Well, Mr. Jordan, I'll let you get to your measuring. I'll be in the kitchen. Just holler if you need anything."

"Will do. Thanks Dottie."

This house is huge; where the hell's the kitchen, he wondered.

Al feigned measuring as he scoped out the rooms with windows facing the pond. After the living room, there was a cozy library/den, then a formal dining room, and, off that running the width of the house at the south end, a formidable state of the art kitchen where he found Dottie polishing silver.

He badly wanted to explore the upstairs, but could find no excuse to do so. That would have to wait.

"Dottie, I've got what I need, and will be going now. It was nice meeting you. No need to see me out, and please, if you talk with Gail, don't mention my being here. Glenn loves to surprise her. So mum's the word, OK?"

"Absolutely, but I just want to know where you decided to put the window seat. Personally, I'd want it in the den. Do you have a key to get in to do the work? I won't be coming again until they get back."

Oh God, how to answer her? Al hadn't thought of that detail, but he somehow managed to provide the perfect response.

"Whew, Dottie, I'm so glad you said that. Glenn told me you would only be here today and to be sure to get a key from you. I completely forgot. Oh, and by the way, you'll be pleased to know the window seat is going to be in the den.

Dottie beamed, hearing about the window seat location, then grabbed her keys which were nearby on the counter and removed the one tagged Ward, handed it to Al. As she did so, Al noticed another key tagged "Baker."

Oh if only I could get that one too, he thought. *This Dottie is so incredibly naive and trusting, she might even give it to me,* Al mused.

"One other thing," he said, "on my way out, I better have the electrician show me how to disable the security system so I won't set off any alarms when I come back to do the work."

"Good thinking. Bye now. I'll look forward to seeing the window seat," Dottie responded.

This woman is thicker than two coats of paint, Al decided, as he headed toward the garage.

Babs felt much more at ease now that the FBI was involved and surveillance had been initiated. Agents Dell and Light emphasized the importance of confidentiality to Babs and George. They must tell no one about the FBI's involvement or the surveillance measures; no relatives, no friends, no one.

Babs respected that warning, but did manage to have some fun with the situation. When a friend called, and she said, "this call may be monitored," etc. like they do when you call Customer Service 800 numbers. She'd really only done it once. George overheard her and didn't think it was at all funny.

"Gad, dear, lighten up," she said when he glared at her.

The agents didn't think it was funny either. Soon after, she got a call from one of them advising her to take her situation a bit more seriously.

And she did, especially when Dottie called to see whether she should come to clean the following Tuesday. They got to chatting, and Dottie told her about the surprise Glenn was planning for Gail and the really nice man who came to take the measurements. "He had these incredible eyes, and the rest of him wasn't bad either," Dottie said rather giddily. "Do you know him? His name's Pete Jordan, and he said he's a friend of theirs."

"I've never heard of him. But remember Dottie, the most we have in common with the Wards is you. I don't really know them or whom their friends are. What surprises me is you let this man into the house without asking for identification or somehow verifying Glenn had sent him. I'm sure it's all on the up and up, but please be more careful. I would hope you'd not let anyone in our house when we're not there. Unless you were told by us they were coming. There's too much evil lurking out there these days, and we all need to be more proactive about our personal safety. Geez, Dottie, I gave you an earful. Sorry, lecture over, still friends?"

"Of course, and I know you're right, Babs. Anyway, I'll come on Tuesday. I know you'll be working, but will George be home?"

"Not sure of George's day. But before I forget, I'll be leaving a new house key for you under the chair cushion nearest the door on the porch. It's to the back door. We've decided to use that entrance to the house for a while for reasons I'll explain later. Look for a note on the counter about what needs doing and how to lock up when you leave in case George isn't there," Babs concluded.

"That'll be great. Oh, and I'll probably be leaving a little treat for you and George. Have you ever had chocolate brickle? I recently got the recipe from a friend, and it's to die for so fattening, so sinful, and so good! On that note, I'll say bye bye," and Dottie hung up.

As it turned out, George would be away on Tuesday. George had been asked by Bab's brother, Tom, to join him for a day long trip to attend a boat show in Cleveland. Tom was recently engaged (at the age of 68) and could see boating as an added pleasure for him and his fiancée. He considered George a boating guru and the best person to have along when a serious purchase was probable. George eagerly agreed to go because, besides Babs, his true love was anything on the water.

Al was ready to strike big time. All he needed to be successful was a steady focus, Bab's complete cooperation, no mechanical or electrical surprises, and a foolproof getaway when his mission was done. Toward that end, he already had his plane tickets and a new alias.

Tuesday dawned bright with no snow storm. Babs left for her nanny job at 7:50 a.m., and George was leaving at 8:00 a.m. with Tom. Sam would be in his crate until after 5:00 p.m. when Babs returned. It would be the longest Sam had ever been caged up during the day, and they prayed it wouldn't spell canine disaster.

Al drove to the Bakers a little after 9:00 a.m. to confirm no one was home. *Perfect*, he thought. But he still had to figure out how to get into the house. Today was the day he somehow was going to abduct Babs and hide her at the Ward home.

He'd been chain smoking since he got up, was all sweaty, and hadn't been able to eat anything, he felt euphoric and hoped the strange contrast spelled a winning combination.

It would work out; he just knew it. One of the tricks up his sleeve was good old chloroform. He was ready to put a soaked cloth of it over Bab's nose to render her limp and pliable. That would make the rest of the transition easy as pie. Part II of the scheme was to leave George scared shitless when he comes home and finds that his wife has virtually disappeared into thin air but is actually right across the street and up a few doors.

After a brief search around the grounds, Al brazenly, but cautiously, entered the Baker's porch. He couldn't believe his luck when he quickly found what looked to be a house key under the cushion on a lone porch chair. His excitement dimmed when he found it didn't fit the front door. Hmm. Could it be for a side or back door? He decided to find out even though it was a huge risk in case the dog sensed a presence and started to bark. Working quickly, Al found it fit the back door. With that intelligence and no canine interruption, he sped away to get the original key duplicated, returned, replaced the original key under the cushion. Then he hastily left to bide his time until around 5:00 when Babs should be getting home.

Since his arrival on the Baker premises early in the day, unbeknownst to Al, there was a major goof in FBI surveillance. For some reason-a computer glitch probably—surveillance of the Baker's and surrounding area had been suspended for several days, including this one.

When Babs did return, and Al watched from a distance as lights were turned on, the dog was let out, and best of all, Babs and Sam emerged for an obvious walk. Al hadn't anticipated this added advantage to his scheme. As soon as they were well on their way, Al hurried with his kidnapping "kit" to let himself in the back door, which to his utter surprise, she had not locked. Just inside the back entrance was a small half bath where he decided to hide until it was time to enact his plan. He felt an odd combination of excited and terrified and wished he had thought to bring a joint to temper the agony of anticipation.

Then it all happened rapid fire. After they returned through the front door, Babs put Sam in his crate, then could be heard in the kitchen, opening the refrigerator, opening cupboards, etc. Al couldn't have orchestrated better timing. Babs' had her back to him when he stealthily exited the bathroom into the kitchen, swiftly grabbed her from behind and clamped the chloroform soaked cloth on her face. She was "gone" in an instant. He lowered her to the floor then dealt with Sam. All it took was a treat to gain his favor, then as he came out of his crate, clamp the chloroform on his snout. He succumbed so quickly that Al fleetingly wondered if the dose had been excessive. He didn't really care, he just wondered.

A half hour later, Babs was still out of it when Lee dumped her on one of the many beds at the Wards. She wouldn't come to for hours, and when she did, he'd enjoy taunting her unmercifully. Meanwhile, he'd enjoy her panic and loved imagining George's distress over her absence from their idyllic little existence. Poor George; what a wimp; they deserve each other."

Chapter Twenty

New Revelations

"Adelaide Stubbs, Handwriting Analyst." Addie answered quickly on the first ring. No lazy, nonchalant 'wait-'til-the-third-chime; I am so cool I don't need to *fake* a slow response. I'm a high energy, go get'em lady.

"Mrs. Stubbs, this is special agent John Longworth calling from the Boston office of the FBI." John's deep voice echoed over the telephone.

"Good morning John, how are you?" responded Addie.

"Very well, thank you." John said. "Mrs. Stubbs, we are touching base with you to see if you have heard anything more from Jake Proctor."

"Oh Gosh, John may I call you John? I would certainly let you know if I had. I am concerned about my friend Babs in Lakeside, but I have done as you've told me and not contacted her. Did you contact her? She really is the one who can recognize him. I have never even seen a picture of him. In fact, do you think I should see a picture? Do you have a photograph of him that I could see in case he poses as a delivery man?" Addie really didn't want to see his photograph, just like she didn't like to see the handwritings of severely emotionally disturbed people, but she knew it would be prudent.

"That is an excellent idea, Mrs. Stubbs. I'll have my assistant scan the photo and e-mail it to you."

"Well, I have your phone number near my desk, in my car, and on our boat. I promise I will stay in close touch," Addie said laughing. "Can I call Babs?"

"No, please don't. We have our reasons and are in control of the situation. I realize she is a good friend of yours and you're concerned about her. But no, please do not contact her at this time. Is that perfectly clear?" John's voice was firm and filled with authority.

"Yes, it's perfectly clear. Please send me that photograph. I will keep in touch, don't worry." Addie felt like a child. She didn't like being talked to with that tone of voice, but recognized that Special Agent Longworth was under some pressure.

"How is the new boat?" Asked Agent Longworth.

"It's absolutely marvelous. We will honor our promise to you and get you out for an afternoon of fishing." Addie said her goodbyes and promised to look at the transmitted picture.

Butch walked into the office. "How about taking a bike ride? It's warm enough, and we could use the exercise. It is a lovely spring day especially if we dress warmly. They had both promised when they were married to each other to try to keep in as good a shape as possible.

"Sounds great, I'm ready for a break. Oh, the FBI just called. They are going to send me a picture of Jake Proctor just in case he shows up here posing as a delivery man or something." Addie looked at Butch whose face suddenly went sullen. He had quickly lost his usual lighthearted smile. Addie loved looking at him. Even at sixty-six, he was handsome with bright blue eyes accentuated by his white hair.

"I will be so glad when they catch this guy. He is starting to interfere in our lives, and it's beginning to irritating me." Butch exclaimed. "Maybe I will move my gun case up into the front hall to show him I mean business. He'd better not mess with my little girl," they both laughed.

Addie glanced at her computer. "Oh great, here is an e-mail from Agent Longworth's assistant. Let's see what this guy looks like. I want you to see his face as well." Addie drew the cursive down to the appropriate entry on her screen. "Oh my god! Butch, I think this guy was here. Remember several months ago when I got that terrible pornographic handwriting sample? I think this was the delivery man. I remember he had a tattoo on his wrist and the delivery was not made in a Federal Express truck. I mentioned something to him about not having his truck, and he said it was in the shop. God almighty, I am so freaked out. I better call Agent Longworth." Addie reached for the phone.

"Are you sure this is the same guy? Why would he come all the way from Memphis to deliver a package to someone he doesn't know?" Butch looked at the photograph.

"Because the guy is crazy, bonkers, wacko tacko, sick, that's why." Addie could here the phone ringing as the call connected on the other end. "Good morning, this is Adelaide Stubbs. May I please speak to Agent Longworth?"

"Agent Longworth." John answered.

"John, this is Addie Stubbs. I just got the picture of Jake Proctor and I am pretty sure he came to our house last fall posing as a Federal Express delivery man. He brought the pornographic letter. The one thing I remember is he had a tattoo on his left wrist which was partially covered up by his watch.

He was also in a black, Chevy pickup truck and not a Federal Express truck. When I asked him about his vehicle, he said it was in the shop, and making the delivery as fast as possible was more important than arriving in a company vehicle. He had a Southern accent. I know most of the delivery guys because we use Fed Ex a lot for our work. Oh man, I am shaking."

"Mrs. Stubbs, thank you for calling me so quickly. Would you know the exact date of the delivery, and have you seen him since?" John inquired.

"I should be able to look in my files and tell you the exact date, which I will do, then e-mail you. But no, I have not seen him since. God, how expensive is that to fly all the way to Boston to deliver a letter?" Addie felt better just talking with Agent Longworth.

"Well, it's very difficult to understand what this type of person does on any level." John answered.

"I totally concur with that. I'll look in my files and e-mail you that date. Man, I am freaked out." Addie took a deep breath.

"Is your husband around? He isn't traveling or anything, is he Mrs. Stubbs?" asked Agent Longworth.

"No he's not traveling, thank goodness, and we do spend a lot of time together. I will let you know if anything else happens."

"Thank you Mrs. Stubbs. We're just a phone call away." John hung up the phone.

"Can you believe the nerve of that guy? Or, maybe I should say, lunacy. He must have spent a pretty penny in travel fees. Glad we are married and you work at home so much. Do you think we should get a dog?" Addie looked at Butch.

"Oh probably, but that is a major commitment of time, not to mention the boarding expense when we travel. You haven't seen him since that one time in the spring, have you?" Butch looked at Addie.

"No, I haven't. Oh gosh, this situation is creepy." Addie physically shuddered.

The temperature had dropped by evening. When it was just the two of them, they had dinner on trays in their den in front of the fireplace. Each evening, Addie bathed around 7:00 and changed her clothes before dinner. Her blond hair, now carefully colored, was well combed and she wore the Channel No. 5 Butch had given her for Christmas. She loved these evenings together. More often than not, she would have a recipe or two for Butch to try. She would wait expectantly for his reaction to the dish she placed in front of him. Addie knew instantly, from the look on Butch's face, whether the dish met with his approval. The real killer was Butch's remark that the dish was "interesting." They would then both laugh, and Addie would say, "You hate it."

Butch took a sip of his martini. "How would you like to go to Provincetown next Thursday night? We could take the boat, do a little fishing on the way over, eat at some good restaurants and spend the night."

"Oh honey, I would love to do that," responded Addie. "I like being on the boat, and I haven't been to Provincetown for years. This will be a great time to go before the height of the summer season. Besides, when all of our children and grandchildren arrive for the summer, I think a trip that long would be too much for the little kids. I think I'll send an e-mail to Agent Longworth, tell him we are going to be out on the boat, and let him know our plans. I am not sure he has our cell phone number on the boat. That was smart to get another cell for the boat. We are going to be out on the high seas a lot this summer."

Butch stood up and through another log on the fire. "It probably is a good idea to contact the FBI and let them know where you are at all times. This Jake guy is casting a cloud over our otherwise happy life. I don't like it one bit. One would think they would have been able to catch him by now. It is interesting when you think, that we have never been able to disappear. I mean, we inevitably run into people at an airport or restaurant when we are traveling."

It was a crisp day when the Stubbs set out for Provincetown. The sky was bright blue, and, although the weather was a bit nippy, they both felt invigorated being on the ocean. "When we get to Stellwagen, we can do a little fishing. With any luck we can bring home some bluefish!" Butch said with a confident smile.

It took them about forty-five minutes to reach Stellwagen Bank. This undersea sandbar in the middle of Massachusetts Bar descended in depth from ninety feet to two hundred-fifty feet, making it an ideal breeding ground for fish of all sizes. The shipping channel crosses a portion of the area, so it is customary to see large tankers, whale watching boats, and commercial fishermen bringing up their catch.

Addie was intrigued. She had heard about Stellwagen Bank for years but had never been there. Despite the fact you could not see any land there was so much activity, one hardly felt removed. "Oh Butch look there are whales over there, do you see them? My gosh, they are magnificent! Where is our camera?"

"It's down in the cockpit. Here, man the helm, I'll get it," said Butch dashing down the stairs to find his camera.

"Oh look, thar she blows!" Said Addie laughing with glee. "They are such magnificent animals. My gosh, look that one is blowing a huge spray of water in the air." Addie was ecstatic.

"The whale is feeding," Butch said, pointing his camera in the direction of the large mammal. "Look there is another one." A large whale watching vessel carrying hundreds of people was also circling.

"I am going to set a few lines. Keep us heading 140 degrees southwest."

Addie took over the helm. The boat was moving very slowly. Butch rigged two lines with shiny metal lures.

"How about making some sandwiches for lunch? We can fish for a bit and then high tail it over to Provincetown. We are about half way there now." Butch looked at Addie and slowed the pace of the boat. They were trolling on auto pilot.

She knew he wanted to fish, and she was very happy to have lunch onboard the boat. She descended into the cabin and made some ham and cheese sandwiches.

As she brought the plates topside, she said, "you know, of course, once we start eating our sandwiches we will get a strike. It's just the laws of the universe; it is that Zen energy of releasing what you wish for!" Butch looked at her and started to laugh. They began eating their sandwiches. Suddenly, one of the reels began to spin.

"What did I tell you, Butch? I knew we would get a strike as soon as we took a few bites." Butch jumped up and started to reel in the rod. Addie slowly brought the boat to a standstill and turned off the engine. Quickly, she ran to bring in the other line and get it out of the way while Butch landed his fish.

"Oh my gosh, it looks like a big one." Butch kept his rod tip high. "Yup, there he is, did you see him? It's a nice bluefish." He reeled the fish and quickly brought him into the boat. The failing fish twisted franticly in the air until a few swift hits of Butch's bat rendered him lifeless. They caught two more fish before deciding to head to Provincetown. Butch cleaned their catch close to the harbor so they could put the filets into the refrigerator onboard.

After securing the boat at the dock, Addie and Butch walked along the wooden pier into town. Addie looked at Butch and said, "This wild and crazy place liberates my repressed New England Puritan core," she took his arm and gave him a quick kiss.

"Check mate, babe. This is the New Orleans of New England. A total shocker, a place so out of character with the rest of Yankee conservative thinking that it broadens our personalities and gives the most uninhibited credence to our dark side." Butch laughed and kissed her back.

At best, the New England spirit is a complex and multi-faceted one. The Pilgrims' Mayflower landed in Provincetown Harbor in 1620. Never in their wildest dreams could this desperate group of God-fearing, Bible-toting, half-starving band of ocean survivors have imagined a community composed of people with alternative life styles. It is a haven for artists, musicians, good food, and unrestrained expression.

"Oh look Butch, there is the sign for a fortune teller. Maybe we should go." Butch looked at Addie in disbelief.

"You have got to be kidding. I am not going to one of those places. They are just hoaxes; you can't be serious." Butch snorted.

"I am serious. Oh Butch, I am so worried about Babs, please let me go and see if the fortuneteller has anything to say. Look, there is a marine supply store on the other side of the street. Let me pop in here, and I will meet you at the marine supply store in a few minutes. Oh please honey, I love you so much. Just grant me this one little wish. Oh please." Addie could be ridiculously coquettish when she wanted, and Butch knew there was no use arguing with her when her mind was made up.

"Ok honey, but I think it's a waste of money," Butch retorted. He really wanted to spend some time in the marine supply store, so Addie's desires were not all bad.

"Oh thank you, sweet heart." Addie dashed into the store front. The banner read: LULA'S PSYCHIC READINGS. A young woman met Addie at the front desk. Or at first glance, Addie thought it was a young woman, but upon closer examination she was not quite so sure. Never mind, it didn't matter. "Do you wish to have a reading?"

"Yes, please. I don't have an awful lot of time." Addie pleaded.

"You are in luck. We just had a cancellation. That will be fifty dollars." Addie quickly took two twenties and one ten out of her wallet and placed them on the counter.

"Thank you very much. Please come this way." The young woman took Addie back to the office and opened the door. A woman in her fifties sat behind a desk. Behind her was a long bookshelf filled with books, and on top of the book shelf were a series of crosses.

"Welcome, my name is Lula. I am a psychic reader, but I want you to know that my gifts come only from God." Lula sat erectly in her chair. "Shall we begin?"

"Please." Addie sat in a chair on the other side of the desk.

Lula began closing her eyes. There was dead silence for the next few minutes.

"You have come to me because you are very worried about something." There was another silence. "You have come to me because you are worried about a friend." Silence. "Your friend is far away. She is in great danger." Lula stopped talking for a few minutes.

"Is she alright?" Addie blurted out.

"I am very sorry, I can not continue this reading." Lula rang a buzzer, which was underneath her desk. She stood up abruptly. Her assistant entered the room. "Please give this woman her money back," she said to the young woman.

"I do not feel very well. I am afraid I may not continue. Please forgive me." She then left her office abruptly. The young woman led Addie out of the rear office and refunded her fifty dollars.

Addie was shell-shocked. She wandered across the street to the marine supply store to find Butch. He was in the third aisle looking at cleaning equipment.

"Well, that didn't take very long," he looked at Addie who looked extremely upset.

"It was so weird," she said. "She thought I came to see her because I was worried about a friend, then she just stopped and said she didn't feel well and had to leave. The good news is, she refunded my fifty dollars."

Butch began laughing. "Honey, it's a fraud. She probably had to take a pee."

They both burst out laughing. "I am going to get these brushes. I think they would be great for scrubbing down the boat, and then let's go get a beer."

"Sounds great, Oh there is The Lobster Pot, one of the restaurants mentioned in the guide book. Let's go there. The book mentioned they have a bar upstairs." Addie felt relieved. She was very frightened and worried Babs could be in some sort of danger. She thought she might phone her, but then remembered that she had made a promise to Agent Longworth.

Butch and Addie sat at the bar. The couple on the left of Butch had just returned from a visit to Prague. They had a timeshare in Provincetown and came to the city once a year every spring. On the other side of Addie were two young men, both quite good-looking.

One of them looked at Addie. "Oh my gosh, you have the nicest blue eyes, and, look at your husband, his eyes are even bluer." Now everyone in the bar was looking at Addie and Butch. "Do you have any children?" The other young man asked.

"Well, we actually have four children but from previous marriages." Addie was a little stunned at the question, but couldn't help herself from responding.

"Are any of them gay?" The taller of the two men asked?

"No, not at all," said Addie.

"Oh Fuck, that's too bad." answered the young man.

The Stubbs ate at a Portuguese seafood restaurant that night.

Addie and Butch tried different entrees so they could taste each other's meals.

They wandered back to the boat before the rain started. Their cabin was cozy and comfortable. They had no trouble sleeping after the full events of the day.

They headed back to Manaport early in the morning. Butch caught a beautiful fifteen-pound bass on his way home. They decide to stop fishing because their refrigerator was getting full. Stellwagen was a bit foggy which made Addie slightly uneasy. "Let's put on the radar."

"Not a bad idea," agreed Butch. As the day progressed, the fog cleared. They reached Manaport Harbor at three in the afternoon.

"One thing I love about a powerboat as opposed to a sailboat, is that it doesn't take a long time to clean up," said Addie as she was snapping one of the canvas protectors to the cabin windows.

"Here, here," agreed Butch. "Besides, we couldn't fish if we had a sailboat."

They picked up their mail from the box at the end of their driveway. Mousetrap was very happy to be released from the basement. The Stubbs would leave him alone with food and water if they were going to be away for twenty-four hours. Addie glanced at the telephone. The message light on the phone was flashing.

"Butch, want to listen to our messages?" Addie picked up the phone.

There were four messages. The fourth was the most shocking: It was George Baker.

"Why on earth did he call?" Addie looked at Butch. "Oh my gosh, I hope nothing happened to Babs."

"Why don't you call him and find out?" Butch suggested.

"My thoughts exactly." Addie quickly dialed the number. She could hear the phone ringing several times.

"Hello, this is the Baker's residence, George speaking." Addie could hear his deep voice, which sounded worried, on the other end of the phone.

"George, hello, this is Addie Stubbs. How are you, and how is Babs?"

"Well, I don't know, I haven't seen her for twenty-four hours. I just thought she might have called you or contacted you. Do you know where she might go? I just don't understand it. I am so worried." George sounded on the verge of crying.

"No, I haven't heard from her, George. I am so sorry. Butch and I have been out on our new boat for the last twenty-four hours. When was the last time you saw her? Have you contacted the police?" Addie asked quickly.

"Yesterday, I went to the Boat Show in Cleveland with Tom, Babs' brother. I got really worried when she didn't answer the phone last night. But I thought she had probably gone out with her friend Mary and forgotten to bring her cell phone.

"How about Sam, your dog? That's his name, isn't it?" Addie's mind was racing.

"He is fine. He was in his crate when I got home." George sounded so sad and upset.

"George, you need to contact the police or even the FBI. Please, even if there is some misunderstanding, I think it is important that you contact them. Please, I will let you know if I hear anything. I'll call you tomorrow." Addie said.

"Don't worry, I got them involved right away. I just thought, being such good friends, she might have said something to you about something I knew nothing about."

"George, I know Babs loves you very much. I wish I could give you some more insights, but unfortunately, I don't have any. I'll call you tomorrow and see if they found her. This must be ghastly for you. I am so sorry you have to go through this." Addie hung up the phone.

"Butch, did you hear that? Babs is missing, and you thought the fortuneteller was a hoax. Oh my god, this is really bad."

Chapter Twenty-one

Who Did This and Where is She?

As Babs slowly came to, she had a sense of euphoria . . . of floating somewhere outside herself off in the distance. It was a delicious sensation, but one that began to dwindle as she regained consciousness and reclaimed her senses.

The first thing she noticed was her eyes were covered and so was her mouth. She could open her eyes slightly under the blindfold but couldn't open her mouth at all. There was some kind of tape on it. The next thing she noticed was how she was lying . . . on her back . . . with her wrists bound together underneath her. It was uncomfortable, but tolerable. The same went for her legs which were crossed and bound at the ankles. She could move them up and down or sideways only about an inch and envisioned they must be elaborately tied to a footboard or other sturdy structure.

As Babs continued, with relative calm, to assess her predicament, she decided it was in her best interests to remain perfectly still and quiet for as long as possible. If she was being watched, she felt her best defense was to appear to be asleep. Fortunately, her nasal passages were clear and she could breathe easily through her nose.

Where am I? How'd I get here? She had no memory of what had happened to her. She didn't seem hurt in any way; *that was good*, she thought.

Wherever she was, it was eerily silent except for an occasional furnace-type sound or the faint engine noise of a car going by.

After what seemed a long time of lying there listening to the silence and struggling to remember, Babs distinctly heard a door close somewhere nearby followed by footsteps and someone coughing. Next she heard another door close and, soon after, a flushing sound. Then footsteps again, now coming her way.

Any feelings of calm and euphoria Babs had experienced up to this moment completely vanished, and she was scared to death.

Her memory had returned full force, and she knew the approaching footsteps had to be Lee's. He had a distinctive gate she would have known anywhere.

He entered the room, all stealth and cunning, and stood at the end of the bed, grinning broadly as he looked down at her still form.

It's been hours, and she's still out of it, he observed, testing his surmise by saying in a hushed, sardonic tone, "Babs, oh Babs, wherefore art thou, dear Babs?" When she didn't stir, he added, "I'd have to say, in a weird way, chloroform becomes you. Keeps you quiet, at least, and gives me time to think."

Lee flashed back briefly to a few mornings ago when he was at the library looking up chloroform on the internet. He felt it would be perfect for subduing Babs but had no idea if it was legal or where to get any. He only knew it was easy to administer, was immediately effective, and left no traceable odor.

His research quickly revealed that use of chloroform as an anesthesia on humans was discontinued years ago due to its toxicity. He further learned, however, that one could make synthetic chloroform by mixing chlorine bleach and nail polish remover. The website even listed the amounts of each to use. Bingo!

However, what the recipe didn't include, however, was how much was safe to use, or how long it would remain effective once administered. As he thought about these omissions and continued to observe no movement from Babs, he began to worry. "What if I used too much? Suppose she doesn't wake up?" he said half out loud.

Lee had little to recommend him as a human being, but he wasn't a murderer. That he knew.

Hearing Lee's last comment, and unable to bear the rapidly escalating discomfort of her captivity, Babs decided to make her living presence known. She emitted a brief groan and lifted her head slightly.

By now she had a nasty headache, an unbearably dry mouth, and an urgent need to use the bathroom. *He'll probably let me wet the bed and get a huge kick out of his depravity,* she thought. What she really wanted the most was to have the tape removed from her mouth. There was something about being reduced to one orifice for breathing that was very frightening to her. She minded the blindfold the least because with it on she didn't have to look at him. His beady eyes, pencil thin lips, cleft chin—all menacing features which, during a period of her past, had translated so differently.

When Babs moved, Lee almost told her how relieved he was, but instead, grabbed one of her feet and said in a menacing tone, "hello, Babs. Sorry I didn't get a chance to say hello properly when last we met. I was too busy subduing you and your dog. Quite the challenge, I must say. I do hope your dog didn't get too big a dose of what I gave you. If George only knew where to find us, we could ask him about the dog."

Babs gasped at the thought of any harm coming to Sam. She also couldn't fathom that after two decades, Lee would have it out for her to such an extreme. *He always was unstable, but now must be truly off his rocker. I need to be very careful,* she thought. Then her thoughts quickly flashed to George, dear George; he must be sick with worry, or is he even back from Cleveland yet? She had completely lost all sense of time. For now she wouldn't give Lee the satisfaction of asking what day, or time of day it was.

Babs was hungry; her bladder was bursting. She wondered what she could do to get him to provide any amenities. She thought back to their long ago relationship and the things that worked in the dysfunction they shared. *Appeal to his ego,* began like a mantra in her head and repeated itself until she had an *aha* thought: *Ask him for a cigarette. He always was pissed when I quit smoking and wouldn't smoke with him.*

But wait a minute. I can't even talk. I've got this tape on my mouth. She mustered the entire ventriloquist in her and said very slowly, "hey Lee, no hard feelings; how about taking this tape off and letting me have a smoke?"

After a few repeats, he managed to understand her garbled request, smiled a crazy smile, and gingerly removed the tape from her face.

Once the tape was off, Babs braved asking if, before the cigarette, she could please use the bathroom. To her amazement, he cooperatively complied. He untied her but left the blindfold on and led her to the bathroom. She could tell even with the blindfold there was not much light in any of the house, wherever she was. *Must be he has to keep the place looking inconspicuous,* she thought. Once they got to the bathroom, he gave her privacy.

"I'll be right outside the door so don't try anything funny," Lee warned. Babs had no intension of any shenanigans. She needed all hers smarts to outwit this wacko.

When they got back to the room, she smoked the cigarette. Why, she even inhaled it. The drags felt god awful going into her lungs, but she enjoyed the activity for its value in relieving her of worry and tension. Hopefully, she'd never have another one. She'd already quit at least ten times, and the agony of doing it again was less than appealing. After the cigarette, he tied her up again, much to her disappointment. But he did, thankfully, leave the tape off. Her next challenge was to cajole him into providing some food. She was starved.

Now that Babs felt less threatened and more conversant with Lee as a psycho project, she actively wondered where the hell she was. He was being nice to her now but, knowing Lee, he could turn manic at any moment and put her in real danger. *How could she alert George without being detected?*

"So Lee, what have you been doing for the last thirty odd years. I have to commend you for your dramatic entrance. But then, you always did have a flare for the theatrical." Babs tried to give a little half laugh. "I must admit you brilliantly took me by surprise. Why did you track me down? Was it you who put the canary in my paper?"

"Of course, it was me, bitch. Didn't you watch any Mafia pictures? The dead canary goes to the person who squeals." He grabbed her arm and shook it violently. Babs didn't answer. She took a deep breath and then answered slowly.

"It was because," Babs slowed her speech and said softly, "I loved you. I was worried about your drinking. I wanted you to stop and knew that you couldn't without help." Babs kept thinking over and over again, *play to his ego, play to his ego.* "You are a bright person. I knew you were capable of being someone." She hesitated. Lee didn't say anything. "I am sorry if I hurt you."

"Hurt me, you called in my fuckin' boss. What if that had been you? What do you think that did for me at the company? Did you ever think of that?" He shook with rage.

Babs managed to answer slowly, "I am sorry Lee. I am really sorry. Hey, I'm starved. Is there any chance of getting something to eat? Maybe we could talk things over the way we did in the old days? What do you say?"

"Lucky for you bitch I'm hungry too. If you try to do anything I'll go after your dog, and that ape size husband of yours." He retired Babs to the bed. "I'll be locking you in here for the night."

Did this mean it was now evening, she wondered? Anyway, that announcement really boosted her spirits.

When Lee came back with crackers and peanut butter, untied Bab's feet and hands and let her sit up, putting pillows behind her back. "Remember, no funny stuff," he said, "I'm watching your every move, and if you so much as put a hand anywhere near your blindfold, the food's history and I'll hog tie you. "As it is, I'll be locking you in here for the night."

Babs was tempted to say "*what* night?" but caught herself and remained silent.

"Hey Lee, remember the healthy food you introduced me to in the old days. I was this young impressionable women and a fast food junky. Peanut butter is pretty good for you, isn't it?" Babs could never figure out his interest in good nutrition when he abused himself in every other way. *Try to establish a relationship*, she thought, as much as, *I hate this bastard.* "you were into whole grains, soy." Anyway, she was thankful for his offering this night.

Imagine being thankful to this idiot. As she reviewed the litany of horrors he committed like the dead bird, casino visit, etc., what was she thinking? What a dichotomy and how telling about how sick their relationship had been. Now, she was letting it trickle into the present. George would be aghast, and rightfully so.

After Babs ate, she realized she was falling into Lee's spell; he had that much influence over her after all these years. It repulsed her and gave her new resolve to right the situation. By now George must be frantic, and her whole focus turned to getting home and letting him know she was ok. For God's sake, there were the children and grandchildren as well. This was serious, and she felt terrible that she had allowed herself such a laissez faire attitude with a madman in her midst.

Lee tied her up again, this time he stretched her arms and legs out lengthwise. He secured the ropes to the bed posts. "I'll be back in a little while." He walked out the door and turned the key.

Babs lay awake, afraid to sleep.

George was beside himself with worry after two days and no word from Babs. The police and FBI were involved since her disappearance and were in constant contact but had no leads or new information. They had interviewed friends, neighbors, the mailman, and also gone over every inch of the Baker's house, property, and both of their vehicles. As a last resort, George had even called Addie, but she knew nothing. It was as though Babs had disappeared into thin air. As George stewed, he also managed to focus on Babs' amazing strength and resilience and imagined that she was all right but just unable to let him know.

The dog was a wreck too. He seemed to constantly be looking for Babs in the house and couldn't settle down. But earlier, when George came back from Cleveland, Sam's behavior had been quite different; he was lethargic and seemed very disoriented, *as though he might have been drugged*, George thought. He mentioned this to the police, but they dismissed the idea, saying Sam's behavior was just due to being alone without food or water for so long. George wasn't convinced and wished he'd had Sam checked by the vet right away.

Another thing George noticed about Sam was that he would cock his head every now and then as though listening to something. Then he would let out a little whimper, look at George forlornly, sigh, and start pacing around the room, always ending by the front door. "I sure wish you could talk, my boy, because I believe you know something about our Babs," George said lovingly to Sam during their second evening alone. "Maybe tomorrow, you and I will play detective. I haven't even taken you for any walks; it'll be good for both of us to get out of here," he added.

Chapter Twenty-two

Stan Gets Chatty

Memphis was beginning to get warm. FBI agent Sanderson picked up a free copy of *The Memphis Flyer* on his way into the bureau office. Sanderson had a few days of free time coming up and wanted to plan a fun weekend with his girlfriend.

"Good morning, officer Sanderson," said Lilly Johnson, at reception.

"Good morning Lilly. It's beginning to get warm out there." Sanderson walked past the reception desk into his office where his partner Bill Freidman was already checking his computer.

"Hi Bill, anything exciting going on?" Jim Sanderson put his copy of *The Memphis Flyer* on his desk.

"Yup, this looks interesting. There is a woman in Lakeside, Pennsylvania who has disappeared. They think she may have some connection with Jake Proctor. The chief wants us to interview Stan again." Bill turned away from his computer. "Hey, is that the new issue of the *Flyer*?" He picked it up off Jim's desk. "I want to read that review of Michael Moore's new movie, *Sicko*.'"

"Help yourself," said Jim, turning on his computer. "Isn't Stan awaiting trial now?"

"Yup, I have already called the prison and set up an interview for 2:00 p.m." Bill was leafing through "*The Flyer*."

"How long has the woman in Lakeside been missing?" Jim asked.

"Only forty-eight hours, but she is was old girlfriend of Jake's. The Pittsburgh office has already interviewed her according to this bulletin. The report states her husband hasn't heard anything from her for the last forty-eight hours. He says they are usually in constant contact. Maybe Stan's memory has changed now that his accommodations have been greatly improved."

Officers Sanderson and Friedman arrived at the federal penitentiary precisely at 1:45 p.m. They were ushered into a holding room where, about fifteen minutes later, Stan was brought in handcuffed.

"Morning Stan, how have you been?" Officer Sanderson started the questioning.

"Terrific. Three free meals a day, television, access to a weight room, and all the accommodations of a Hilton Hotel. Jesus, you have to get me out of here—the other inmates are weird." Stan slouched in his chair. "Any chance of getting a fuckin' cup of coffee and a cigarette?"

"We might be able to get you a cup of coffee, but this prison is a smoke free zone, except for designated areas, you know that Stan." Officer Friedman piped in. He got up and returned momentarily with three coffees from the nearby vending machine.

"Stan, it seems as if there is a woman missing in Lakeside, Pennsylvania." Officer Sanderson began talking slowly and calmly.

"How could I have anything to do with that, fellas? I've got the perfect alibi. Besides, who in their right mind would want to go north in this weather?" Stan offered, and all three men laughed.

"Have you heard anything from your friend, Jake? Seems kind of mean that if you were partners he is letting you take the full rap for this." Officer Friedman said.

"How long have you been doing this job? Do you really think he is going to contact me in the Federal Penitentiary, Officer? You really have some sense of humor." Stan said, amused by Officer Friedman's statement.

"Guess you have a point there, Stan. Did he ever mention a woman named Babs?" Officer Sanderson inquired.

"Babs, yeah, now that you mention it, he did. He really hated her. Said he wanted to get even with her about something. I think they dated after college or something like that. Jake was pretty wacky, but he really liked studying about the Civil War. I think he met this Babs chick at a conference and they both liked history. Sounded like she jilted him a long time ago. He drove me crazy slowing down the production room machines looking for stuff that might go to Lakeside. He could be a fuckin' pain the ass, if you know what I mean." Stan was looking more alert and was beginning to enjoy the break in his prison routine by answering questions.

"Well, Babs has disappeared and the fact that Jake has also disappeared is an uncomfortable coincidence. Can you think of anything else that could help us find where they are? Did he ever mention a cabin, hideaway, or an escape plan?"

Officer Sanderson stirred the sugar in the bottom of his bitter coffee.

"Hell no, this little theft ring was going to help finance our retirement. I have only fifteen more years, and with Social Security going the way it is, I thought I better plan for the future on my own. Besides, working for the postal service is god damn boring. This became a fun little game to see who we could outsmart." Stan was quite proud of his scheme. Their racket had lasted more than a year.

"Hmm, was there anyone else he ever mentioned?," officer Sanderson inquired for the third time. "Anything at all he told you that might be helpful?" Interrogators are trained to ask the same questions repeatedly and pick up any inconsistencies.

"The only thing I can think of, that I might not have mentioned before, was that there was a package Jake stole from a handwriting analyst. There was a green glass necklace inside going to San Francisco. The return address was this chic who analyzed handwritings. Jake checked out her website and sent her a copy of his handwriting. He didn't want the necklace so he gave it to me. I gave it to my wife for her birthday. It was real pretty, and she liked it. Jake wanted me to get my handwriting analyzed too, but I thought he was full of shit."

"Do you remember the name of the handwriting analyst?" asked Jim.

"Hell no, but I think the postmark was from some place in Massachusetts."

"That could be pretty helpful. What type of cigarettes do you smoke? Just make sure you smoke them in the designated area. I could see that you get a couple of packs." Jim mentioned to Stan compassionately.

"Marlboros would be great, thanks. Say, do you know when I am going to have my trial? This is pretty tough on my wife." Stan raised his eyebrows.

"The wheels of justice turn slowly. The best thing to do from here is acknowledge your misdeeds and be helpful to the authorities. Give as much of the contraband back as possible, and give us the names of the people to whom you sold your merchandise. Stan, you're not a bad guy, you just got a little sidetracked," said Jim. For one split second, Stan looked remorseful.

Stan leaned forward lowered his voice and looked Officer Stanhope in the eye. "I have given all of that information to the police already. But do you think the fences don't have connections inside this place? It is more fuckin' dangerous to be in here, in some ways, than it is to be on the outside."

"Stan, thanks a lot. You have been helpful. I will mention it in my report."

FBI officers John Longworth and Mike Addleborough drove up the driveway to the Stubbs property. Addie was hardly surprised when she opened her front door to see the two men.

"Good morning, gentlemen, I have been half expecting you. Do come in. I'd like to introduce you to my husband." They followed Addie into the living room where Butch was having his morning cup of tea and reading the newspaper.

"Sweetheart, these two gentlemen are Officers Longworth and Addleborough from the Boston FBI. I told you about them." Butch stood up and shook hands with both of the men.

"I guess you have heard that Babs is missing," Officer Longworth said.

"Yes, it is terrible. I feel petrified for both Babs and her husband. George, her husband, called me the other day. I wish there was something we could do. Would you like some of our good Chinese tea, by the way? We just made a large pot," Addie asked.

"I would very much like that," said officer Longworth, and Officer Addleborough nodded in agreement. Addie disappeared into the kitchen.

"Do you think my wife is in any danger, officers?" Butch asked with understandable concern.

It is hard to know. I think it's a time to be cautious. It is my understanding that you are semi-retired and spend a lot of time at home," replied Officer Addleborough.

"Yes, we are very close, and I don't want anything to happen to Addie. When I travel, she usually goes with me. I won't leave her alone for a night until this guy is caught," said Butch as Addie returned from the kitchen with a tray, holding a large tea pot and two cups.

"It is quite impossible to discuss anything without a cup of tea!" exclaimed Addie. "I was looking at Jake's handwriting, or Lee's handwriting, or whomever . . . and I was trying to think of any characteristic I may have missed. He is cunning, very good at detail, and sexually deviant. He focuses on smaller venues rather than large ones. He is very possessive: pathologically so. God, I hate to think of what he is doing or planning to do to poor Babs.

If he used one alias when he sent me a handwriting for analysis, wouldn't that be a pattern? I mean, one would guess he is probably now operating under another name than Jake Proctor, right? He used the name Jake P. Hunt when he was writing to me. Maybe the name he is using now has some connection with his past.

"Thing that surprises me most is that the Bakers have a dog. Well, I guess their dog is still a puppy, and even if he barked, I guess he didn't deter abduction. I suppose we don't even know whether or not Babs was taken from her house. Lakeside isn't that big of a town. How many places could he take her? I guess, of course, he could be taking her back to Tennessee. Sorry Officers, I always wanted your job." Addie stopped talking and looked at the three men who had slightly amused looks on their faces.

"No, this is good," said officer Longworth. "This is exactly the type of dialogue we have when we are sitting around trying to solve a case. The FBI does have personality profiles for different types of criminals."

"Really? Well what is the profile of an abductor?" Addie asked. "From my perspective, Jake feels he is so much smarter than other people that he feels constantly misunderstood. He thinks his plans are quite brilliant. The tragedy with someone like this is that he did have the capacity to have achieved in a lawful segment of society. My guess is that he is close by and right in Lakeside. There is nothing in his handwriting that shows me that—just simply a hunch. Babs has lived in Lakeside for a long time. Have all of the media been alerted? She knows half the town and has so many friends there." Addie was beginning to talk more rapidly.

"Yes, the Pittsburgh office is right on it." Officer Longworth took a sip of his tea. The phone rang. Butch picked it up and looked at the telephone number, "Unknown caller" he said. "Those damn telemarketers, I am not even going to pick this up."

"What if it is Babs, and she is trying to signal us? Or Mr. Wacko is calling to torment me?" Addie exclaimed.

Butch handed her the phone. Addie put the receiver on speaker, "because of your superior credit rating . . ." Addie hung up the phone. "You were correct sweetheart."

"I love it when she says that," Butch looked at the two officers who were laughing. "Mrs. Stubbs, this is a routine question, but I know you were very close to Babs Baker. Is she happily married?" Officer Longworth asked.

"Oh yes, my impression is that she is very happily married. Both of us had been married previously and then single. One never really knows about someone else's relationship, but we both talked a lot about how happy and lucky we were to have such wonderful husbands." Addie looked at Butch.

"Well thank you very much, sweetheart." Butch looked at Addie with affection. "I will keep a close eye on her and let you know if we see anything suspicious."

"Is there anything we should do, or can we help you in any way? Is it ok to make phone calls to George? I know this is a tough time for him." Addie asked.

"I am sure he would appreciate your concern. The best thing is to try to keep the phone pretty open and not tie up his lines for understandable reasons." Officer Longworth suggested. He stood up, and extended his hand. "Thank you very much Mrs. Stubbs for all of your help. We will be in touch. You have all of our phone numbers. I don't need to remind you that you can call us anytime day or night."

"We have your phone numbers next to every phone in the house, in our cars, and not to mention, programmed into our cell phones," exclaimed Addie! "You are very reassuring and I am sure you will find Babs and Mr. Wacko."

"We are certainly giving it our best effort."

Chapter Twenty-three

The Rescue and Flight

After locking Babs in for the night, Lee went downstairs to grab a smoke and think about his next move. He had to feel his way carefully as there were only a few lights on in the house: the ones the Wards programmed to be on in their absence. He didn't dare turn on any more.

Following some fumbling around, he found his cigarettes only to discover that the pack was empty. "Jesus H. Christ," he fumed. "I can't believe it!"

Lee without cigarettes was like a dog without a bone. He had to get some smokes even if it meant leaving Babs and risking detection. Hell, it was nearly midnight, but it isn't like he'd be the only car on the road, and he figured he could be gone and back in less than 10 minutes.

He approached the nearby 24/7 convenience store; it appeared dark. Getting closer he could see some kind of note on the door. *Closed due to a death in the family*, the sign read. *Will reopen Saturday.*

This was Thursday.

"Oh that's just great," he murmured to himself as he got back in his car. "Now I've got to add another ten 'friggin' minutes to this quick little errand." And off he sped to the next closest convenience store his mood as dark as the moonless night.

While Lee was on his nicotine mission, George had decided not to wait until morning to take Sam for an overdue walk. Both of them were restless, and some exercise would hopefully help ease George's mounting anxiety and distress over Bab's disappearance. He needed to eat something too, but when he had tried earlier, he just couldn't. He was too upset. He promised himself he'd force something down when they got back from their walk. Sam hadn't been eating normally either.

"Come on, little buddy," George said to Sam as he grabbed the cell phone and keys, and opened the front door to the porch. Sam shot past him as if out of a cannon, then repeatedly jumped on the porch door until George finally got him to sit still long enough to put the leash on. He attached it to the prong collar which had proved a great training tool for Sam. A quick pull for correction was very effective, and as a result, Sam learned early on who was in charge on walks. Sam also wore a cloth collar with a glow strip so he was visible in the dark. George made sure he could be easily seen as well wearing a light tan windbreaker and light grey sweats and carrying a flashlight.

George planned to take their usual walk north toward the lake then circle the neighborhood's perimeter, about a half hour traveling at a brisk pace.

But Sam had other ideas. The minute they were out the door he began with frenzied determination to pull George hard to the left, or south. He pulled so hard, the prongs digging into his neck elicited some painful yelps, and George nearly lost his footing.

Sam's obstinacy proved overpowering, and George decided to follow his lead feeling with some uncanny, fresh certainty that they were on the way to finding Babs.

George loosened his grip on the leash giving Sam the needed slack to put his keen nose to the ground. Sam looked up at George as if he were saying, "thank you for trusting me, I truly am onto something here."

In less than a minute, they were entering the Ward's driveway. Sam's pace had accelerated and was very deliberate. No wasted motion he was definitely on a mission. He led George into the garage, through one of two bays that were opened, then stopped abruptly in front of the door leading into the house where he began sniffing frantically and barking.

"What is it, Sam? What is it?" George could barely contain his excitement, and was suddenly infused with feelings of hope. To his relief the door was not locked, and they entered with Sam still barking and sniffing, and then suddenly, he was quiet, his ears forward.

They both heard it . . . a female voice far off but definitely somewhere in the house. George could barely see where to go, even with the flashlight. He located a light switch, flicked it on and saw that they were in a large living room with a hallway and staircase beyond. Sam was pulling so hard by now that George wisely let him go.

If dogs could fly, Sam suddenly had wings. He leapt up the stairs with the swiftness of a gazelle, then bounded down a long corridor. The voice they heard earlier was now close by, very familiar, and clearly calling out for help.

George couldn't get the words out fast enough, tears filling his eyes, "Babs honey, we're coming. 'You all right?"

"Yes, thank god, darling, I am. But you must hurry. Lee locked me in this room, and I have no idea if he's still around. He's very unpredictable and could be dangerous. Can you find a phone and call for help?"

Her voice was steady and her delivery very matter of fact. George was amazed that she could sound so even-keeled under such frightening circumstances. *That's my Babs,* he thought with admiration.

While Sam and Babs "talked" through the door, George called 911 and gave the needed information. The operator promised help within five minutes and cautioned him against any heroics to free his wife by knocking down the door. "Just stay right where you are," she said, "the police are on the way."

George felt that if Lee were still around, Sam would have flushed him out by now. He relayed that thought to Babs, who found her husband's supposition very reassuring.

Even before Lee turned onto the street going back to the Ward's, he had a strong sense of foreboding. What if Babs got loose somehow? Suppose she found the notebook and personal stuff he carelessly left in the kitchen? His imagination ran wild, nearly imploding when he saw from a distance the house was ablaze with light, and there appeared to be cop cars in the driveway. He wasn't sure about the latter since he was approaching the back of the property and the driveway was in the front.

Sure or not, he instinctively knew his "fun" with Babs, and stay in Lakeside, had to end, abruptly, swiftly, and immediately.

"Thank god, I've got the cover of night," he thought. But that was little consolation when reality hit, and he realized he couldn't risk returning to the motel for his belongings, turning in the car, or showing up anywhere in the area for that matter. The only thing going for him was his new identification papers. They were sewn into the lining of the windbreaker he was now wearing.

His mood lightened somewhat as he thought about the new credentials and his new name: Elliott Q. Woodrow. *What kind of weird ass name is that?* he mused as he cautiously exited the neighborhood and headed out of town going east. It was 1:00 a.m., and he had a lot to accomplish before daylight.

Using back roads and attracting as little attention as possible, Jake felt he needed to get as far from Lakeside as he could while it was still dark,. He knew he couldn't go too far though without getting some gas. *How will I pay for it?*, he anxiously thought. *As Elliott, using his credit card? How can I get some cash when I need it if I don't have Elliott's pin number? Have the authorities linked this car to me? Do they have a picture of me?* These questions and other unsettling thoughts gave him a headache, and he longed for a joint to ease mounting tension.

Instead of a joint, Jake was going to be drinking a lot of coffee and maybe even popping some No Doze. When the gas gage registered a quarter tank, he began in earnest looking for an open service station. He realized he might have to venture into a more populated area to find one. Before he did that, however, he stopped briefly on the side of the road to remove "Elliott" from his jacket lining.

It was now near 2:00 a.m. and Jake found himself in the town of Dunkirk, New York. Pretty desolate at this hour, he observed, but there appeared to be no lack of business at the all night Kwik Fill where he pulled in, pulled up to the least conspicuous pump, pulled his cap down over his forehead, zipped up his jacket, and cautiously got out.

His new identity worked like a charm, and by 2:15 a.m. "Elliott" was back on the road with a full tank of gas, a super size coffee, a carton of cigarettes, an assortment of junk food, bottled water, and some No Doze. He wanted to get a New York State map too, but was afraid that might arouse suspicion or make him memorable to the clerk if the police visited.

As Jake drove on into the night, he felt strangely calm, as though none of the chaos in his life had really happened. He let his thoughts drift to his family and was again overcome with longing to connect with his daughter. He thought of his parents, long dead, and wondered how much his life was shaped by *their* chaos and dysfunction . . . and poverty. He remembered the "candy" his mother would make for him and his sisters out of stale bread and sugar water. He also remembered going to school with the soles of his worn out shoes slapping as he walked.

After a while, he didn't want to remember anymore and checked to see whether anything good was on the radio. He settled on a country music station and began tapping on the steering wheel in time to the beat. He had no idea of his destination or what he would do when daylight came.

Chapter Twenty-four

Sam Becomes the Savior

Duty Officer Williams, with the 2nd precinct in Lakeside, had just poured himself a cup of coffee. He looked at the clock and saw it was close to midnight. "Another calm night," he said to sergeant, O'Brien. "This is the sort of job where you come to work and hope like hell nothing bad happens." Williams and O'Brien, veterans on the force had been partners for the last twenty years. They were dedicated to their profession and cared deeply for the people in their community.

At that moment, a call came in from the 911 operator. Her voice was clear. "George Baker has found his missing wife, tied up in an empty house five doors down from his 228 Bayview Drive home. The owner of the house is Ward. The address looks like 220 Bayview."

"We are on it. Tell him we are coming, keep him on the line, and keep us informed." Williams leapt up and called dispatch. "Calling all cars in the Bayview area, Baker has found his wife at 220 Bayview. She is tied up and gagged. We do not know if the kidnapper is still on the premises."

O'Brien nimbly zipped up his bulletproof vest, and grabbed the telephone number of FBI agent Miles Dell. "I'll call the FBI agents and let them know what is happening on my cell phone." Officers O'Brien and Williams grabbed their coats and were in their police cruiser within minutes. The night air was cold and O'Brien could feel his adrenaline pumping. He dialed Dell's number. "Hi, Miles, the Baker woman has been found by her husband several houses down from her house. We are on our way over there now. I'll keep you informed."

Miles Dell and Bill Light were on duty that night. Miles had just finished up some paper work. "Roger, keep us informed." He turned to Bill and said, "that was Lakeside police officer O'Brien. Babs Baker has been found several houses down from their own residence. The officers are on their way over there."

"Excellent, looks like we will be going to Lakeside, that Jake is one stupid guy. Not only will he be wanted for robbery, but now he is also wanted on kidnapping charges. Was he in the house with her?"

"Officer O'Brien did not know. In fact, he was just on his way there and didn't know much. He was just alerting us. Good officer cooperation."

Williams radioed two cruisers headed over to Bayview Drive. "We'll meet at the corner of Sagamore in the parking lot of the 7-Eleven store. We'll have no sirens to alert the assailant. "O'Brien was driving as fast as was safely possibly. He rounded the corner of Sagamore and pulled in the lot. The two other cruisers, with two police officers in each, followed within minutes. All six officers jumped out and congregated in a circle.

Officer Williams took the lead command. "Here is the situation as we know it. I think you have all been previously briefed on this case. The assailant, Jake Proctor, has allegedly kidnapped Babs Baker. She has been found at the Ward house at 220 Bayview. Her husband discovered her there when he was walking their dog. We do not know if the assailant is still in the house.

"Homes and Reilly, you take the rear entrance, O'Malley and Donavan cover the sides of the house, and O'Brien and I will enter through the front door. O'Brien is going to call the Fire Department and an ambulance. Will someone call Sharon and get her over here." The police department always included a female officer when there was a woman involved in a case.

Homes volunteered to contact her and called her cell phone. Unmarried and new to the force, he had a crush on Sharon, who was also single. "Sharon, they found the Baker woman. Come over to 220 Bayview ASAP." He hung up the cell phone without waiting for an answer. He knew she'd be there.

The officers surrounded the house, each taking positions assigned by Williams. All officers had drawn their weapons. George had managed to turn on as many lights as possible. Babs was locked upstairs in one of the bedrooms and George ran down and opened the front door. Sam was barking loudly.

George yelled: "Don't shoot! Don't shoot! I'm George Baker, my wife is locked in a room upstairs." Sam was excitedly jumping up on Officer Williams. "Down Sam, down." George yanked the lease and Sam sat obediently.

Officer Williams approached George. "May I see some identification?"

"Yes, of course, but you have to understand my wife is locked in a room upstairs. I have no idea what condition she is in." George fumbled for his wallet in the back pocket of his trousers. "Here's my license, but *please* it's my wife that I am concerned about."

"I understand sir. Do you think the assailant is still in the house?" Williams asked George.

"I don't know for sure, but I don't think so. I was taking Sam for a walk and he dragged me over here. I figured he knew something I didn't. So, I let him take the lead. He drew me right to the back door, which was open, so we went in. Sam pulled me upstairs. I have talked to my wife, but please, can't we try to get her out of there?"

At that moment, the Fire Department and ambulance arrived. The Fire Chief ran up on the porch of the house along with the ambulance driver. "Can you show the Fire Department which room your wife is located in?" He asked George.

"Of course," George walked around to the east side of the house. "It's that room up there."

"There is a kidnapped woman locked in the room upstairs. See if you can get her out of there." The police officer said to the fireman.

The Fire Department quickly assigned a hook and ladder team to the second floor. They broke a pain of glass, reached in and opened the sash lock. One of the fireman and a female EMT climbed the ladder and entered the room.

Babs lay in bed. Her arms were stretched upwards and her wrists were tied to the top of the bedpost. Her legs were tied to the end of the bed. She was covered with a small blanket.

"We are here. Don't worry ma'am, your husband is right outside this door." The firefighter, clad in a helmet, large boots, jacket, and carrying a pick ax looked at Babs. "I will remove those ropes, Mrs. Baker, Ok? I know you want to see your husband. He is right outside." The firefighter forced his body against the bedroom door and broke the lock. George came running into the room and gave Babs a big hug. Sam was right behind him barking.

"Oh honey, we will get these ropes off you as soon as we can. How do you feel?" George looked lovingly at Babs stroking her face with his hand.

The fireman was undoing the ropes at the bottom of the bed. "Excuse me sir, I want to remove those ropes at the head of the bed as well." George reluctantly stood back.

"Thank God you are still alive. I have been so *worried* about you." George's eyes welled with tears as he looked at Babs.

"I am so glad to see everyone, thank you." Babs shed a tear of joy.

"It was really Sam who found you. He kept pulling me in the direction of the Ward's house." George laughed.

"Excuse me," said the EMT. "Could I please examine your wife just before she gets up? I know you are anxious to see her, but we have to follow some careful procedures here. If you men don't mind waiting outside for a few moments, it won't take very long."

"I'll be right outside honey, I promise." George walked into the hallway followed by the fireman. George's face was ashen. What would he do if she had been sexually violated? How would he feel or react? Would that change their wonderful love life? His breath shortened and his chest felt tight. Officer O'Brien had reached the top of the stairs and interrupted George's train of thought.

"The assailant does not appear to be anywhere in the residence. Have you noticed any unusual cars or strange people in your neighborhood?" O'Brien asked George. The officer noticed that George looked stunned, and understandably disoriented. "Sir, why don't you come down to the kitchen for a few minutes? The EMT will be with your wife a few minutes longer. That is standard procedure in a case like this and we just want to make sure she is alright." George felt shell-shocked, angry, confused, and upset. How could anyone do this to his wife? How could he have allowed this to happen so close to his own home?

The EMT was very sensitive to Babs. "Mrs. Baker, my name is Jane and I am going to give you a short exam. Please tell me how you feel—any pain in your body? Do you feel comfortable sitting up?" Babs felt a little more disoriented than she realized. The full shock of what she had been through was beginning to take hold.

Jane helped Babs sit up. "Thank God, you found me," she heard herself say.

Jane placed the heads of the stethoscope in her ears and listened to Babs heart. Her heart was beating quickly; she looked at Bab's wrists which were red and bruised from the tightly tied rope. "Here," she said taking out vitamin e cream from her bag "let me put some cream on these bruises. It will promote healing. Is there any pain, in these areas?" She looked at Babs.

"They are a bit sore. I don't know how I'll feel when I take a bath." Babs looked at Jane admiring her compassion. She almost felt as if she were going to cry. She had held on for so long and been so brave. She had been calm in front of so damn much adversity. But now, somehow in front of another woman, she felt suddenly safe to let go a bit. Tears fell down her cheeks, and she could not talk. She felt worn out, just so very, very worn out.

"I am going to roll up the blanket and put some of this ointment on your ankles. Just lie back, for a few minutes." Jane was wearing rubber gloves. She carefully messaged Babs' ankles which were marked and sore looking. "As I suggested before, keep an eye on these. If you start getting blisters call your doctor immediately. We want to avoid infection."

Jane put her hand on Babs's arm. "Mrs. Baker this is a very difficult question to ask, and more difficult to answer, but it is very important we know the truth." Jane paused, and took a deep breath. "Were you sexually assaulted or abused in any way? You realize this is nothing for you to be ashamed about. You were in a terrible situation which was out of your control." Jane was half of Babs's age. Babs looked at her and wondered with admiration what this young woman's working life was like and what challenges she met everyday. How many women had she examined in similar circumstances?

"No, no, I was very lucky. Nothing like that happened that I know of. I think I was drugged. I just remember waking up feeling very groggy and having a terrible headache. I was at home in my kitchen when someone grabbed me from behind. The next thing I know, I woke up here in this bedroom. Where am I anyway?" Babs asked.

"You are at the Ward's house at 220 Bayview just a couple of doors down from your own house, Mrs. Baker." Jane looked at her.

"Gosh, the Wards are going to die when they find out what happened here. They just live here in the summer. I have only been on the first floor in this house.

"One very ironic thing, that is that we share the same cleaning lady." Babs put her head back on the pillow.

There was a knock on the door. "Come in," said Jane.

Police Officer Sharon Smith entered the room. She was wearing a dark blue uniform with trousers, heavy armed belt, and wool coat. She took her coat off and approached the bed.

"Mrs. Baker, I am Officer Sharon Smith. Call me Sharon, please. Can you try to remember the events of what has happened to you in the last two days? I know it is going to be tough, but these early impressions are so important for us. We want to find the man who has done this to you as fast as possible." Jane had short, cropped hair and was trim. Babs guessed she was in her middle thirties. Her countenance was one of strength and was seemingly very under control. Her face was void of emotion.

"I was just telling Jane, I had just arrived home at 228 Bayview. It was the end of the day. George, my husband, had gone to Cleveland to the boat show. There had been several strange incidences and I felt uneasy, but I wanted to take Sam, our dog, for his walk. I heard a noise and then he grabbed me from behind. From the strength of the grip, I knew it was a man. The last thing I remember was having something over my mouth. When, I woke up I had a terrible headache and Lee, this guy I knew a long time ago was sitting beside my bed." Babs looked at both of them.

"Mrs. Baker, I am going to urge you to go to the hospital. We want to give you a thorough examination; especially when you feel you were drugged." Babs sighed. She felt awful. Going to the hospital was the last thing in the world she felt like doing, but she understood the importance of cooperating.

"Mrs. Baker, when was the last time you had seen Lee?" Sharon had a small notebook out and was writing down Babs's answers. "Oh along time ago, I guess you know that the FBI visited me about this guy and warned me he was wanted for questioning in a series of postal robberies. Last week, I got several calls and hang-ups in the middle of the night. I assumed it was a wrong number. Then, I received a newspaper with a dead canary wrapped inside." Babs was sitting up now.

"We have informed the FBI you have been found and we have put out an alert with his description to police in neighboring towns. The FBI does have a postal employee picture of a Jake Proctor which we would like you to look at when you are finished at the hospital. Do you feel as if you can walk downstairs, or would you like us to bring up a gurney for you?" Officer Smith inquired.

"No, no, I am fine. I will walk downstairs." Babs stood up and felt weak. "Can you please hand me the rest of my clothes on the chair?"

"When was the last time you remember eating anything, Mrs. Baker?" asked Jane.

"Come to think of it, Lee gave me some food yesterday, or today, I don't know, I can't seem to remember much at this point." Babs responded.

"Here Mrs. Baker, sit back on the bed for a few minutes and drink this can of Ensure. It is high in calories and will give you a little quick nourishment. But first, let me take a quick swab of the inside of your mouth." Jane took out a long stick and gently went around the roof and tongue of Babs's mouth.

"Can my husband please ride with me?" Babs pleaded.

"Of course he can. But it might be better for him to bring your car to the hospital, the he can drive you home after the examination," Officer Smith suggested. Jane handed the Ensure to Babs who drank it and began to feel better.

The three women walked slowly downstairs.

Officer Smith talked with Officer Williams: "We are going to take Mrs. Baker to the hospital for a complete physical. Mr. Baker can follow in the car so he can drive her home afterwards." Jane held Babs by the arm, and George came over immediately to give Babs a hug.

"Honey, I'll drive our car over so I can drive you home after the examination. I'll follow you over to the hospital. How are you doing?"

Babs, looked at him tearfully, "I am so glad you are here."

Officer Smith spoke to Officer Williams privately. "They have the same cleaning lady. I wonder if that's how he got access to this house. It has a burglar alarm which did not appear to be set."

"Our thoughts exactly, we'll get in touch with her first thing in the morning." Officer Williams continued, "We did find a small black book with some handwriting at the kitchen table. The FBI works with a handwriting analyst, they should be here any minute."

"Run this guy Lee Roberts and see if you come up with anything. Have we got a picture of Jake Proctor? He might have tried to alter his looks. Doesn't he like aliases? I could stop by the station and with your permission get the photograph to take to the hospital. We are going to give Mrs. Baker a complete exam. She was drugged and doesn't remember much of what happened to her." Officer Smith was good at follow-up and taking initiative.

"The picture is in the file on the left-hand side of the desk. Go for it, and report back to us after she has looked at the photograph. We are going to wait here for the FBI," Officer Williams replied.

George walked back towards their house to get the car. He was shaken and decided to call an alarm company the next day. As George walked down the street, he saw a neighbor coming towards him aroused by the noise of the police cars.

"George are you alright?" Jack Anderson, his next door neighbor inquired. "I heard all the commotion. What the hell happened? Have they found Babs?"

"Yes, thank god. They found her tied up in a bedroom on the second floor of the Wards' house. I have to go down to the police station now." George didn't want to tell Jack that Babs was going to the hospital. "But they've not found the person who did this. Make sure you lock up your doors."

"Is there anything I can do for you?" asked Jack. George appreciated his offer.

"Thanks Jack, not at the moment. I will let you know." George walked into his house not feeling as if he could handle a more in-depth discussion at this time.

George gave Sam a biscuit. He patted his head and put him in his crate. Picking up the keys to his car, he kept on a hook beside the back door, he glanced at the bouquet of flowers on the counter. *That is so like Babs to always have fresh flowers in the house,* he thought. It is ironic to think how dramatically a life can change within moments.

After locking the kitchen door behind him, George opened the garage with the automatic door opener and climbed into the front seat. He backed out the car and made sure he had activated the switch to close the door behind him.

The emergency room at the hospital was empty. *Well, there are some advantages to coming to the hospital at 3:00 a.m.,* thought George. There was a friendly looking woman at the admissions desk who looked as if she enjoyed a few too many chocolate malted milk balls. Hello, my name is Mr. George Baker, my wife Babs Baker was just brought here."

"Yes, Mr. Baker, your wife is in one of the examining rooms. Could you please give us some insurance information? Mrs. Baker told us you were on your way."

George took out the insurance card from his wallet and gave the necessary information to the clerk.

FBI agents Miles Dell and Bill Light arrived at 220 Bayview after 3:30 a.m. Officer Williams was in the kitchen.

"Thanks for coming, guys. Wish I could offer you a cup of coffee." Officer Williams said to them. "Thanks, we stopped at a Dunkin' Donuts on the way. Where is the Baker woman now?" Asked Dell.

"She is at the hospital getting examined. Her husband was out walking the dog, who kept pulling him in this direction. You know, they live just a couple of doors down the road. Mrs. Baker was locked upstairs in the bedroom, but the assailant was nowhere to be found when her husband entered the premises.

"According to our female police officer, Sharon Smith, who interviewed Mrs. Baker, she was drugged and couldn't remember much. The assailant tied her arms and legs to the bed. We have gone over the house thoroughly, but I am sure you will want to conduct your own search. One thing we did find is a small black book with some notes." Officer Williams handed it to Officer Dell.

"We'd like to make copies of these pages." Said Officer Dell.

"Take it and leave us the copies. After all, this is a federal case." Officer Williams laughed. Dell and Light searched the residence. They found no additional clues, where the assailant had gone or why he had left.

"Let's go back to the station for copies and I'll fax some of the pages to that handwriting analyst outside of Boston to verify it's Proctor's. We might also catch a couple of hours shut eye at that Motel Six and meet you around 8:00 a.m. later today." Dell suggested to Williams. "Will you contact the Wards and tell them what happened to their house?"

"I'll call them tomorrow. Oh, did we tell you, the Wards and the Bakers shared the same cleaning lady? We will be able to interview her at that hour. We will also prepare a press statement and make sure the other police departments in our area have received the APB and received a picture of Proctor" added Officer Williams.

"Excellent," Dell wrapped it up.

As tired as Lee was, he knew he was in big trouble. He had rented his car which needed to be returned by next Sunday and today was Saturday. He had seven days before the Alamo Rental Car Company would report the car missing. He took a long drag off a cigarette and another swig of coffee. He felt high on nicotine and caffeine. *Man did Babs look scared!* He laughed ghoulishly to himself. *I better change my appearance,* he thought. Upper New York state is desolate, but he realized from the road sign on the highway he was near the Vermont boarder. A large green sign read Route 7, Middlebury. Shortly thereafter was another sign for an all night truck stop in twenty miles. *Perfect,* he thought. *Those places may have someplace to eat and maybe even a pharmacy where I can buy some hair dye.* He turned on the radio and began singing along with one of his favorite country and western songs: 'They Aren't making Jews like Jesus Any More.' He actually laughed out loud. He hadn't heard Hickey Friedman and the Texas Jew Boys for about thirty years.

The all night rest stop was everything he had hoped for and more. He passed six trucks pulled up along the parking lot with men probably sleeping in them. There was an all night garage with men changing oil on three big rigs.

Jake parked and wandered into the restaurant. He could smell bacon and hot coffee. He sat down on one of the stools at the counter.

A waitress in her early thirties carrying a big glass coffee pot in her hand was approaching him. "Can I pour you a cup of coffee?" She asked.

"Thanks, yes." Jake responded.

"Oh my, you sound as if you are a long way from home darlin' with a Southern accent like that," the waitress teased.

"Yup, I reckon so." Jake looked at her large breasts.

"My name is Agnes, and I will be your server this morning." She gave him a big smile. "Would you like to see a menu?" Jake nodded.

The server went to the other end of the counter. He had forgotten about that damn Southern accent. He'd better see if he couldn't tone that down a bit. The fellow next to him at the counter said, "Man, isn't that ridiculous? Whatever happened to 'waitresses'? Now all of these broads are 'servers,' I really don't care what you call them as long as they have big boobies like this chick." He spoke under his breath to Lee and they both laughed. "Hey, where are you from?"

Starting a conversation was the last thing Lee wanted to do, but it was too late for that now. He thought to himself, *I should have sat at a table, damn it. What was I thinking of? Better give a fictitious answer,* so he answered nonchalantly. "Oh every place really, I am one of those Army brats who grew up all over the country, most recently a little town in Georgia." Lee noticed the guy was eating a piece of pie. *Good,* he thought, *maybe he wouldn't be around long.*

"Georgia, eh? Yeah, that's a nice state; nice temperature now. Better than this area, for sure. I have driven a truck through every state in the union. I'm going back to Iowa now." He finished his last bite of pie and stood up. While putting a bill on the counter for the waitress, he said to her. "Thanks a lot, honey. See you next month. You take good care of yourself now, won't you?" He walked out of the restaurant.

Thank god, he thought. He grabbed yesterday's newspaper and tried to look engrossed, to avoid further encounters. When the waitress returned he ordered a "Number 5:" hash browns, and two sunny-side-up eggs over steak and toast.

"Wheat, rye, or white?" asked the server.

"Wheat, I guess. Say, is there an all night pharmacy or motel near here?" "There most certainly is. If you go about three miles down the road there is an all night Rite Aid, and then in another five miles is a Motel Six. A lot of the truckers stay there. There is a swimming pool which a lot of the men like. They get so stiff sitting in those trucks all day that the swimming really helps them."

"Thanks," Lee responded. He finished his breakfast and left her a tip. *Wonder what it would be like to tie her up,* he thought. He found the Rite Aid and bought some hair dye and scissors. *I'll get some shuteye and then change my appearance a bit. I always wanted to be a blonde anyway.*

He checked into the Motel Six. His waitress was correct they did have a pool and a lot of big rigs were in the parking lot. "Truckers are good advertisements for restaurants and accommodations," his father had always told him. He undressed and sank into the bed exhausted.

Addie and Butch woke early on Sunday. They usually had a big weekend breakfast of eggs and bacon or sausage. "Too bad the *Journal* isn't published on Sunday. I love that paper. I hope that Murdock doesn't ruin it, but I can't say that I have much hope," Addie said. She was sitting at the kitchen table while Butch was preparing breakfast. They could hear the fax machine running upstairs in their office.

"Hmmm, that's a bit unusual to have a fax come in on a Sunday, isn't it?" Butch was beating eggs in a large bowl for the scrambled eggs.

Addie's business phone rang and then her cell phone. "Maybe there is some news about Babs." Addie stood up and answered her line, which had a distinctive ring from their home phone. "Good morning, Adelaide Stubbs. May I help you?"

"Good morning, Mrs. Stubbs this is FBI Agent Light, from the Pittsburgh Office. We found Mrs. Baker in a house five doors down from the Bakers house last night."

"Oh, that is such a relief. Is she all right?" Addie said putting the hand held telephone on speaker so that Butch could hear the conversation.

"She appears to be doing well. I can't say much more than that." Agent Light responded.

"I understand. How can I help?" Asked Addie.

"We found a notebook. We have copied a couple of pages, and faxed them to you. It looks like Proctor's handwriting, but we wanted to make sure. Can you give it a quick look and get back to us as soon as possible?"

"Of course I will. I will get right on it. Shall I call your cell phone?"

"Yes, that would be great. The reception should be pretty good up here. If you have trouble contact Officer Williams at the Lakeview Police Department. His telephone number is: (805) 767-2340. Speak with him directly." The agent hung up.

"Here honey, these eggs are done. Taking a few minutes to eat will make your brain cells work more efficiently." Butch spooned two eggs onto each of their plates. He removed the bacon from the microwave and picked up two pieces of toast on his way to the kitchen table.

"This is delicious, sweetheart. You are so good at making Sunday breakfast. My god, thank goodness they found Babs." Addie took a quick bite out of a piece of toast.

"How is she?" Butch asked concerned.

"Well, you heard Agent Light, 'she appears to be doing well.'" Addie lowered
her voice mimicking the F.B.I. Agent. She quickly polished off her breakfast. "Will you forgive me . . . ?"

"I will forgive you for leaving the breakfast table early, and not sitting here reading the paper with the man you love!" Butch looked at her and smiled.

Addie rushed upstairs to the office. She looked at the two faxed pages. She was almost certain that it was the same writer but just to be sure, she went through her files and pulled out her three other samples: one from Jake P. Hunt, the letter Babs had given her from Lee Roberts and the writing Bill Deluth had sent from Jake Proctor.

She carefully read the information in the new sample which listed several names and the telephone of Alamo Rental Car in Lakeside. She picked up the phone and called FBI Agent Bill Light. "Bill. It's Adelaide Stubbs. Call me when you can." He instantly called her back. Addie saw his name on her caller identification screen, and felt there was no need for an introduction to their conversation. "Yeah, it's his handwriting all right. Did you notice that he has a telephone number for Alamo Rental office in Lakeside and several other names?"

"We did indeed. Thanks for your help." Agent Light spoke quickly and then hung up.

Addie went downstairs where Butch was reading the paper. She picked up the teapot and asked if he was ready for another cup.

"Was it the same guy?" Butch asked Addie.

"Not only is it the same guy, but he had the telephone numbers of Alamo Rental on the first page." Addie refilled Butch's cup.

"Oh no," Butch laughed. "That's funny. I am sure the police will be able to catch him now."

"I really want to call Babs and George. They must be so relieved. Maybe we should turn on the news and see if there is any national coverage."

Addie grabbed the remote control and turned on the news.

Mary O'Donnel, Addie's favorite newscaster, was giving the 9:00 a.m. report. She had just finished covering another car bomb in Iraq and a flood in China.

There were the usual adds for cereal, hemorrhoid treatment, and trucks. Then Mary O'Donnel began the story Addie waited for:

"*They say a dog is man's best friend, but for an Upstate Pennsylvania woman, it was a dog who was woman's best friend. Babs Baker was kidnapped from her home in Lakeside, Pennsylvania, and was held hostage in a neighbor's summer residence. When her husband tried to walk their dog Sam, he pulled him towards their neighbor's home. Sure enough, Mrs. Baker was tied up in a second floor bedroom.*

"*The assailant was not in the house. He is still at large and considered dangerou*s." A picture of Jake Roberts filled the screen.

"Oh my god, did you hear that?" Addie was so excited. "Butch, he is still at large. I can't believe that. I think I might know which house that was too. That is just unbelievable. I'll try to call Babs later. I just have to hear her voice and know first hand that she is alright."

Butch, who was always the voice of reason responded, "Now that his picture is broadcast all over national television, the authorities should be able to catch him. Don't worry honey, and Babs is alive and safe."

Chapter Twenty-five

A New Beginning

Once he hit the sack, Jake slept a solid nine hours and woke up feeling wonderfully refreshed but acutely aware that he had a lot to accomplish in a short time. The first order of business was to change his appearance, and checkout time was a scant two hours away. He splashed water on his face, swished some mouthwash around his cigarette stale mouth and headed to a McDonald's down the road to grab some coffee and an Egg McMuffin. He didn't dare go back into the truck stop restaurant as much as he'd enjoy getting one more look at Agnes's ample breasts. *Heck, she's probably ended her shift by now anyway.*

Jake's trek to McDonald's took twenty minutes of his precious time but provided fuel he badly needed. Dying his hair would take at least another half hour, and the finishing touches for his disguise would eat up whatever time was left. He had to stay completely focused; with renewed manic energy, and no pot to calm him down, that would prove a challenge.

"Ok," he said, staring into the bathroom mirror, "here we go." The dye smelled terrible as he worked it through his thinning hair. The wait for it to "take" seemed endless. So, he spent the next twenty minutes distracting himself checking the television and weather. The forecast called for unseasonably mild temps in the 60's, with partly cloudy skies. The national headline news was relatively uneventful, and the local news was downright boring, the highlight being the crowning of Tammy Wainright as Miss Springtime of Campbell County. "Good for her, and lucky for me," he commented out loud. He wondered just how competent federal authorities were if no one seemed to be looking for him. He knew, though, as long as he held on to the rental car, he was really pressing his luck. He had to ditch the damn thing . . . soon!

Checking his new appearance in the motel mirror one last time before leaving the motel, Jake flashed a thumbs up at his image and exclaimed, "lookin' good, Mr. Elliott Q. Woodrow, lookin' good!" What pleased the most was the color of his hair-no longer a mousy gray brown—now more of an ash blonde with a little gray. Trimming it short and getting rid of the comb over he'd had for years gave him a more confident, less uncertain, countenance if that made any sense. And he felt the wire rim glasses added just the right hint of intelligence, while softening the intensity of his somewhat startling eyes.

He had prepaid for the room and just left the room key on the dresser, made sure to wipe off any fingerprints, and took all his cigarette butts with him. He was going to be extremely careful of every move, especially until he could ditch the car and score a fake photo ID.

If all went well, by late afternoon Jake would be setting up camp somewhere in Vermont's Green Mountain National Forest. First, he had to get the camping gear and enough provisions to last a while. About a week, he was thinking. The trick would be getting in without having to register. If he registered, they'd require a license plus the fact most campsites also make note of your car registration. "What to do?" he pondered as he drove along. He thought back to his wilderness camping days during the '70's, and suddenly struck the answer: he'd hike and camp carrying everything on his back. Anybody who saw him would think he was just a day tripper. Now, where to ditch the car? He'd figure that one out he made his purchases. Could he be lucky enough to find a mall where he could leave the car and get local transportation to the forest area? He knew it would take more than just luck to pull off this one.

Brimming with excessive confidence, Jake pulled into the Green Mountain Shopping Plaza which just happened to have a Dick's Sporting Goods store and a line-up of what looked to be shuttle-type buses alongside an open shelter. He drove up to the bus stop first and got out briefly to grab several fliers from an assorted "take one" rack. Back in the car, he quickly perused them and found that, yes, he could carry out his plan just as he'd envisioned.

The only problem with Dick's was a scarcity of sales assistance, but Jake quickly acclimated himself to the layout and rapidly filled his cart with everything he'd need to stay comfortable and dry. He made sure all the items would fit easily into the backpack he selected allowed space for the food he would purchase next. The most cumbersome item would be the tent, but he was pleasantly surprised to find a one man model made specifically for hiking and camping. The poles ingeniously telescoped, similar to the way collapsible drinking cups work. The whole thing folded up to the size of a baby pillow which he could easily carry strapped to the backpack. At the checkout, he was pleasantly surprised to have spent less than $200. Yea, Dick's!

Groceries presented a different challenge. This limited his purchases to things like peanut butter and jelly, tuna fish, sardines and chocolate bars. Hopefully, there'd be a place near his campsite where he could buy milk, eggs, and meat in small quantities. Come to think of it, a number of trading posts were indicated on a tourist flier he had picked up.

By now, it was only 3:00 p.m. Jake had plenty of time to scout an inconspicuous place to leave the car, head toward the transit shelter, and catch a shuttle which apparently left every half hour to 5:00 p.m. He made a mental note to catch the 3:30.

The only thing Jake didn't want was conversation; he'd pretend he was a deaf mute if anyone tried to talk to him. He carefully sanitized the car wiping prints and throwing his belongings and cigarette butts into a mall trash bin. He then drove the car to the opposite side of the mall and left it in a full parking lot. By the time he arrived at the transit shelter it was just 3:25. He hopped right on a bus and buried his face in a magazine.

An hour later, he had his little tent set up and was foraging for firewood. Jake picked a site way off the hiking trail where he hoped no one else would venture. He did worry a little about four-legged invaders and made sure to dispose of any food wrappings or scraps by burying them. In the morning, he'd venture to the nearest trading post for more provisions and find out if anyone was looking for him. But for now, he was just grateful to have gotten through the day and wanted to get some shut eye.

The next morning, he awoke to a brilliant sun filtering through the tall conifers and teasing his face. He thought it must be very late, but it was only 7:30 a.m. He had decided going to sleep, that today would be a day of exploration and testing if indeed he was safe in his chosen, temporary retreat. He wanted some reading material and was psyched to cook over a campfire; headed out early to the trading post he figured was about a quarter mile away. When he got there, it was closed, with no sign indicating when it would open; he decided to check out the nearby hiking trails and come back later.

After hiking for a couple of hours, Jake returned to the trading post and found it open. By then Jake was ravenous and ended up buying more food than he could possibly eat: sausage, eggs and frozen hash browns. It turned out, he did eat practically all of it, an buried the rest. Although, he was tempted to toss the leftovers out into the woods and see what critters showed up.

Fortunately, caution ruled, and Jake realized the importance of his next move onto a new life but of seclusion. For the rest of his time in the woods, the challenge was to remain "invisible" but, at the same time, gain intelligence whether or not he was being actively sought by authorities. So far, there were no indications that he was. No "wanted" posters on telephone poles, no special news bulletins on the radio or TV, no nothing. This truly amazed him, and he suspected it was just the calm before the storm. He was a fugitive and something of a celebrity after all. *You betcha*, his ego bellowed, *those fuckers would just love to catch my wily ass!*

On Jake's fourth day in the woods, the adventure's novelty was wearing thin. He was very jittery and desperately craved pot. He hadn't made any headway planning his next move, the few clothes he had were getting pretty rank, and he was bored, bored, bored. He felt tired and defeated. Cigarettes didn't even help. He crawled into his tent early in the afternoon and immediately fell asleep. When he awoke four hours later, his demeanor had completely changed. He was bursting with manic energy and excited because an idea came to him in a dream.

In the dream he was at the trading post buying some items and noticed an area with postings of things people were selling, and looking for, and stuff like that. One of the ads, was looking for someone to drive a car to Virginia, another was for cleaning help, and one just said: "if you like adventure, call Larry before 6 p.m. weekdays at (802) 397-8824."

How weird, how vivid, Jake thought, and he felt sure the dream was pointing him in a direction he had to pursue. He checked the time and felt he could get to the trading post and back before dark with enough time even to do a load of laundry while there. Things were looking up; no more Mr. Stinky, and maybe a way out of the woods—literally.

Heading to the trading post with a pillowcase full of laundry slung over his shoulder, Jake's mood was buoyant. Like a child, he walked along pretending he was Johnny Appleseed and the laundry pillowcase was a sack of seeds. He remembered during a rare, happy interval in his turbulent childhood doing the same thing. He actually had the role of Johnny in the 6th grade school play. Soon after that, everything in his world started to turn to shit. Now bad memories overtook the good and, by the time he got to the trading post, his mood was glum.

He cheered up immediately though when he saw there was indeed a community board with all sorts of postings. *Gawd, that's uncanny,* he said to himself. *I dream about it, and here it is.* Before checking it out, he got his laundry started then went back to the board and began reading everything on it. There were four sections: Community Calendar, Job Openings, Services and Want Ads. He'd remembered to bring a pen and some paper and was soon jotting down several interesting possibilities. He'd come back and make calls them tomorrow after he figured out the best way. Would it be safer to use a phone calling card, or a cell phone? He wasn't sure. He still had plenty of cash and could buy either one.

As his laundry dried, Jake went outside, sat on a bench, smoked, read and re-read the ads he'd written down. He kept going back to one looking for a temporary installation work crew for an underground sprinkler system at a new golf course in the Adirondacks at Blue Mountain Lake. "No experience necessary. Housing provided." Another intriguing ad said: "Need the impossible? Call Paul at 802 824-7777. No questions asked." And finally, there was: "share ride from Green Mountain area to Adirondack Regional Airport on April 7th. You pay for the gas." It was now April 4th. Jake considered this last one meant to be since he had originally intended to stay in Vermont for only a week. April 7th would be a week to the day.

He found it hard to settle down back at the campsite. "Oh for some pot" he lamented. After making a meal over a small campfire of baked beans and hot dogs, Jake began to relax and spent the next hour daydreaming about events he hoped were just around the corner.

Up bright and early the next morning, Jake tidied up the campsite then timed his walk to the trading post to coincide with its 9:00 opening. He was still unsure about his choice of phone method, so he just flipped a coin to make his decision. The cell phone won, and he bought one with 30 minutes for just $15.99. *That should be plenty,* he thought.

Outside the trading post on the same bench where he sat the day before, Jake first called the sprinkler system help wanted ad and was pissed to get an answering machine. "If you're calling about the job openings in the Adirondacks, please call back after 3:00 p.m. Eastern Standard Time. Thank you," the male voice said.

His second call to Paul was more fruitful and led to a 10:00 a.m. rendezvous the next morning to score some pot. If all went well, this might also be his source for getting a false ID. They were to meet at Pine Bluff Lookout about 10 minutes from Jake's campsite. Paul would be on foot and wearing a forest green windbreaker, jeans, and a plain black baseball cap turned backwards.

Finally, Jake called the "share ride" number and was amazed to discover the advertiser was Sharie, a woman, fairly young sounding. She didn't seem at all wary of Jake and said he sounded like someone fun to ride with. He asked her if he could have until the next morning to think it over and get back to her. "Sure, no problem. I haven't had any other calls yet. So right now, you're it," she responded with a slight 'come hither' timbre in her voice.

"How could I be this lucky? Am I dreaming?" he asked as he hung up.

The next seventy-two hours of Jake's life were beyond his wildest imagination.

Paul turned out to be a rich resource far beyond scoring pot. As they talked and Paul gained his trust, Jake ventured into other territories, asking whatever Paul knew anything about a woman named Sharie who was offering a ride to the Adirondacks.

"Sure do. That would be 'Sharie Share a Ride'. She'll want to give you more than a ride though . . . You know, a good bang for your buck if you get my drift. And if you're on the run from something, as I suspect you are, she'd be the one to help you. Go for it, I'd say, and tell her Paul sent you. She'll know."

Jake next told Paul about the ad for the temporary work crew at Blue Mountain Lake. Paul was unfamiliar with the project and suggested Jake might be wise to wait until, in that area to pursue other job opportunities further. By now, Jake felt certain Paul had his own reasons to lay low and that his advice was worthwhile.

After Paul left, Jake didn't waste a minute to call Sharie back. She answered on the first ring, and he ridiculously imagined she'd been waiting for his call. He felt newly lustful and knew he'd have to temper his appetite if she was going to be of use beyond sex.

"Paul," she said after Jake told her of their meeting, "Why ain't that funny? I haven't seen him for quite a while, but he's been on my mind the past couple days, and now I know why." Their conversation continued very comfortably and they agreed on what time and where to meet on April 7th, just two days away.

Jake knew he'd just hung up with someone chockfull of street smarts, exactly what he would need to navigate the next chapter of his crazy life. *It's gonna work out just fine,* he thought as he walked back to his campsite.

The next day he busied himself as best he could, but the hours dragged. He'd been getting by with sponge baths in a nearby creek since he arrived and now felt the need for a real bath. The creek water was brisk, but nothing he couldn't tolerate if he was quick about it. Jake hadn't shaved since his arrival because he wanted to see his beard color. It was grey, but not too great a contrast to his new blond hair, so he decided to let it grow. He thought it fit pretty well with his new mountain man persona. What didn't seem appropriate was the Elliott Q. Woodrow identification he carried, but he'd worry about that after he found out how much Sharie could help. In the meantime, he thought of giving himself the nickname "Elk," but quickly dismissed it as too unusual and memorable.

Before settling down for his last night in the little tent, Jake double-checked there'd be no trace of his presence when he left at dawn the next morning. He slept little and fitfully, but didn't care. He was entirely pumped up to meet Sharie and move on.

Her instructions were to meet at the Beaver Falls Lodge at the west end of the parking lot at 7:30 a.m. She'd be in a 2003 beige Honda Civic sedan with an "I love my Pit Bull" sticker in the back window. She assured him she didn't really have a Pitt Bull but found the sign came in handy for protection sometimes. Jake got a kick out of that.

To get there by 7:30 walking, Sharie suggested he allow an hour, and she'd wait until 7:45 in case she'd misjudged the distance. He knew from his map the lodge was only about a half mile past the trading post and figured he'd have plenty of time.

It turned out he was 10 minutes early, but there was the Honda, and there was Sharie, in all her blonde, buxom glory, standing beside the car smoking a cigarette. "Pinch me, please," Jake muttered under his breath in admiration as he walked toward her. He wanted to say, "Where have you been all my life, gorgeous?" but contained himself and simply said "Sharie?"

At first their conversation was a little awkward but any verbal kinks quickly smoothed out, and they chatted easily. She gave him a few housekeeping rules like no smoking cigarettes or pot in the car and o please let her know if he needed to stop for the bathroom. One thing she couldn't tolerate was grown men peeing in their empty pop cans to avoid a pit stop. It had happened too many times, and she thought it was absolutely gross!

Jake found Sharie amusing and very attractive. Although she had an aspect of appearing "rode hard and put away wet," there was also a soft innocence below the rough surface. He liked that. He liked her. For someone with a long history of treating women badly, this was quite a change for Jake, and he sincerely wanted to be along for more than the ride with Sharie.

Two short weeks later, Jake not only had a new 'old lady' who put her former life on hold to be exclusively with him, he also had a photo ID and a job. The ID was easy: he simply joined Sam's Club, a retail store chain which requires a photo card for membership and a small annual membership fee. He kept the Elliott identity and did use the nickname "Elk."

"It suits you, darlin'" Sharie said.

The job had been the hardest part. They ended up at Blue Mountain Lake, which was his original destination, but he never pursued the golf course job. By then, Sharie knew enough about Jake's past to know he couldn't apply for anything involving background checks. He respected her advice on this and limited his search to things like line cook, dishwasher, handyman and those sorts of unskilled positions. Even so, without her connections it probably would have been a lot longer before he found a job.

As it turned out, Jake ended up as a laundry attendant at a 24 hour Laundromat. He was fortunate to get first shift, and it really wasn't so bad. He and Sharie rented a place together from one of her "associates" for some ridiculously small amount, and over the next four months he grew to feel safely hidden and his past truly behind.

Chapter Twenty-six

Camping in the Spring

A little more than a year had passed since Babs had been kidnapped. She dealt with her experience by taking a course in self protection. Along with Sharon Smith, the young female police officer, who had attended to her that fateful evening, the two give lectures to women's groups on safety. Babs enjoyed this new role and had become somewhat of a celebrity in Lakeside. However, her brave outside appearance did not show her anxiety which often manifested itself in terrifying dreams when she would scream for help. George was there to comfort her.

Despite the added monthly expense, George insisted upon installing a burglar alarm. He was very upset with the law enforcement agencies for not apprehending Lee or Jake, or whoever that guy was calling himself these days. It was impossible to go even one day without discussing their situation.

"I'm going to call Agent Longworth every single Monday until they find that guy," George said every Sunday evening. "I hate living with this notion he could be out there and re-appear at any moment."

"I know sweetheart, I do too. It is the uncertainty that is so terrifying. I find myself looking over my shoulder everywhere I go." Babs was always trying to comfort George who seemed to blame himself.

"One thing is for sure, I am not traveling anywhere until this guy is apprehended." George pounded his fist on the dining room table.

"I may not let you leave ever again." Babs reached over and held George's hand for a brief second.

Lee, alias Jake and Al, now "Elk," had enjoyed one of the better years of his life. His job at the Laundromat had worked out well. A bit boring of course, for someone of his brain caliber, but he contented himself with readying detective novels and seeing how fast he could fold laundry. Going to the library was too risky, so Sharie picked up books at one of the second hand book stores in town. Unlike the other women in Lee's life, Sharie liked his possessive nature. She had been abandoned by both her parents at the age of four and brought up in an orphanage. She rather enjoyed his controlling nature which made her feel loved and needed. Sharie could always find him pot and knew how to handle his fits of rage before they escalated to violent behavior.

As for Addie, she finished her book analyzing the handwritings of the presidents of the United States. She had found a publisher mid-May. To celebrate, she suggested to Butch that they take a camping trip.

"Oh honey, that is a great idea. I was just about to suggest that to you. We could go to this new camp ground in Vermont I heard about from Will Boatsman on our last hunting trip. We could camp for a couple of nights and then spend three days at the Norman Forest Bed and Breakfast. By then, we will be anxious for a hot bath." As usual, Butch was sitting in front of his computer answering e-mails.

"I can think of nothing better. What a relief to have finally finished that book. I feel as if I have been working on that for half of my life!" Addie stretched her arms up above her head and yawned. "Let's see, today is Saturday, can we leave on Monday? That way, we can avoid the crowds, if there are any. Will that give you enough time to get the camping gear organized?"

"Avoid the crowds? You are a scream. Honey, it is the middle of May. We will probably be the only ones in the campground." Butch laughed.

"Oh, I guess you are right. I wonder if I should call the FBI and let them know where we are going?" Addie said, thoughtfully.

"No," responded Butch, "don't bother them. They have enough to do. They have both our cell phone numbers. They can track you down if they need you."

"It just seems so amazing that they have not been able to find Mr. Wacko, doesn't it?"

"I agree," concurred Butch. "Maybe, they have given up trying. After all we are living in an age of terrorists and looking for a two bit kidnapper just isn't that important."

"Poor Babs, I know she has to deal with recurring nightmares. Did I tell you, she is now lecturing on women's safety with the police officer who helped rescue her?" Addie said proudly.

"You didn't tell me that. Good for her. That is a very positive way to deal with a horrible situation," Butch added. He turned off his computer.

"Where are you going?" asked Addie.

Butch laughed. "Getting the camping gear in order, where else?"

On Sunday, Addie went to church while Butch played tennis. It was their standard routine. Addie loved the Episcopal Church she attended in Manaport. By Monday the car was loaded with enough equipment for a transcontinental expedition. At the last minute Addie added a table cloth and candle sticks.

They found the camp ground without any difficulty. Butch was right; they had the park to themselves with the exception of three young men whose site was quite a ways away. It didn't take them long to set up camp. They had a wonderful tent from L.L. Bean which went up in no time. Butch brought two canvas chairs with drink holders in the arms. Addie spread the table cloth out on the long wooden bench. Next, she gathered evergreens on site and placed them in a plastic container in between the candle sticks. The scent of the freshly cut branches filled the air.

"Oh my gosh, it doesn't get much better than this, does it?" Asked Addie.

"Nope. This campground is a wonderful spot, I must remember to thank Will for giving us this tip." Butch was getting some firewood out of the car. He placed it into the fireplace.

"Those steaks look marvelous. I'll start marinating them now. The weather certainly is cooperating. It is a lovely temperature." Addie took a deep breath. "I love the early spring. Look at how beautiful those small green leaves are. They look good enough to eat."

They cooked the steak over the fire and had the large salad Addie had prepared in advance. Butch had brought a bottle of red Chilean wine to go with the meat. They talked long into the night. It was clear and the far away stars seemed brighter without the interference of city lights. Butch and Addie slept well in their double sleeping bag over an air mattress.

Butch and Addie rose early the next morning. They planned to go into town and have breakfast before the day's hike.

Addie was straightening up the inside of the tent. She had a bottle of hand lotion and was smoothing some of the mixture on her hands.

Butch had just returned from the camp lavatories down the road. He crept up to the tent and made a loud roaring sound, "Grrrrrrrrrr! I'm coming to get you!" He peered into the tent with arms raised and hands spread in claw like fashion.

Addie roared with laughter. "Oh my gosh, you are too scary. Gads, look what I've done. I've spilled this lotion all over the sleeping bag. How stupid of me. Maybe there is a laundromat in town."

Butch was rather cavalier about such matters. "Oh honey, it will dry by the end of the day, don't worry about it."

"This is our brand new sleeping bag. Lotions don't really dry. I bet we can find a laundromat in town and wash this while we are having breakfast. Please, let me try to do this. We just bought this bag. If we can't find a place to wash it out, so be it, we haven't lost anything."

"Ok, but let's get going. I am anxious to take a hike. This weather is wonderful.

We are very lucky it is so warm, so often May can be chilly." Butch was putting a few of the cooking supplies into a large plastic box.

The town of Churchville was typical of many Vermont villages. There was a white wooden church in the center of town overlooking the green. Cute shops lined the main street with several restaurants. To the right of the Always Welcome Coffee Shop was indeed a laundromat.

"I'll run in and quickly put the sleeping bag into the washing machine, and come back. It won't take a minute." Addie said to Butch as she got out of the car. She entered the laundromat and was pleased to see it was clean. *It is surprising how often laundromats are not clean,* she thought. There before her, was a large white bulletin board. On the bulletin board in bold distinctive handwriting were the hours of the establishment and the rates for having your laundry washed by Elk, the laundromat attendant. "Slick as a smelt, have your laundry done by Elk!" Addie starred at the handwriting. She had seen this handwriting so many times. She knew it belonged to Lee. It somewhat amused her to think that he was now calling himself Elk. There were two young women folding laundry and gossiping. Addie didn't want to run into Elk, so she left quickly.

Butch had settled himself in a booth and was looking at the menu. Addie slid in across from him, pulled out her dark glasses and raised the menu in front of her.

"Butch, my god, I think Lee Roberts is the laundromat attendant next door. I went in there and I saw his handwriting on the bulletin board. I don't want him to see me." By now, Addie was almost sliding under the table. "It is quite funny, actually. He has this little advertisement which says, 'Slick as a smelt, have your laundry done by Elk.'"

Butch roared with laughter. "Are you sure? It sounds as if he has changed his name to Elk. You've got to love this guy. Clearly, he has a great sense of humor." Butch turned around and looked in the direction of the laundromat.

"Careful, I don't want him to see us. He might run away. He could be dangerous, maybe have a gun stored with the extra soap. I better call the FBI in Boston. Oh my god, I am just shaking." Addie was breathing very hard; her hands were beginning to perspire. She couldn't help but laugh at the same time. She took out her cell phone, and dialed the FBI number on her speed dial. She could hear the phone ringing.

"Good morning, this is the FBI." The woman's voice was alert.

"This is Adelaide Stubbs, could I please speak with Agent Longworth or Agent Addelborough?" Addie said urgently.

"Agent Longworth," John always sounded tough on the phone.

"John, this is Adelaide Stubbs. My husband and I are in Churchville, Vermont on a camping trip and we came into town to use the laundromat. The handwriting on the bulletin board is Lee Roberts's or Jake Proctor's or you know, the guy that kidnapped Babs Baker. I haven't seen him and I don't want to. He is calling himself Elk these days and has an advertisement that goes something like, 'slick as a smelt, get your laundry washed by Elk.'" Now Addie, couldn't help herself from laughing and so did John.

"We'll be right on it. Whatever you do don't let him see you. This guy could be desperate and we have no idea how he will react. I'll call you on your cell phone when I know more." Agent Longworth hung up.

"God, those guys never say good bye." Addie looked at Butch. "He wants to make sure that Mr. Wacko doesn't see us. I wonder if I should dye my hair?"

"Oh good idea, you'd look great as a red head. Maybe I'll dye my hair too!" Butch could not stop laughing. "Let's order breakfast first, it may be our last meal. Why die on an empty stomach."

"I agree-just hate when that happens. We will be hiking most of the day, so I am not holding back. This "Number 3" looks good: bacon, eggs, toast, and home fries." Addie laughed.

"Hm. Sounds good but I think I'll have the hash instead of home fries." Butch responded.

"Oh my god, look what's outside?" Addie took out her Boston Red Sox hat from her knapsack and pulled it down around her ears. "There's a police cruiser pulling up to the laundromat." Several other people in the coffee shop looked around. This was just about the time the two local police came in for their morning coffee. But the two men did not come in the coffee shop; they went next door to the laundromat. It seemed like ages that they were in there.

"May I take your order?" A young girl asked, note pad and pencil in hand.

"I'll have the "Number 4" and my wife will have the "Number 3." We'll both have tea and wheat toast." Butch smiled at the waitress.

"You can't help but think this is exciting. Can you?" Addie said excitedly. "Maybe I should call Babs and tell her."

"No. Don't do anything until the FBI says it's alright. You don't know what is going on. It could be a coincidence." Butch cautioned.

"Oh there he is. My god, he must have been in the back room when I went into the laundromat. I am so glad he didn't spot me." Addie was straining her neck to look out the window. "He looks like he has dyed his hair blonde. Hm. Can't really see him that well." The officer put the man into the cruiser and drove off.

By now, most of the coffee shop was watching the drama outside. The older woman, who appeared to be the owner, was working the cash register. She looked over to one of the waitresses, "That's odd, looks like they took Elk off to the police station."

"He always seemed pretty quiet and kept to himself; never talked very much when he came in here for coffee. He had kinda of a funny accent . . . almost Southern," said the young waitress.

"It may be something routine, maybe a license issue. Who knows? It isn't fair to criticize until we know the truth." The owner told her employee.

"You are right." The young woman replied.

"Did you hear that?" Addie asked Butch. "I like that. That woman is correct. That is the way our American system is supposed to work. These Vermonters are good people. Butch, do you think we should spend the night in the hotel tonight?"

"Honey, Mr. Wacko does not even know we are in town number one, and number two, the police just took him away." Butch gave her one of those looks, which she knew meant there was no use in talking him out of it.

"Well, I guess you are right." Addie took a big sip of her tea and a deep breath. "This was quite a lot of excitement for one morning. Wouldn't it be terrific if this man is Lee, alias Jake, alias Elk! The name does have a ring to it, doesn't it?"

"Wish I could have gotten him to do our laundry just once." Butch laughed.

"I think we'll just hope that lotion dries and forget about any cleaning." Addie conceded. "I am looking forward to some hiking."

They poured over some local maps describing trails in order of difficulty. Addie liked to hike but didn't really like to challenge herself with steep uphill grades for long distances. They had a good day and found trails the correct level which was difficult enough for Butch not to be bored and easy enough for Addie to be comfortable.

They listened to the car radio as they returned to the camp ground. There was no mention of finding the now infamous Lakeside kidnapper. Despite the fact that Addie wanted desperately to call Babs, she knew Butch was right. It would not be smart to contact her old friend.

The next day they broke camp and loaded up the car. They had another wonderful day of hiking on different trails. The weather cooperated and was warm.

"As much as I love camping, I have to admit, I am really ready for a nice long hot bath." Addie confessed.

"I wouldn't disagree, my love, although for me, it is a long hot shower." They drove into the Norman Forest Bed and Breakfast driveway. "They said in their advertisement that this is the oldest B&B in northern Vermont." The large white rambling wooden structure had deep green shudders and a cherry red door.

"Oh you are right, Norman Forest Bed and Breakfast, northern Vermont's oldest B&B founded in 1845. Hmm . . . Just think, that was before the Civil War." The large central hallway had a fireplace in the center of the room. Fresh daffodils filled the vase on the front hall table. They checked in and went to the second floor to room 212. There was a comfortable looking queen size bed in the middle of the room and a pretty view of the mountains outside the window.

"Mind if I turn on television and get some news. I am amazed we haven't heard anything about Mr. Wacko," Addie said. "I am also amazed I haven't heard anything from Agent Longworth."

"He's busy honey, he'll get back in touch with you. I am sure he wants to make sure he has all of his ducks in a row." Butch sat on the bed and was taking off his shoes.

The 6:00 o'clock news was about to come on. "Good evening, this is Emmet Cleveland, with your local WRT news. Churchville residents were surprised to learn that a local Laundromat attendant was the man who kidnapped a Lakeside, Pennsylvania woman a year ago. He had many aliases and was known currently as Elk. He gained a reputation of being a fast laundry folder and coined the phrase, *slick as a smelt have your laundry done by Elk.* This will be a useful skill he can continue to use in the state penitentiary. Now, news from our state's capital, Montpelier . . ."

Addie jumped up from the bed and muted the television. "Did you hear that? They caught him. It was him. Oh my gosh, I am going to call Agent Longworth." Just at that moment her cell phone rang.

"Mrs. Stubbs, this is Agent Longworth. I have tried to call you several times today, but guess you were out of range. Coverage isn't great in that area of Vermont."

"Oh it is so good to hear from you. We just checked into a B&B and heard the evening news. I am so relieved. Especially for my friend Babs, I know this has been very difficult for her. Thank you for all of your help. We were serious about that offer to take you fishing. Boating season is coming up."

"Thank you Mam, for all of your help and cooperation; we couldn't have found this guy without you. And yes, I would like to take you up on that offer for fishing."

"I assume it is alright for me to call Babs now, isn't it?"

"Yes M'am, it is."

"We'll be in touch and let you know when the boat goes in the water. Thanks again." Addie could hardly wait to call Babs. She dialed her number with excitement.

"Bakers residence." Babs answered cheerily. Addie could hear the relief in her voice.

"Oh Babs, it is Addie. You must have heard the news. Butch and I were camping up here in northern Vermont. I spilled some hand lotion on our new sleeping bag and wanted to get it washed. So we went into this little town called Churchville. When I went into the laundromat, there was Lee's distinctive handwriting on the bulletin board. I almost died!"

"Oh my god, did he see you?" Babs was aghast.

"No, are you kidding? I was so scared I ran out. I was terrified and did not want to see him. I quickly called Agent Longworth at the Boston FBI. Oh Babs, I am so relieved for you."

"I must admit I am thankful. Now that it is over, I feel a hundred years younger and think I'll get my first good night's sleep in a year."

The End.